# THE COFFEE SHOP CHRONICLES OF NEW ORLEANS

## PART 1

DAVID LUMMIS

River House Publishing
www.riverhouseINK.com

River House Publishing
New Orleans, LA 70117
www.riverhouseINK.com

To purchase copies of *The Coffee Shop Chronicles of New Orleans*, please visit www.coffeeshopchronicles.com

Printed in New Orleans, LA by Garrity Print Solutions, Inc.

Grateful acknowledgement for reprint rights is made for the following:

Excerpt from THE GRAPES OF WRATH by John Steinbeck.
Copyright 1939, renewed © 1967 by John Steinbeck.
Used by permission of Viking Penguin, a division of Penguin Group (USA) Inc.

Excerpt from p. 72 from YOU CAN'T GO HOME AGAIN by Thomas Wolfe.
Copyright 1934, 1937, 1938, 1939, 1940
by Maxwell Perkins as Executor of the Estate of Thomas Wolfe.
Copyright renewed © 1968 by Paul Gitlin.
Reprinted by permission of HarperCollins Publishers.

Excerpt from "What a Wonderful World."
Written by George David Weiss and Robert Thiele.
Copyright © 1967. Renewed 1995 and assigned to Quartet Music, Inc.,
Range Road, Abilene Music LLC c/o Larry Spier Music LLC.
NY, NY. International Copyright Secured. All Rights Reserved.
Reprinted by permission of Larry Spier Music LLC,
Range Road Music, Inc., and Hal Leonard Corporation.

*For Csaba Lukács*

# The Coffee Shop Chronicles of New Orleans
## Part 1

# Mellifluously Mixed Metaphors

## Tuesday, August 16, 2005 – 10:45 a.m.

S itting in CC's all by myself, as long as you don't count the other people, sipping a double cap I don't want ever to end and committed to getting started on this book (okay, guidebook) with no further ado. At the same time I must say I'm mildly distracted by the possibility Catfish will come strolling in right about now since that could result in our following up on his weekend in the slammer with several hours (if not days) worth of deconstructing the roots and ramifications of racial injustice in the U.S. correctional system, something I can ill afford to do what with this first draft deadline looming. On the other hand, at this juncture I believe it's fair to say that this whole "grave-robbing" business has just gotten a tad bit out of hand, and that a little explanation is in order here. Because while it's one thing for some over-Cialised southern cracker of an assistant D.A. to arrest a perfectly innocent man, it's entirely another for Catfish to have more or less chosen to spend the weekend in Central Lockup, where I suppose he'd still be had it not been for some fancy footwork by me and Infinity Feingold, Esq.

I mean you tell me, what was he thinking, using his one phone call to alert not me, or Infinity, but *Tess*! All I can say is it's a good thing my housemate Naomi was watching the evening news Friday night and that she bounded across the breezeway to drop the bomb and that I then managed to track down Infinity in Vegas. Because while I was half-assuming she'd already be on it, Catfish's own attorney was even more in the dark than I myself. She was also furious over having her hubby's big 7-0 blowout interrupted. She and Morty had just checked into a high-roller suite at the Bellagio for a long-weekend spree, and there was (and I quote) no way in hell they were going to turn right around and come back. Nevertheless, she set the legal wheels in motion via Blackberry and took the Sunday evening red eye back to New Orleans, with me standing by to pick Catfish up while she continued to pull strings in the Halls of Power.

Needless to say, by the time Catfish came through that metal security door yesterday morning I wasn't exactly exuding bonhomie. In between phone calls to Infinity I had, after all, just spent two days earmarked for cranking out deathless prose staring off into space, a silvery strand of spittle dangling from one corner of my mouth like a disconnected electrical cord. And of course I couldn't help but suspect that this was just one more of Catfish's trumped up sociocultural psychodramas. Even so, as he closed the short gap between us and his image sharpened through the windshield of the PT Cruiser I lunged across the passenger seat and flipped open the door. With his matted-down hair and damp Brooks Brothers button-down, he looked sticky and exhausted and excessively thin, yet even more delicately handsome than usual, his face at once pale and impenetrably dark, as if some starved organ existing inside him had absorbed all the exterior color and light.

"You okay?" I said as he folded and swung his long limbs into the car.

He donned a thin smile. "I am now. Sorry it took so long."

I upped the AC a notch. "Why didn't you call Infinity?"

"Uh, this morning?"

"No. Friday afternoon. As soon as it happened."

"Oh. Infinity didn't tell you?"

"Tell me what?" The unintentionally turned up back of his collar was making me want to scream. I reached over and yanked it down.

"I called Tess."

"Yes. I know. Why?"

"She's my mother."

I glared at him.

He blew a weary sigh my way. "I tried."

"Great. Did she?" Heavy with sarcasm, the words clunked out of my mouth before I could swallow them.

He slumped down in the seat and stared forward. "Whatever. Could we please go?"

Given Catfish and Tess's gory history, "whatever" was right.

I shifted into drive and pulled out onto one of the bleak streets surrounding the Criminal Sheriff's office compound, pretending I knew the way back to Tulane Avenue. A couple absurdly long blocks crawled by while Catfish sulked and I tried to distinguish north from south, pretty sure I was going the wrong way. Perdido, a crooked street sign advised.

I made a call and turned right and proceeded two blocks, then made another call. Sliding up on the right was the razor-wire-topped fence of Central Lockup's jolly neighbor, Orleans Parish Prison, whose acquaintance I'd had the pleasure of making earlier that morning during a similar incident of directional impairment. A three- or four-story cinder-block affair with staple-sized windows and aqua blue accents, it was everywhere I'd never wanted to be and, the thought occurred to me, possibly Catfish's next stop if he decided to pull another stunt like this.

"Tulane's over there," he quietly advised. "But Gravier's one-way, so you have to go around."

I took the cue thanklessly, then made the hair-raising swing onto Tulane, a sea of maniacs all talking on cell phones and gobbling fast food as they darted between lanes in their determination to beat the upcoming light.

Less than half a block later, I slowed to a stop.

"I really am sorry," Catfish said.

The light winked from yellow to red.

"It's fine," I said.

He observed me a beat, then put his head back and focused on the road.

The traffic situation failed to improve. And as we managed to hit every additional red light possible while halving the distance to City Hall, there were at least a dozen burning questions I refused to ask. As usual, however, my irritation was ebbing prematurely. I stole a peek. That ropy neck tendon of his was throbbing like crazy, but would he go in for a stress test?

"Infinity's going to skin you alive," I finally said, the scrawniest olive branch I could find.

He nodded, then turned. "Thank you, B."

"For what?"

"She said you just kept on calling."

"Well somebody had to do something. You could have been killed in there."

"It wasn't that bad."

"Are you out of your mind?"

"Okay, okay. It's just that... I mean, I really did think..." He dead-ended in a way that made me want to pull over and hug him.

"You could have called me, you know," I said.

He reached over and gave the back of my neck a squeeze. "I know. Rain check?"

"Ha ha."

"How did you find out?"

"Naomi saw it on TV. It was all over the news. Beaucoeur heir arrested for possession of stolen cemetery ornaments. 'Grave robbing,' they called it. Like you were digging up bodies and snipping off ring fingers. She was pretty freaked out. We both were. Thank God Infinitely Irritating deigned to check her messages."

"Georgia's still out of the country though, right?"

I confirmed that he was. Given what Georgia—Catfish's long-time friend and my and Naomi's landlord and housemate—was going through, that kind of stress was the last thing he needed. During the seven years I'd been renting from him, Georgia had been to the ends of the earth trying one experimental protocol after another in order to beat back the cancer he'd been diagnosed with the same week I'd moved into his subdivided antebellum manse. Somewhere in there, his lavender PT Cruiser had become the household's community car, since even when home Georgia rarely ventured beyond the French Quarter and neither Naomi nor I had a car of our own.

The I-10 overpass flashed us with shadows, signaling the remaining distance to City Hall as only a few blocks. And I was about to become last-minute inquisitor when Catfish sat up straight in the seat and crossed his arms. "I was the only white guy in there," he said, thrusting me instead into the role of student as Professor Charles Beaucoeur launched an unrehearsed but no doubt statistically unassailable assault on the correctional system in America, where blacks account for 39 percent of all prisoners compared with their 12 percent share of the U.S. population, with 13 percent of black men in their late twenties in jail or prison, and with black women incarcerated at rates between ten and thirty-five times the rates of white women in fifteen states, leading one to conclude that African-Americans are either: 1) far more likely than white people to commit crimes or 2) far more likely than white people to be arrested, convicted, and dealt harsher sentences due to a deep-seated, systematic bias in the U.S. justice system not only against people of color but against all citizens unable to afford a motivated attorney. With the professor in full support of the second theory (and backing it up with a wealth of additional data I won't go into), from there on out I thought it best to keep my own middle-of-the-road mouth shut, in part because I knew Catfish was essentially right and in part because the lecture seemed to have lifted his spirits, infusing his bony cheeks with a bloom I found reassuring.

On the other hand, I found Infinity's plan to "play the race card" in his defense unconscionable. I'd heard the threat muttered before, but during our final interstate exchange she'd vowed to make good on it. "Cut-and-dried," the café-au-lait skinned consigliere had reveled, reminding me that Catfish was one of the most vocal white-skinned proponents of civil rights New Orleans had ever seen, while our newest assistant D.A. was a virulently anti-affirmative action Good Old Boy Republican (talk about redundancy). "You do the math," she hissed into her Blackberry between hands of blackjack. And I did, and it didn't add up. No, far more likely than covert racism was the unbridled ambition of Mr. Tucker. A former justice of the peace from southwestern Louisiana, Tucker had gotten where he was by invoking the name of Jay-sus every five minutes during every public appearance. And now that he was ensconced at City Hall, what better way to make a quick name for himself as a hardnosed guardian of all things moral than to nip in the bud, as spectacularly as possible, this latest spate of cemetery thefts? At its last flowering, the pilfering of angels, cupids, urns, and benches from New Orleans cemeteries had made headlines from coast to coast, culminating with the shocking arrest and conviction of an antiques-dealing sugarcane scion much like Catfish. Otherwise, given the paucity of evidence, it really was hard to explain why the D.A.'s office had become fixated on Catfish this time around, even if New Orleans is a place that's always been, shall we say, overzealous about its dead.

Like Venice, New Orleans is one of the few great cities of the world that admits it is living on borrowed time, with rising waters certain to one day call in that overdue loan. And perhaps no city integrates this inevitability as enthusiastically as the Big Easy. Here, those supposedly polar opposites of Death and Life promenade arms linked, while New Orleanians—far from avoid-ing that Dark Priestess and her underage paramour—sashay into their arms for a full-tilt ménage à trois, as drunk on Her promise of absolute care-lessness as they are determined to celebrate whatever time's left. And after that fling? Who gives a hoot! Because here God's the moment you're in and Satan each tick-tock. Night and day, death hangs draped over this riotous corpse-to-be of a town not like a shroud but like the cape of a carnival king, a cape that flutters and flaps along thronged parade routes in time with music that won't ever give up the ghost, for long after New Orleans has joined Atlantis under the waves the African heartbeat of those tunes will still pound.

What's more, in New Orleans life and death *literally* cohabitate side by side. Because like the cemeteries of Paris—Montmartre, Montparnasse, Père Lachaise—the graveyards of New Orleans are on top of the earth. Here, in sprawling cities of the dead rusty crucifixes tilt toward the sky as angels survey row upon row of sun-bleached mausoleums clustered in familial neighborhoods, their outer walls crumbling stacks of "oven-style" vaults that host the dear departed of centuries and decades and merely days past. This configuration embraces both style and function, recalling the beehive-like catacombs of ancient Rome while thwarting this area's high water table, which during floods or even hard rains still manages to snatch the occasional coffin and send it bobbing through town. In all, New Orleans proper is home to more than thirty historic cemeteries, from the ancient St. Louis No. 1 downtown to the rambling suburban Metairie Lawn, with crypt designs ranging from basic box tomb to posh Pyramid, Society, and Temple. And yet not even this abundance can readily contain all those consigned to perpetual rest. Thus, "reburying" is not uncommon here, a custom by which coffins are emptied and their mortal remains stuffed in burial bags inside the tombs, or pushed back on their slab using flat-topped wooden rakes, until they tumble down a narrow shaft into a grim chamber beneath. Around midday these cities of the dead sometimes harshly glare, especially in summer when the callous southern sun seems determined to blast to cinders those princely tombs. But by early afternoon the shadows have begun to creep back and the living to come—the families, and the friends, and the just plain curious. And no wonder these cemeteries are among New Orleans' most popular attractions! For if you meander in any direction you may find a table laid with white tablecloth and silver, with offerings of red beans and rice being ladled into fine china, or a jazz band traipsing respectfully (but not quite mournfully) up and down those outdoor corridors, tiny shells crunching underfoot, and maybe even some hoodoo going on. And yet for all of their sacred and historical glory, these same cemeteries are routinely neglected in terms of rudimentary municipal maintenance and security. *Don't go there alone!* the locals are quick to warn, because no, you will not find police officers patrolling those grounds. And it's this well-known absence, along with the cemeteries' lavish adornments and opportunities for concealment, that makes New Orleans graveyards both unsafe and easy to plunder. And in part because of this negligence, cemetery theft has been going on here for generations with hardly any notice, with some cemeteries—including poor old St. Louis No. 1—stripped almost to the bone, so to speak. So when in the late 1990s this thievery touched directly upon some of New Orleans' most prominent families—the Brennans, the Brocatos, the Louis Primas—it behooved the City to make a great show of its outrage.

It was late November 1998 and I'd just become one of the Big Easy's newest borrowers of time, still puzzled and blinking over how fate had managed to drop me into the most fantastic apartment imaginable in a plantation-style house a stone's throw from the Quarter. The week before my arrival, Peter Patout, a renowned expert in Louisiana antiques who traces his lineage from one of the state's first sugar planters, had been handcuffed in his Royal Street shop and carted off to jail, where not just a book but a whole library had been thrown at him, including charges of theft, possession of stolen property, obstruction of justice, desecration of graves, and criminal conspiracy. In the context of the same "conspiracy theory," a number of other well-known locals were also arrested, including Dr. Roy Boucvalt, a wealthy anesthesiologist whose historic French Quarter home, a regular stop on the annual preservationist tours, was found loaded with cemetery-style benches and urns; Aaron Jarabica, another local antiques dealer, who stood accused of "passing along" a marble statue worth $30,000; and Andy Antippas, a former Tulane professor who in the late 1970s did time for stealing rare maps from Yale University, and who had since recreated himself as a French Quarter business owner, including an art gallery and Marie Laveau's House of Voodoo. In the case of Antippas, the police raid resulted in an especially interesting array of items, including a collection of human skulls and bones, animal carcasses, an old prison electric chair, a self-portrait by executed serial killer John Wayne Gacy, and a jar of eyeballs. Nevertheless, Mr. Antippas was arrested and released. And perhaps because the City was more focused on making its point than its case, in a joint trial with Patout, Boucvalt and Jarabica both were acquitted, with Patout alone being sentenced to prison: a brutal six years of it. But not definitively. Because in mid-February 2002, after serving 18 months in Dixon Correctional Institute in Jackson, Louisiana, the verdict was voided by the Fourth Circuit Court of Appeals and Patout was freed pending a new trial, which has yet to occur. As a result, some people suggest that the blue-blooded New Orleanian was little more than a sacrificial lamb for a City trying to sanitize its own reputation, even if Patout's courtyard did yield a marble Madonna whose base "matched like a puzzle the jagged piece on a tomb," as *The Times-Picayune* put it. Not surprisingly, among those people are Mr. Patout himself, who maintains his innocence to this day, and who proclaimed it most famously during a pre-trial press briefing held near the tomb of his great-great-great grandparents in St. Louis Cemetery No. 3. "I am astonished and outraged at the easy assumptions being made regarding my integrity," he lamented to a cluster of onlookers, which included the two NOP detectives heading up the investigation. As for the Our Lady of Lourdes also seized from his residence, Patout went on to instruct that the statue was "made of plaster of Paris, not marble, and therefore could never have been used out of doors anywhere, much less a cemetery" (Associated Press). It was the biggest and most blatant cemetery heist New Orleans had ever seen—the populace, powerful and poor alike, were incensed. And during the run of that investigative tour de force, which turned up hundreds of stolen artifacts worth close to a million dollars, there were antiques store raids from the French Quarter all the way up Magazine Street, including of Catfish's erstwhile shop on the corner of Chartres and Dumaine, which of course came up clean as a whistle.

Not that Catfish and I had time to rehash any of this by way of reassurance as I taxied him over to City Hall. In fact, I didn't even get a chance to wish him luck with the D.A. since the instant we pulled up in front of that grimy white Sixties Functional fiasco Infinity was all over us like scalding water, yanking open the car door and hoisting Catfish out by the elbow.

"You! Inside!" The circular saw blades whizzed horizontally forth while neither her lips nor her eyebrows budged a hair. There's no way a person can speak at that low of a decibel level and still be heard, but she always does, and she always is. As usual, she was impeccably dressed in designer styles too expensive to identify, which might work for her were it not for the inevitable bauble or two too many.

She launched a freshly sharpened saw blade at me, the gist being that I was to stay the hell right where I was, then hustled Catfish up the steps and into the building.

But this is a no parking zone, I reasoned.

Before I could reconnoiter, however, she was back, her lips gleaming between the symmetrical scythes of her ebony coiffure, not a bead of perspiration daring to sully her precise maquillage.

"Is everything okay?" I inquired as she poked her head in through the passenger door.

"Peachy," she purred.

Then the blades really began to whirl as she alleged with the crippling force of almost absolute silence that her own failure to anticipate Catfish's arrest and incarceration was all *my* fault since as the person who spends more time with him than anyone else I should have seen it coming, having apparently forgotten that *I* was the one who alerted her to the crisis in the first place and spent the past 48 hours running after her while she and Morty continued their intergenerational love fest in Sin City! Adding insult to injury she then proceeded to inform me that she was holding me personally responsible for Catfish's welfare from here on out!

Which is why, I'm convinced, I ended up scraping Georgia's

car on the way home. I was distracted. Okay, deeply resentful perhaps, but definitely in need of a double cap. So I made a quick stop in the Quarter, which from the standpoint of weekday parking restrictions plainly was not quick enough. Instead, the five minutes or so I spent inside CC's was exactly enough time for the City to hitch up the Cruiser and haul it off to the impound, a Dante-esque place beneath the raised section of I-10 that destroyed the economic and social foundations of Claiborne Avenue and dealt a blow to the African-American small business community from which it has yet to recover. As a result, the rest of my morning was spent tracking the vehicle down and paying a $160 towing charge before side-swiping an ill-placed directional device in my haste to get out of that chamber of horrors.

Whatever the case, let me just say that Infinity's low-volume tirade did not go over well with yours truly, and that I had every intention of giving the woman a piece of my mind. However, by the time I'd managed to hoist my jaw up off the floor mat she was already disappearing back inside City Hall, which was the last time I saw her—or ever will. That's right, I don't care how far back she and Catfish go or if she is one of the sharpest legal minds in the Gulf Coast region, Infinity Feingold and B. Sammy Singleton are through, just like I'm through letting myself get side-tracked by this ridiculous legal posturing (grave robbing and race-card-playing indeed). As unsettling as this ordeal has been, it's over, thank goodness, and Catfish is fine. He's also, even I must concede, receiving superlative legal counsel, since narcissistic personality disorder aside Infinity knows the labyrinthine loopholes of Louisiana law like the back of her own bejeweled hand. "I'm sorry..." I shall therefore feel justified in telling Catfish with a clear conscious should he show up, laying down this new boundary gently but firmly, the most effective manner of engagement undoubtedly being, as it so often is, the casual appearance of a complete absence of bitchiness.

I mean it, no more distractions.

Bringing me back to the task at hand.

Where was I?

Oh yeah, sitting in CC's, gearing up for some serious wordsmithing here, sipping a double cappuccino I don't want ever to end, a wisp of mocha-colored foam adorning my upper lip, a sweet shadow of...

Hold on a minute.

Are the grande caps at CC's always this small?

I'm sorry but I just really don't think so. In fact, as I sit here staring ruefully at the remaining inch of liquid in the bottom of my cup I find myself constitutionally incapable of dismissing the possibility that this particular cappuccino was on the stingy side to begin with. To the contrary, the longer I ponder that eventuality the more distinct it becomes, like a subcutaneous tumor swelling up before the lens of a time-lapse camera.

Oh dear. I'd hate to think it has anything to do with Carla over there, who tends to be overly generous with her café crèmes, connecting rather blatantly customer satisfaction with the heft of her tip cup. A brooding Latina about my age with an armful of prison tats and difficulties making ends meet, she was so solicitous when I cozied up to the counter a short while ago, stopping right in the middle of chopping up lemons to make me the beverage in question—which is indeed about to come to an inglorious end, forcing me to interrupt this gentle musing on behalf of a refill, a cup of Kenya perhaps, which as dusky and complex as it will almost certainly be will be nothing like this first double-shot of the day. Then again, what cup of coffee is ever comparable to that inaugural one, just like that first cigarette used to be, made all the more delectable by life's fragile...

But I digress. And the mystery of this first cup lingers on. Was it something I said, or didn't say? Some unconscious slight of which I'm not aware? A facial tick, perhaps? Surely not. Don't I always go out of my way to act as if that infinitely awkward unspoken fiscal inequity between upscale-coffee-shop worker and patron, between those who spend $7-$10 on a cup of coffee and a scone and those who make that much in an hour, if they're lucky, does not exist?

Does it really even matter?

You're darn right it does!

Because B. Sammy Singleton takes his coffee seriously.

And not just that. As a sober person and rabid ex-smoker I not only love coffee, I need it, the way other people need air. And as far as overpriced sustainable-crop dark-roast blends go, Carla's my mid-morning dealer of choice. So heaven forbid I should have done anything to offend the poor woman, who makes no more apology for having spent a chunk of her youth in the System than she does for that rose and dagger tattoo oozing blood into her cleavage. In any case, to be on the safe side, moving forward I'm going to be careful not to repeat whatever it was I did, or did not do, to possibly offend her.

How?, one might wonder, since I haven't the foggiest what that might have been?

A logical inquiry and one for which I, as yet not fully caffeinated, have no facile reply. However it's still early in a day in which all things are possible. At least that's how I see it, because, well—*me voila!*—in a trendy coffee shop on New Orleans' ever fabulous Rue Royale, where shades of olive and taupe combine so tastefully as to take the edge off the worries of any man, with a virtually unlimited supply of caffeine at my disposal [USE IN BOOK]. And as this first cup of life-sustaining elixir courses through my veins I find myself filled with energy and enthusiasm and limitless optimism (not to mention humming old Helen Reddy tunes) as I prepare to dive into a miniature magnum opus that could very well, all modesty aside, lead to something sublimely sensational despite the stifling constraints under which I'm obliged by my uninspired editor to toil, like a twenty-first century Baudelaire restricted to sunny themes, or a Deep South Sedaris sans satire, nonetheless determined to overcome—nay, to smash and transcend and transform all established literary molds— possibly unleashing a whole new genre, one in which alliteration and run-on sentences and mellifluously mixed metaphors are de rigueur, as well as a new way of looking at life and love and *la condition humaine*—all within the context of the modern-day coffee shop experience, of course, and yet with a style, a flair, a *je ne sais quoi* that will make the dreary little lives of Lucky Dog Press guidebook readers everywhere a bit brighter, their steps a bit lighter...

Oops! Time for another cup.

Ah. Better.

And no disgruntlement chez Carla beyond the signature scowl, although I'm still not convinced something's not slightly off there, coffee shop workers being as they are a thin-skinned and inscrutable bunch. Nevertheless, like Catfish's prison polemic that's a line of scintillating sociological inquiry that will have to wait until another day.

Because like I said before, *no more distractions.*

(Hm, still no sign of him…)

And so, Dear Reader, at long last, let us begin:

*The Coffee Shops of New Orleans*
by
B. Sammy Singleton

**2**

I'm Not Saying
I'd Fall Apart

## Thursday, August 18, 2005 – 11:15 a.m.

The day before yesterday while sitting in CC's pondering subtly subversive departures from the usual guidebook fare I decided to commit to a program of physical fitness, not having gone jogging since my inguinal hernia repair a few months ago and appreciating the need to be in tip-top form for endurance writing. I don't care what anyone says or how many gracefully aging starlets proclaim from supermarket tabloid covers *"IT'S FAB TO TURN FORTY!"*, it's now a number of years since I did and despite my fair share of heroic effort I can unequivocally state that I've yet to uncover a single positive thing about that so-called milestone. Up until then I'd never been sensitive about crow's-feet and such; had even been a mite critical of those who were. But the Big 4-0 blindsided me completely, rattling the impeccably organized china cabinet of my world view with mid-level Richter scale reverberations.

Taking the cue like a Nazi soldier my body immediately began to fall apart, behaving like a stranger who for no apparent reason had it in for me. Minor aches and pains once barely noticeable or easily dismissed were now each a painful foreshadowing of a future full of far greater corporeal woes, most of them undiagnosable and impervious to bulk orders of highly toxic prescription medications. And yet the prospect of unspeakable physical anguish paled in comparison to the cosmetic ramifications of that most grievous of birthdays, and rightly so. Indeed, practically every day now it seems, cursed with exceptional eyesight as I am, I'll catch a glimpse of some rapidly mutating part of my body—a fold of flesh hammocking beneath an upper arm, an ear or nasal cavity populated by wiry black or (inestimably worse) downy gray hairs—biological oddities that individually might seem benign but which taken together assume Learning Channel proportions.

Anyway, like I said, in my case the highest-priority calling card of advancing age was an inguinal hernia, the repair of which I had, in all fairness, been putting off for nearly a decade. I first noticed the little mound during early sobriety, back in the mid-1990s when I was still living in "The City" (aka New York), during that unfortunate sliver of time when spandex was in again and I thought I looked good in it (talk about pink clouds), even if I did have to periodically excuse myself and stagger discreetly off somewhere and slip my hand down my pants and push the bulge of intestines and what-not back inside my body so as not to disrupt the sleek lines of my bicycle shorts or cause undo alarm among the overly observant, as people in 12-step recovery programs tend to get, especially once they actually start working the steps. Of course, at that low-budget stage of the game formal medical intervention wasn't an option. Nor would it be until seven years after I finally sobered up enough to become terrified of not having health insurance and bent over for Blue Cross, where any pre-existing condition more serious than dandruff means you may kick the bucket waiting for exclusion periods to expire. Anyway, about five months ago my "procedure" was at last approved. And after some doctor I don't know and received no follow-up from sewed my insides back in I proceeded to fill out a bit, ergo the new leaf.

Grittily determined I heaved myself out of bed yesterday morning, pulled on the baggiest jogging clothes I could find, tucked a $10 bill into my sock, and headed for the great outdoors, dangling before myself the promise of a post-workout triple cap. No need to push it though. So after bursting out onto the sidewalk I downgraded to warm-up walk the three or four blocks to the trail atop the Moonwalk levee and joggled pluckily forth, daring a slowly advancing thunderhead to rain on my parade. No sooner had I crossed the railroad tracks and mounted the levee steps, however, than a cloud roughly the size of Asia started spurting unseasonably cold globules as a vertical wall of water a bit further ahead arched my way. "*Bring it on,*" I snarled, putting my head down and plunging into the maelstrom, recalling an exhilarating beachfront experience I'd had in my thirties and telling myself I was nothing like those fools in *The Perfect Storm.*

Now whereas jogging in downpours may be considered crazy fun when you're in your teens or twenties or even thirtysomething, with half a century breathing down your neck and spoon-sized raindrops laterally battering your body, I think it's fair to say that some basic recategorization is in order. Nevertheless, I persevered for the entire abbreviated version of my pre-surgery run—once rather than twice around Harrah's casino—such that by the time I'd dog-paddled back to St. Philip Street and gushed into CC's I felt entitled. I paused inside the door and inhaled deeply, a willing host to the legion of earthy dark roast spirits grappling for my soul. *Good morning, America!* I mentally bellowed in response to the flickering eyes of a few patrons no doubt awed by my allegiance to holistic well-being as I squelched to the counter—only to find that none of my regular brewmakers were there. Instead, a fierce creature with purple hair and great pendulous breasts unfettered by anything other than an organic cotton T-shirt was planted behind the register, discussing natural childbirth with a liberally pierced and tattooed character who could obviously ill afford (and had almost certainly not been charged for) the $5 latte she was slurping. Far worse, in their absence of basic human decency both parties were either oblivious or indifferent to the fact that they were holding up the entire line, which was me.

Dripping wet, my T-shirt plastered against my goose-pimpled flesh in a way I understand could not have been attractive, I did my best not to appear rude or impatient, merely drumming my fingers atop the pastry case while refusing to succumb to the temptation of so much as a peek inside. And yet the two energetically self-absorbed she-devils, neither of whom could possibly be older than 25, nattered on.

Aware of a tendency in myself to be slightly judgmental and resolving not to be discernibly so, I trained upon them a veiled eagle's eye, quickly assessing that, yes, perhaps they were tight-skinned and full of that come-what-may/devil-may-care/world's-your-oyster defiance of youth. But give it a few years. Sooner or later they'd find themselves, figuratively speaking at least, exactly as I was now: an out-of-shape, caffeine-jonesing, fortysomething nursing an ugly crotch scar. From beneath an arched eyebrow I studied the haughty Amazonian service worker—Inga, her name tag read, how appropriate—and pictured her fifteen years hence: hump-backed and slaving in some coffee shop not nearly this nice, her youthful conviction gone, rushing her tips home to an emotionally abusive lesbian lover who demands the money and roars "That's all?!" before storming out to blow every last cent on brewskies and cigarettes and easily impressed baby dykes who snicker at old Inga behind her back. Inga's present-day umbilical-cord-chewing disciple, meanwhile, will have fared no better, having been mowed down by a Hotard tour bus operating illegally in the Quarter on her way to collect a Lotto windfall, which might have been enough to sustain her indefinitely had it not been for the crippling medical bills that eventually landed her in a state facility on Judge Perez. And what of the illustrated girl's statement-making tattoos then? Well, all I can say is, remember Silly Putty?

While light-hearted musings such as these are in most cases sufficient to keep me entertained at length, without any caffeine in my system I found myself distracted by the aroma of freshly ground beans. And I was on the verge of inserting my selfish needs into the conversation when Susan, one of the assistant managers, emerged from the storage room at the rear end of the service counter. A chin up kind of girl with dish-pan hands and thinning hair, she and I had recently bonded over a quick exchange about Paxil, which I felt she might want to consider since the crystals weren't working.

"Hey, Susan!" I cried. (As in, "Yo! Inga! See who you're ignoring here? Not some Bourbon-Street-or-bust tourist but a *regular*!")

Which is when I ran into a hitch. Because whereas in the past Susan had always given me her undivided attention, even when bluer than blue, today she whizzed right on past, eyes bolted forward, a bucket of soapy water sloshing at her side as she made it from one end of the bar to the other in record time.

Not about to give up that easily, I waited for her to land, then unleashed a wall-to-wall windshield wiper wave.

She blinked, smiled. "Hi, Sammy. How're you?"

"Fine! Really good!"

She nodded, then snatched a sponge out of the bucket and dropped down on all fours behind the counter, going at something only she could see.

Determined to maintain visual contact, I put both hands on the counter and leaned forward. "Where's Catfish?" she was bound to inquire, or "How's the book coming along?" Or perhaps a friendly jab about my new watersports look.

Not a word.

Nevertheless, my ploy had apparently worked to some degree in that Inga's companion was skulking away, with Inga herself observing me with that all too familiar 20-something concoction of defiance cloaked in disinterest, daring me to give her the least bit of attitude.

Not about to afford her that satisfaction, I greeted her cordially. "Grande cap with an extra shot," I then rattled off, using the insider lingo which, in case there was any lingering doubt about my position in the unstated pecking order of the coffee shop universe, was sure to remove it.

She held my gaze a little too long, then punched in my order and nodded toward the LED screen. I fished out the drenched bill and slapped it down. She peeled it off the counter and rendered my change.

"Wet out there?" she said as I made the obligatory tip cup clink.

Not waiting for an answer, she crab-stepped over to the espresso machine…and my heart sank like a rock. For with Carla having apparently overslept again, as she tended to do on the outside, I'd been hoping for the ministrations of Susan, who as a bipolar person understands the equilibrium-related role of caffeine not so much as a beverage as a *raison d'être*. But alas, there Susan still was, scrubbing away, by this time fully prostrate on the honeycomb mat.

"Sir?"

*Her* again.

"Yes?"

"Here or to go?"

"To go," I surrendered as the last bit of hope for a decent cup drained out of me and the amoeba of rainwater surrounding my feet completed an impressive divide. What could this person, young enough to be my daughter were I not far too pragmatic for procreation, possibly know about the finer points of making a cappuccino?

Did she understand that the frothing cup must be cold but the shot glass warm?

Was she awake during orientation as it was explained that at least some milk must be poured into the cup first, so that the freshly pumped shot can be immediately immersed?

Did she get it that it took at least a minute for the foam to separate, following a few hardy taps of the frothing cup?

Yeah right, I concluded with an unintentionally audible snort.

Nevertheless, with the AC raging and my teeth starting to click, I was in no position to quibble. As in, I'd take pretty much whatever Ms. Inga managed to sling my way. Plus I supposed there was still some chance she knew what she was doing. Aiming to increase those odds by whatever means left, I hovered as she pumped, letting her know that I, for one, was paying attention.

Coffee shop workers have an almost metaphysical way of going and coming, appearing from or disappearing into back rooms and bathrooms and side doors leading to dubious destinations. And that's exactly what happened next. For while Susan was all at once no longer visually apparent, suddenly Carla was next to Inga, slicing lemons.

Perhaps all was not lost...

"Hi, Carla!" I enthused.

She stiffened as if a stranger had blown in her ear, then slowly looked up. "Oh. Hey."

And that was that. For whereas on any other day that salutation would have, at bare minimum, been followed with a basic "how are you?", today this was not the case.

Today B. Sammy Singleton was the invisible man.

A big fat wet one.

Then, Inga spoke: "Want that extra shot?"

"I beg your pardon?"

She nodded toward the lonely fourth shot glass of espresso on the drain tray, which is so often tragically discarded in the making of a three-shot drink since most machines can only produce shots in even numbers.

"Sure! Why not!" I panted as my new best friend dumped it into my cup (which by the way she *had* first filled with a dollop of milk) and topped it with a perfect foam. She slipped the cup into an insulator and placed it on the counter.

"Excellent," I commended, dragging the word out in a surfer dude drawl I'm way too old to get away with but you only live once.

I proceeded to the amenities counter for the obligatory two and a half NutraSweets, then test sipped.

Ah! Excellent indeed!

I lifted the cup in salute toward Inga.

By this time, however, the stunningly efficient coffee goddess had gone back to her friend, with me back to being the invisible man.

Or was I?

Because Carla, I now realized, was furtively watching my every move.

Jealous?

Guilty?

I didn't know about her but I certainly hadn't forgotten about that sad little cup she'd pawned off on me a couple days ago, pre-Inga.

And well, like they say, payback's a bitch.

Not that I have a vengeful bone in my body.

Nor was it my fault that Carla just so happened to still be watching when I threw my head back and took a rapturous slug off my quadra-cap and let out a bliss-filled moan, then twirled right back out into the rain, feeling not a day over 25.


Of course that was yesterday and this is today, a day during which the Jennifer Convertible sofa I finally got around to Uhauling down from some storage place in Hoboken a few months after moving to New Orleans is definitely feeling the love. Ever since I woke up I've been lying here on its slightly thigh-burned classic twill so sore I can barely move, unable to fathom that a mere few months without exercise could result in such a vehement muscular protest to such an irreproachably well-intentioned gambit. Further suggesting that I may need to suspend such pursuits until further notice, after strutting home from CC's yesterday morning I found myself so worn out that it was all I could do to drag myself into the shower and scrounge up something to eat before tumbling back into bed. Nevertheless, there I valiantly began to mentally triangulate the first coffee shop review on my list: *The original cup of fresh-roasted premium CC's coffee, which is today roasted, brewed, and served by the Community Coffee Company, was sold out of Henry Norman "Cap" Saurage's country store in 1919. Today, CC's shops are a welcome feature of the Louisiana landscape, from Baton Rouge to New Orleans to Lafayette...*

But slumber swiftly took me. It was therefore noonish and with only that sprig of a start when, as I was once again foraging in the kitchen, somebody rapped on the door.

The silhouette through the curtain was tall and male.

Well, it was about time.

"Hey! Come on in!"

*Rap-rap.* "Hello...?"

I yanked my T-shirt and boxers into presentable form, then opened the door to reveal not Catfish but Naomi's assistant Jay, an actual heterosexual with whom I rarely exchange more than a low-key "hi how're you." We get along well. His hair's straight too, and usually in his eyes. He swept back a lock and blew out a jet of air. "Man, you've *got* to come over there."

"What's up?"

"She won't stop IM-ing me. I haven't gotten anything done all morning."

"But I just…" I gestured toward my kitchen table. Although the array of leftovers was meager, it was well presented. Plus the table itself was impressive: an emerald green faux-marble-Formica-topped 1950s jewel with coordinated chairs that came with the apartment and instantly made this my favorite room.

Not even a blink.

"Alright," I caved. "I'm on my way."


Living in a multi-family home comprising a number of other apartments and tenants has its ups and downs, and as a person not prone to communal living I tally up the plusses and minuses on a regular basis. On the plus side, with my own balcony and run of French doors overlooking a crape-myrtle-filled courtyard, my apartment—one of two second-floor units in the *garçonniere* dependency behind the main house—is both ridiculously charming and the deal of the century. On the minus side, because a central breezeway is the primary point of entry for all of the apartments, the occasional knock on the door by a housemate when you're just so not in the mood is not that unusual. In my present mode of post-workout recuperation, now was one of those times, even if that sentiment did make me a terrible person since, knowing how Naomi tended to fret, I'd neglected to update her since slipping Georgia's blemished automobile back into the driveway Monday afternoon.

I was therefore not sprinting as I entered the breezeway and noticed that the curtains to Georgia's bedroom in the adjacent main house were open, which was unusual.

Was he back?

I slowed to a halt beside the French door. Even though Georgia had been gone much longer than usual this time, I'd barely given his homecoming a second thought since Naomi had reminded me it was imminent last week. Following an especially brutal chemo backlash the week after 9-11, the then eight-months-pregnant Naomi had moved in with Georgia, and since then she'd had everything under control.

I peered discreetly inside.

A cool gray light coverleted the chunky four-poster bed.

Fresh linens.

Lavender hydrangeas.

Yes. The room was immaculate, ready.

But no pill bottles or garment bags.

And like the curtains, the door through to Naomi's front bedroom was open.

I picked up the pace.


Naomi's former apartment on the riverside of the house—now her office—is a reversal of the layout of my flat in that its kitchen is at the back, facing the garden, while its bedroom is at the front, with a window onto the breezeway. On both sides of the rear dependency narrow balconies and multiple pairs of French doors make it possible to enter any one of three rooms. But for both apartments the official entry point is through the kitchen. As I stepped down onto Naomi's balcony I glimpsed her through the door to her former bedroom, which she now calls "the lab" because of the product trials, even though it's still fully functional as a spare bedroom. Ankles in air, a pair of headphones engulfing her ears, she was lying on her tummy at an angle across the bed, banging her laptop with feral gusto, the baby alligator of a loose braid asleep on her back. I proceeded down the hip-width balcony to the former kitchen, which is now an art studio, its doorless cabinets stocked with paint cans and plaster of Paris. In the center of the room was a table equipped with a lazy Susan loaded with crayons and colored pencils, and seated at the table was Naomi's toddler son Dylan.

The soon to be four-year-old looked up as I entered, crayon in hand. "Finally," he said, sweeping back a wheaten strand of almost shoulder-length hair in a conspicuously Jay-like manner.

"I know. Whatcha doing?"

He gestured toward the sketch before him.

I walked over and inspected it, an abstraction of purple stripes inhabited by a lone stick figure.

"Nice."

He nodded and indicated two converging lines. "Guess what that is."

I pursed my lips. "A path?"

"How'd you know?"

"'Cause you're good."

"That's true."

"Where's it going?"

"Huh?"

"The path."

The child resumed drawing. "You'll see."

As I passed through Naomi's converted living room Jay was sitting with his back to me at an iMac nestled among Port of Call cups, manning one of the three desktops docked atop the room-length counter traversing the inner wall. Above the counter was a shelf lined with abstract plexiglass shapes, with a row of wooden plaques on the wall above those—all business awards, and not just local ones either. Founded in 1997 and currently pulling in annual revenues in the six figures, Naomi's Internet business, Touched by the Lord LLC, had been recognized by over a dozen business and philanthropic groups, as well as by a half-page article in *Entrepreneur* magazine subtitled "Shaping The Way Female Consumers Connect Online *And* Off." Slipping quietly past Jay I stopped in the doorway to the lab and watched Naomi in action. Blogging, instant messaging, viral marketing, I marveled. If it could help to sell an esteem-building product to a large woman surfing the Web—from therapeutic devices to cosmetics to sensible fashion accessories—Naomi was all over it, whereas I had only the vaguest idea how any of those "new media" worked no matter how many times she tried to explain it or asserted that social networking had changed her life. Although she'd toned up in the years since we met, she was still essentially proportionate to a mature kangaroo, with calves and hind quarters that nullified any weakness her petite upper half might imply. The marsupial theme continued in her smallish head and inquisitive snout, as well as in the suede fanny pack she never left home without. She spotted my reflection on the monitor and tore off a few additional lines, then slid the headphones off onto the bed without bothering to pause her chat room music of choice, Gregorian chants.

"Sammy!" She maneuvered to the edge of the bed and sat up. "How are you?"

"Okay. Did you see the car?"

"I did. What happened?"

I recapped, offered to deal with it.

She waved me off. "Wow. I am so sorry. What a day, huh?"

"Yeah."

"What about Catfish?"

"What about him?"

"Is he okay?"

"Oh. Yes." Another minimalist recap.

"I still don't understand why they arrested him."

"Neither do I."

"What did Infinity say?"

I grimaced. "I'd hate to be Tucker."

Naomi nodded, frowned. "Are you sure you're alright?"

"Oh yeah. Have you heard from Georgia?"

Her jaw tensed. "Yesterday."

"And?"

She groaned and fell back on the bed. "You know how it goes. It'll be weeks before we know anything."

"But he's still coming home, right?"

She sat up and smoothed the bedspread around her. "Yes, but still no set day. That's what's got me worried. He's still pretty weak. What if he gets stuck at the airport?"

"Why would he get stuck at the airport?"

"Because it's the middle of hurricane season and there are like a zillion tropical depressions out there? What if he gets stranded and his temperature shoots up and there's no one to…"

I plopped down next to her. "*Stop* it."

"I should have gone over there."

"He didn't want you to."

"I know, but…"

"Do you really think all those doctors would let him make the trip if he wasn't up to it? Or that Georgia would take that chance?"

"You're right. Of course. I'm such a worry wart. It's just that now, between Dylan and Georgia…" She leaned into me. "…and *you.*" We sat there a moment, allowing holy music to uplift our spirits with Bose precision.

Then, into my ear, "You're still coming with, right?"

"To the airport?"

Naomi ratcheted up straight. "No, silly. To the Aquarium. This afternoon."

Could I have spaced that out any more thoroughly?

I lunged for a save.


Situated at the Canal Street end of the Moonwalk next to the ferry landing, the Audubon Institute's Aquarium of the Americas is a tile and glass-panel structure whose silvery top has become a distinguishing skyline feature, tilting toward the river like a colossal klieg light. The main attraction is a 400,000-gallon tank containing stingrays and sharks and other marine beasts thriving around the barnacled pilings of a one-quarter-scale offshore oil rig replica. From there, a ramp swoops upward past additional exhibits featuring everything from sea otters to alligators, before opening out into a simulated rainforest on top. Although Dylan has been there no telling how many times, he can't get enough, though unlike so many children his age he is introspective and undemanding. As a result, by the time we were three-quarters of the way up the ramp Naomi and I had had plenty of time to update one another in between introductions to selected creatures Dylan apparently knew well, including a jaunty colony of warm water penguins.

Naomi touched my arm and motioned toward her son, who was a few steps ahead, conversing with a stingray hovering at eye level.

"He sure does love this place," I observed.

"Oh yeah. Thank you, Sammy."

"For what?"

"For coming with."

"Of course. I wanted to."

"Look at him. He's out of his mind."

"He's an amazing kid."

"He certainly is."

Light spilled down the ramp as the rainforest opened out ahead. Dylan pointed. "Look!"

Naomi and I caught up with him and formed a chain in which the child was the center link, his hands in ours.

A hoot owl whooshed across the glass and metal sky as we

entered the rooftop jungle.

"Wow!" I exclaimed.

Dylan nodded and sighed. "I know."


A couple hours at the Aquarium was usually plenty, but on this day Dylan was in no hurry to depart so we opted for pizza on the way down. Like always, the topping was the only part that interested the kid, and after reducing his slice to a soggy white pile he'd been allowed to drift over to the adjacent play zone while I nursed a French Roast and Naomi sipped tea. The mini food court faced the river, and on the other side of the tempered glass panels seagulls balanced and swayed over the water, fuzzy in the light gray summer drizzle. In Dylan's absence the subject had returned to Georgia, whose current hope was an experimental procedure available only in the South of France. In the seven years since he'd been diagnosed, there had been so many treatments in so many places I'd lost track. But Naomi knew the specifics, along with the timeline of remissions and recurrences, which she'd quietly summarized. While speaking, her eyes, like the gulls, had been sweeping the water, and after a period of silence she let out a lip-flapping sigh.

"I promise I wasn't planning this," she said.

"Planning what?"

"But there's no time like the present, right? So I'm just going to say it. If Georgia dies—"

"Whoa! Georgia's not going to die."

"I know but...hear me out?"

I conceded, sipped.

"If Georgia were to die, we—Dylan and I—would need you."

"Of course."

"I'm not saying I'd fall apart. Not at all. I mean, I hope not. But I might…need a little time, you know? Just a few hours here or there to…" She closed her eyes and swallowed, then resumed. "And it would be important for me to know that…"

"You don't even have to ask."

She lay her fingers across my wrist.

"I'm not asking. I just wanted you to know."

"Okay. Sure."

The fingers remained.

So did the eyes.

"What?" I said.

She pressed her lips into a smile.

"*What*?"

She shook her head.

I took the bait. "Is this about Catfish?"

"Sammy…"

"Because like I said, he's fine. I mean, you should have seen him. Anyone else would have been a basket case. But there he was, going on and on and on about racial discrimination. Did you know there are almost a million black people in jail in this country? Plus, I wouldn't be surprised if the D.A. had already…what?"

"Nothing."

"*What*?"

She patted my hand. "I just hope Catfish knows how lucky

he is."

Dylan straggled over, his head hanging almost as low as his hair. Naomi fished a wet nap out of her fanny pack and cleaned his hands. "What is it, Sweety? Was it not fun?"

A mighty sigh. "No...it was fun."

"Then what?"

He shrugged.

"What is it, Honey?"

He hesitated, then ambled over to me. "Sammy?"

"Yes?"

"Could we *please* go see the penguins again?"

That Second "A"

## Friday, August 19, 2005 – Noonish

S ome people go to coffee shops not just for the coffee but to socialize, greeting one another with affectionate-seeming hugs and double kisses, slapping backs and sloshing beverages, dragging chairs over to tables to which they do not belong, where stories and newspapers, hopes and dreams, are publicly aired and shared, where topics of politics, religion, art, and society are explored ad infinitum.

I am not one those people.

In fact, I go to coffee shops for exactly the opposite reason: to be left to my own devices.

Unfortunately, certain individuals can't take a hint.

Lydia and Nigel Slatter are two such individuals, but because they are early birds this generally isn't an issue. Moreover, on the rare occasions that our coffee shop paths do cross I'm prepared. To wit, whenever I see them perched at one of the tables dead center, waiting for weaker or less willful moths than I to fly into their web, I assume a panicky demeanor and shoot past, ostensibly on an urgent trajectory to the washroom in back. Because Lydia has a penchant for pursuit, at such times I pray that the men's room is unoccupied, since otherwise I risk getting buttonholed in the corridor leading back to the kitchen, where I will be condemned to face at close range the unpeeling of lips from teeth that chew up and spit out the inevitable "Heeey, Sammy! Come sit at our table!" Something about the divergent length and angles of those chompers never fails to bring to mind the image of her launching herself at an unsuspecting prey from behind, clamping teeth into shoulder muscle and flapping like a bicycle streamer as her quarry runs shrieking through the French Quarter, whose residents know better than to interfere. As one of the co-owners of Slatter & Glume, the largest and oldest real estate outfit in New Orleans (perhaps best known locally for the tendency of a few of its agents to snap up the deals before they go on the market and either sit on them forever slumlord-style or promptly relist them for double the original price), Lydia is not someone you want to take on. Rumor has it she was born with both a vagina and the hint of a penis, forcing her parents, who already had two males, to make the ultimate choice. Be that as it may, Lydia is one of only two French Quarter property owners capable of slapping a dormer on a Creole cottage without a permit and keeping it there (the other being Infinity). For years Lydia and Nigel have been trying to curry favor with Catfish while salivating over his real estate. And despite their wily attempts to cozy up to me as well, B. Sammy Singleton remains the self-appointed bouncer at the door to a club they might otherwise have weaseled their way into long ago.

I know, even the slightest possibility of spending a morning listening to Lydia gloat over her latest dog park altercation—interspersed with the occasional "Shut up, Nigel!"—should be enough to make me steer clear of CC's altogether. But I'm a caffeine creature of habit and they're usually gone by the time I get there. Besides, as the Marigny has yet to birth a coffee shop in which I feel completely at home, the Royal Street CC's remains my caffeine procurement venue of choice. What's more, I've promised myself that today I'll be making a dent in the book since the past 24 hours were pretty much a wash, in that I spent the better part of yesterday attempting to recover from my ill-fated jog by eating antioxidant-rich bon bons and catnapping on the couch. Demonstrating both the breadth and depth of my commitment I was up and running (so to speak) this morning a good deal earlier than usual, newly resolved to put all Catfish-related matters aside. It was in fact due to my immersion in possible tie-ins with Kafka and Kierkegaard (Kafkappuccino? Kierke-klatch?) that, upon entering CC's a short time ago, my laptop bobbing jauntily in its naugahide case, I failed to spot Lydia and Nigel in time.

Like a bear trap, Lydia sprang. "Heeey, Sammy! Come sit with us!"

In between the early and late morning crowds, the place was about half full, and over papers and coffee cups a few sympathetic eyes flicked my way.

"Hey, Lydia! Hey, Nigel!" I enthused, throwing up a smokescreen of congeniality as I briefly deluded myself that it might still be possible to pull off the throbbing bladder act.

Then the grim reality of the situation began to sink in.

*Oh Sammy!* twittered the choirboy inside my head, *they're not that bad!*

*They are too!* I fired back, almost taking him out.

Lydia advanced.

"Okay!" I surrendered as she was about to enter my space. "Just let me get my fix!"

She flashed me a salacious grin impaled with a thumbs-up, then withdrew as Nigel's head eagerly bobbled.

Carla was on. As I approached the service counter, she shot a glance over the bow of my shoulder, making it clear that she'd witnessed my consummate entrapment.

"Double cap?" she inquired, almost cheerfully.

"Whatever," I said.

I hoisted my elbows onto the bar and rested my chin on my knuckles, then watched as she flew into action with a degree of enthusiasm so uncharacteristic I immediately suspected what was going on. As payback for my hyperbolic praise of Inga's brew the other day, Carla was now delivering me forthwith into the Slatters' clutches à la prison yard, her retribution sadistic and disproportionate and every bit as effective as a patiently whittled shower shiv.

And yet, what could I do?

*Be nice!* chirped the choirboy.

*Can it!* I snarled.

Like twin brains undergoing shock therapy my eyes started to jiggle wildly about. The Slatters' table effectively blocked the Royal Street door I'd come in, and for all I knew the service entrance at the back opened out into some fourth dimensional *Huis Clos* buzzing with Lydias and Nigels. Hurling chairs through picture windows aside, that left only one other possible route of escape, the side door onto St. Philip directly behind me. Still, I never seriously considered flight until—just like that— what I'd typically categorize as barn-bred rudeness transmuted into a cosmic dare when a jovial group of tourists decked out in Mardi Gras beads and joker hats burst through said side door, not bothering to close it after them. In other words, wafting in right behind me was the sweet scent of freedom American-style, which I smelled every bit as intensely as I did the brew Carla was placing before me.

Keeping one eye on the Slatters and the other on the door, I fingered the cup and replaced it with a five-dollar bill while mouthing the words "keep the change" to a now extremely alert Carla, whom I feared might attempt to impede my escape. Instead, however, she discreetly sized up my would-be captors, then jerked her head toward the exit with the taut, breathless expression of a woman who understands what it means to be caged.

"*Ahora!*" she said.

Eyes met.

Souls connected.

Then, like Clint Eastwood in *Escape from Alcatraz*, Sammy flew.

Which is how I ended up back in the Marigny, in this peculiar *endroit* called Zotz, which I didn't even know existed until I ducked in here just moments ago. Located on the corner of Royal and Kerlerec, sharing a piece of prime real estate with a pea green laundromat that's been here forever, this coffee shop sprang up like a fern from a red brick wall. Either that or I'm even more out of it than I thought, since I must have walked this block at least a dozen times in the past few weeks without noticing it. The food-service section of the building, whose *briqueté-entre-poteaux* mode of construction dates it as circa 1830s, has either been carefully restored or remained uncannily intact, retaining such original features as wide plank floors, a brick hearth, and a charmingly narrow flagstone courtyard along one side [USE IN BOOK]. To top it off, the stork-like woman who works here has just the right mix of F-you-very-much New York attitude and southern demureness, making me simultaneously long for The City That Never Sleeps and bless the day I kissed its steely cheek that final goodnight.

Aiming to get to work right away, I ordered a second double cappuccino (having inhaled the first one on the dash over) and positioned myself at the sole window table. Almost the entire way here I'd been glancing down at my shoulder, half expecting to see an elongated Lydia clamped there à la Edvard Munch, a condition to which pain had somehow failed to alert me, perhaps because I'd proceeded directly into shock. By the time I reached Esplanade, however, there was still no sign of her, and as I continued down Royal I began to breathe easier. Like a witch facing running water, Lydia is one of those Quarter dwellers congenitally incapable of crossing Esplanade, the downriver border street that segregates the Quarter from its less illustrious Marigny neighbor. Thus here I sit, typing this morning's events into this sorry excuse for a laptop. Yes, I know. At some point I'll have to face the discordant music of Lydia Slatter, most likely when I least expect it, in some fog-shrouded alley or, even worse, the Royal Street A&P. In a city the size of New Orleans it's impossible to avoid running into those you most wish to avoid, especially when you live south of Canal. But aside from savoring this currently blessed state of Lydialessness, what can I do?

Not a darn thing. As in: *God, grant me the serenity to accept the things I cannot change, courage to change the things I can, and wisdom to know the difference.*

Aka, screw it.

Now: Time to focus.

To get started in earnest on the book.

Or guidebook.

Or whatever.

The thing is, it really did start out as a bonafide book, and now that the soul has been sucked out, it's taking longer than I'd expected to pull together the many themes and subplots and nuances I'd envisioned—and then eliminate them. Poof! Over! Down the toilet. Because no, dear Winnie Hargreaves over at Lucky Dog Press does not, God forbid, want a provocative examination of New Orleans coffee shop culture, infused with an incisive and well-researched analysis of the manifold social, demographic, and psychographic implications of this genuinely fascinating phenomenon, this new American melting pot where people of all ages, races, and incomes (sort of) come together, a mighty saga of great import and implication, one that will keep the denizens of coffee shops everywhere chattering and self-analyzing for years to come ("Oh my God! He's right! *That's* why I spend so much time in this place!").

And so here I sit, saddled with this stunted Winnie vision, this Mission Impossible of the Heart, this gradual insertion of a bamboo shoot beneath the fingernail of all I hold dear, but one I have nevertheless chosen to accept in my desire to "branch out" as a freelance writer, as it were. To free myself from the bondage of having to take on yet another Handy Stats market research report. Which is, by the way, what I've been subsisting on ever since I got sober in New York in 1995. Shortly thereafter, and long before the fog had fully lifted, I promptly quit my job at *Librairie de France*, the French-language bookstore in which I landed a job right after college and managed for over a decade in my drunken quest to win the Most-Going-No-Place-Job-Ever Award.

Truth be told, it's been quite some time since I came up with the core concept of *The Coffee Shop Chronicles*, an exegesis which I still imagine as an ongoing series of socially evocative musings laced with trivia, history, fiction, poetry, and art (pared-down pop-up editions for preschoolers are not out of the question)—combining to create a new-American form of expository prose germinating not in bookstores but in coffee shops across America, with different versions for different cities (*The Coffee Shop Chronicles of New Orleans*, *The Coffee Shop Chronicles of Baltimore*, and so on). Consider this: there are at least 15,000 coffee shops in America, and if each one sold only 10 copies at $14.95, that would be $2,242,500 which—were I to receive only a mere 40 percent royalty (as in, fine with me)—would be $897,000 pour moi, and $1,345,500 for Starbucks, who would publish and distribute the book in partnership with Barnes & Noble, with which the coffee chain just so happens to have a synergistic relationship.

Simple math, in other words.

Starbucks, however, quietly begged to differ. Very quietly. As a matter of fact, I could not even get Mr. Schulz (or anyone else at Starbucks.com) to email me back. And without Starbucks in on it the whole coffee shop marketing venue thing is pretty much shot. So I ended up sharing the concept with a number of literary presses—St. Martin's, Picador, Random House, Knopf— all of which also failed to seize upon the import of what I'm suggesting here since that was 37 months ago and counting and I've yet to hear back a peep, not even one of those sad little rejection slips of the kind that *The New Yorker* clips to doomed poems, or so I have heard.

Anyway, the point is *nobody* seemed to get my idea. Which is how I found myself sitting in Croissant d'Or commiserating with Lyle Bowser, a fellow Western Kentuckian whom I'd serendipitously run into in a New Orleans AA meeting a couple years back. As Winnie's administrative assistant, he suggested I take my proposal to Lucky Dog Press, a magnanimous gesture I suspected had more to do with the petite baguette and fresh-from-the-oven Royal Brioches I'd just plied him with than any heartfelt concern, but so what. *A publisher's a publisher!* the choirboy yelped as Lyle filled me in and I attentively nodded, periodically reminding myself that authentic French-style baked goods don't pay for themselves.

Besides that, I must confess I was struck by LDP's illustrious history, as well as by preconceptions of Winnie that failed to pan out. Founded by her grandfather, Sir Oliver "Lucky Dog" Hargreaves, and located in one of the tallest structures along the riverfront, Lucky Dog Press was during its heyday an up-and-coming literary press. A week into the crash of '29, however, L.D. rolled sideways off a top-floor window ledge. Although the building remained in the family, it never again opened for business until Winnie, riding high on a Wharton Business School award, decided to make a girlhood dream a reality. Backed by her father Burt, a bullish investor with a duplex office suite in Sears Tower, her business plan included not just saving the Hargreaves building from the wrecking ball but (inspired by a rudimentary slide presentation by then Vice President Al Gore) making it energy-efficient, then leasing out the lower floors to earth-friendly businesses to help pay back the loan and subsidize the revival of LDP on the top floor. Equally impressive, she'd

persevered despite a battalion of road blocks thrown up by the
City Planning Commission, thanks to rabid opposition by a
number of City Council members absolutely not in the pocket of
a massive parking lot corporation that had been trying to get its
hands on the Hargreaves building ever since that had begun to
appear inevitable during the Reagan administration.  Putting the
icing on the cake, less than a year into the renovation Winnie had
fallen for her contractor, who upon learning that she was pregnant
had made off with the balance of Burt's investment, forcing her to
dramatically scale back her plans.  Nevertheless, there Winnie the
publishing savior now was.  And as Lyle shared this with me I
envisioned her as a modern day Jeanne d'Arc for whom LDP's
"conveniently pocket-sized guidebooks with fonts large enough
to engage the senior reader" were no more than a stepping stone
into far greater crusades.  Given how much we had in common,
the woman was bound to see things my way.

A few days later, I was reminding myself of this preordained
meeting of the minds as Lyle steered me past modular cubicles
fashioned out of salvaged door panels on our way to Winnie's
office area at the back of the loft.  Despite the maze of worksta-
tions, business didn't exactly appear to be booming.  Aside from
myself and Lyle and the woman I presumed to be Winnie up
ahead, the place was uninhabited.  It was also freezing, the loft's
solar-powered AC unit humming with smug efficiency.  Oh well,
I reassured myself with a shiver, nothing like an introduction by a
fellow Kentuckian to warm things up.

Winnie smiled as I entered, one half of her face pleasant
enough, the other oddly expressionless.  Aside from that, she
looked damn good.  Frightfully fit, in fact.  One of those young
mothers you see loping along behind a baby carriage with bicycle

tire wheels, ponytail bobbing, wearing a Crescent City Classic T-shirt. Quick tally: firm body, rich daddy, own business, at least five years younger than me. I tried not to hate her, finding consolation in the two-inch black roots of her otherwise Lucy-red bob.

"You mush be Sammy," she said.

I hesitated, waiting for Lyle to jump in and do the honors.

Then I realized he was gone.

To make up for lost time, I rattled off my name punctuated by a bizarre bow-like motion.

The publisher took this under consideration, then motioned toward a vintage office chair in front of her bargeboard desk. But for a Dell laptop and a framed photograph of a sweet- but strange-looking little old man, the desk was clear. She waited for me to settle in, then lifted a blood red press-on to her face.

"Bellsh palshy," she explained.

"Ah," I nodded, professional but caring.

"Lyle filled you in?"

Absolutely, I assured her.

"Sowashagot?"

Fingernail tapping atop desktop commenced.

I began to explain.

Fingernail tapping ceased.

"Twenty words or less?" she half-smiled.

Fingernail tapping resumed.

I did my best, still going way over limit.

Winnie mused, still tap-tap-tapping as her good eye ricocheted around like a stray bullet that could wind up anywhere.

Then the finger froze.

"I like it," she said.

"You do?"

"Yes. I do."

"Great!"

"But…" she leaned forward, "we're all about guidebooksh. Shound bites. Rat-a-tat-tat!"

I made a mental note to send a bottle of Jack to Lyle, to whom I'd made it perfectly clear what *I* was about and who'd assured me the pump was primed. "Thank you but no thank you!" I was about to get a great deal of satisfaction out of making known when Winnie flipped open a checkbook and additional commentary ensued, the gist being this: Down Payment.

At which point I realized I'm not a proud person.

Because well, what can I say?

*Down payment.*

I liked the way that sounded.

And my rent was due.


Much as it soon will be again as I sit here at Zotz and the check that has kept me afloat since that first fateful encounter with Winnie almost two months ago dwindles. Rapidly. Making me think maybe I'm not cut out for this after all. Forcing me to consider that perhaps writing reports intended to help companies find ways to sell people things is not just a resumé bullet point but my unexceptional lot. Leading me to wonder whether Catfish—who's been encouraging this whole "branching out" thing from the get-go, and who has dropped out of sight when I need his moral support most—is full of crap.

I just don't know.

One thing I do know is that I won't be getting another red cent until the first draft of *The Coffee Shops of New Orleans* (the audacious title Winnie pulled out of her poncho) lands on her desk. As in, it's time to get cranking, at least if I want to go on living in the manner to which I'd so very much like to become accustomed. Which is what I've been laboring toward since the day I sold Winnie my soul, heading straight home (post check cashing and Rib Room splurge) and spreading out the examples on the kitchen table—*The Restaurants of New Orleans. The Bakeries of New Orleans. The Bars of New Orleans*—and so on. Trying to identify the common denominator that had elevated each one of those to the ranks of LDP's most successful titles. As far as I could determine, however, the only thing they had in common was catalog-style writing, that and the strict protocol of providing the name, address, and phone number of each establishment at the top of its respective page. The only other requirement was that there be 25 reviews, each two pages long. Given the 14-point type, that meant maybe 350 words per, which one would think any hack could crank out while asleep.

I, of course, remain determined to encapsulate within each one of those nuggets not only hours of operation and range of gourmet blends, but a subtle yet incisive look into the spiritual core of each painstakingly selected venue. Perhaps, then, my failure to conclusively launch (not to mention my psychotic swings between gusto and umbrage) stems from the speck of direction Winnie gave me RE writing style.

"Nothing too critical," I believe is how she put it, jabbing her filthy lucre at me.

"Or bitchy," she winked (thanks a lot Lyle), as if I tended to

*The Coffee Shop Chronicles of New Orleans*

be so inclined.

Okay maybe a little, but that's something I've been working on ever since I got sober lo those many years ago. You know, that whole business about not taking other people's inventory and such? Nevertheless, this writing constraint has, it appears, presented something of a stumbling block, since what's the point of a guidebook if it doesn't offer *guidance*, including away from. Let's face it, some of these places are a little bit scary. So shouldn't there be at least a veiled attempt to forewarn the naïve or unsuspecting?

Which brings me to perhaps the biggest question of all: Is it really even criticism if it's true?

(Oh my God, I just sounded like Carrie Bradshaw.)

As in, isn't that what objective reportage is for?

Oh, and by the way, whatever happened to truth in advertising? I mean, what parallel universe do those "Place Called Perfect" people over at Walgreens reside in? I can guarantee you they've never been to the one on the corner of St. Claude and Elysian Fields. As far as I'm concerned, this is a mystery of biblical proportions, right up there with gay Republicans and small business owners appearing in their own commercials.

But I digress.

The point is, as a preacher's kid and basically decent human being, I cannot in good conscience join the Big Fat Liars Club, even if it means no first draft check. Or for that matter, no publisher. Even if it means picking through cartons of rotten fruit at the end of Marigny Street after the wholesale produce hub closes as the undocumented workers being whisked back to Lowe's look on from the beds of rusty pick-ups, rethinking their own American dream.

That's right. I can't and I won't.

Which is why I have in these last few weeks, in a process superficially akin to procrastination but which is actually the furthest thing from it, devised what I believe to be a possible route around such duplicity, a system for circumventing the creative vacuum that is Winnie Hargreaves. That being this: In compiling my research and making notes, I have resolved to tell the unvarnished truth about each place I visit, calling it as I see it. I can always tone it down in the actual draft. And then if Winnie doesn't like that version either she can do what she is presumably, as not just my publisher but also my editor, getting paid to do. It's her karma. In the meantime, the way I see it, my job is, plain and simple, to tell the truth, the whole truth, and nothing but the truth, letting the chips fall where they may.

Starting right now.

With this place.

No holds barred.

Hm. Perhaps because this latest double cap has yet to kick in, my immediate surroundings are beginning to look considerably less charming. Because while I suppose somebody should get maybe a "B" for effort, the fact remains that that person clearly is not a gay man or, if so, not in any meaningful way. The repurposing of discarded automotive bench seats as interior seating is a dead giveaway.

Oh, and will somebody please tell me, what is this thing floating in a saucer on my very own table? Although I'd initially dismissed the business as something to be bussed, a few minutes ago the stork lady popped over and sprinkled it with Miracle-Gro, so my best guess now is that it's some kind of organism, one with sinister-looking appendages trailing down into grayish water.

And yet I'm far from sure.

A lily pad derivation from which some manner of bloom is projected to sprout?

An addle-brained invertebrate deformed beyond recognition prior to birth?

Do I really even care?

Of course not!  Just get it the hell off my table!

(please?)

Which brings us to Rule No. 1 of coffee shop/foodservice protocol [CONSIDER ADDENDA]:  Never place any not immediately identifiable ornamental article on any table from which food or drink is to be consumed.

Although believe you me that's just the beginning as far as this place goes, oh yes indeedy.  For as I take an even more penetrating gander I find myself literally surrounded by decorative expressions that are stunning as long as they're giddily pondered (oh the joy of creativity!) and then summarily discarded, having shattered to pieces under even the gentlest pressure of elemental good taste.

Where to begin?

Okay.  How about that row of shelves over there by the door, sagging with books, which a notecard identifies as "Lending Library!"  Fine in theory, except in a place like this everyone knows that sign really should read "Next Stop, Dumpster," especially after a quick run through the titles reveals that somebody did a lot of budget traveling before Shirley MacLaine turned to channeling and sudoku caught on.

*The Coffee Shop Chronicles of New Orleans*

Next: A host of plastic dolls indiscriminately integrated into the décor. Because while I suppose there's something "New Orleans" about dolls, in this case we're not talking about anything as interesting as the Anne Rice collection or Mardi Gras king cake babies (the latter of which are additionally thought-provoking in that people occasionally choke to death on them). Nor is there anything even remotely attractive about the dolls now under consideration. No, these are nothing more than poor-quality cast-offs that never should have been mass-produced in the first place, with missing limbs and crayoned faces and torn-out hair, the kind passed over by desperately poor children in thrift stores. Apparently somebody dropped a tab of acid, made a run on Thrift City, raided the kindergarten supplies aisle at Wal-Mart, and went to work on these babes in a way that would do Timothy Leary proud, nailing them to the walls in a final manic burst of adrenalin before lapsing into unconsciousness.

Naturally the unfortunate Chuckie theme extends into the bathroom, which I had cause to visit a few minutes ago. There, the glossy black tub/shower combo made it clear that this place once was (and perhaps still is) somebody's home. But the arts and crafts paled in comparison to what likely also occurred before the windowpane wore off, this being the conversion of the tub portion of the shower unit into, hm…I'm not really sure. Some kind of pond, or aquarium?

Whatever the case, this I failed to perceive until after I'd thoroughly lined the toilet seat and sat down like a gentleman so as not to dribble. So with the side of the tub almost touching my thigh, there I was, doing my best to evade the baby doll art when I glanced over and realized I wasn't alone. Rather, staring up at me from those briny fiberglass depths were several enormous yet starved-looking goldfish, their panic-stricken eyes watching my every move, their pale lips burbling what could only be interpreted as a last-ditch SOS. *Kill us! Kill us!* they seemed to implore, causing my bladder to clamp back as images from the movie *Born Free* threatened to overwhelm me. In a half swoon, I looked from the fish to the water between my knees, suspecting that the sewer pipe I was capping let out in a much better place but unable to bring myself to it. Instead, I buttoned up and careened back to my table, the only flushing being that of my face with shame.

Now, as I sit here attempting to process these manifold traumas via the written word, my weary eyes take in one final blow to elementary good taste, one that's...

Damn! Low Battery Alarm.

(and of course no charger with me...)

Oh how I hate this crappy laptop.

Oh well. Time to wrap it up anyway, I suppose.

Besides, I suddenly find myself feeling mildly depressed, the end result, I suspect, of having taken so thorough an inventory, which despite concerted efforts to the contrary remains an art form for me, one that embraces both the vagaries of human beings and the places in which they dwell. Off the record, though? Appearances do matter. And I'll be the first to tell you that one of the top ten reasons I stopped going to AA in New Orleans was because I felt personally insulted by the décor in the meeting room, which included a carpet that could have been sectioned and sold off as nicotine patches, not to mention the cigarette smoke itself, me being an enlightened ex-smoker and all. Then of course there was also the never-ending guilt over not wanting to mingle, even though I've never been much of a joiner. No doubt, I'd been spoiled rotten by AA Manhattan-style, where the second "A" really does mean something, abetted by the sheer number of meetings (hundreds if not thousands each week) and the natural aloofness of those still clinging to the specialness of their area codes. On the other hand, in the South, AA meetings are more like church potlucks at which you're obliged to sample and love every dish. Perhaps not surprisingly therefore, after three years of almost daily meetings in New York, within a few months of moving to New Orleans I began to taper off, first to a meeting every other day, then to a few times a week, then to once a week and so on and so on. Which if not explicitly recommended seemed at least defensible given that other AA saying: "A bridge back to life."

No one could have been more surprised than I, therefore, when almost two years ago, on the morning of my 8th sober anniversary, I found myself missing it all: the meetings and the people, the certainty of being on the right path even though you have no idea where you're going, the relief of knowing you're no longer alone. After quite a few months without setting foot in a meeting, I hadn't even remembered that it *was* my anniversary until I sat down at the kitchen table with my second bowl of Frosted Flakes, opened my laptop, and saw the date pop up. And even then it didn't instantly register. By that time it had been ages since I'd made a big deal out of my anniversary, so much so that I'd almost forgotten the excitement of those first few sober years, when each new day was cause for celebration, each anniversary a miracle well worthy of being shared during the day's meeting, triggering applause and back slaps followed by lunches with sponsors. So, after a few heartbeats of squinting at the computer, I jumped up and dug around until I found a small book I'd picked up not long after getting sober, a book called *Touch-stones*. Inside the front cover, I was pretty sure, I'd written down the date of my anniversary. And, sure enough, there it was: *August 26, 1995*. The day my world changed forever.

Or had it?

Because eight years later, there *I* was. Still addicted to high-carb foods. Still counting on the cash in my parents' Christmas cards to help pay off credit card binges on eBay items that always seemed infinitely more desirable before they were mine. And yes, still alone, and seeming to mind that less and less. I was also the same number of years older as I was sober and far more set in my ways, making the prospect of a Significant Other seem even further away than it had been when I was drinking, when the range of possibilities—unrestricted by such technicalities as Dysfunctional, Codependent, Unavailable, etc.—was a good deal broader. As for friends, I could count those on the fingers of one hand, including Catfish (who at the time I hadn't spoken to in almost two weeks due to a spat that had yet to blow over) and, stretching the definition a bit, Naomi and Georgia. As for my sober "friends" in New York, within a year of my defection to New Orleans they'd apparently lost my phone number as re-morselessly as I had theirs. Even my cat Rowan had decided she'd rather take her chances as a scavenging outdoor orphan than reside under the same roof with me. So while certain positive changes had been made—such as letting go of a city I was never cut out for and nailing an indisputably cool apartment in an indisputably cool town—in the larger scheme of things, what, really, had changed?

With this in mind there was, I concluded, only one thing to

do: Go to a meeting and share my experience, strength, and hope by announcing my anniversary.

Unlike the cornucopia of options in New York, New Orleans has but one gay meeting spot, which is located in a pleasantly retro but heartbreakingly unoptimized building three blocks from chez moi, on the corner of Frenchman and Decatur across from the fire station. And during my first year or so in New Orleans, it was there that I'd attempted to matriculate, attending the 12:30 Mid-Day Meeting often enough to be considered a member, I suppose. The last two or three times I'd dropped by in the past year or so, however, the turn-over had been complete, with not a single familiar face remaining, which despite the implications had been a relief. Equally welcome in terms of flux, congruent with the group's belated adoption of a no-smoking policy, the carpet had been eliminated and the hardwood floor buffed to a sheen. And I now saw myself with an unobstructed birds-eye view, reflected in that oaken luster as I stuck up my hand and all heads turned. *Who's that*? everyone's understandably frantic to know about the exotic stranger fate has gusted into their midst like a wondrously out-of-season autumn leaf, not quite daring to hope that he's both sober *and* single.

Determined to bring myself in line with that vision, I sprang up from the kitchen table and pounded into the bedroom. Due to my routine (aka late) morning start, I had maybe ten minutes to groom myself for the meeting. But I made wise use of it, donning my baggiest khakis and fashionably wrinkled linen shirt en route to the bathroom, where I mussed up my hair and bared my teeth in front of the mirror, going for all windswept and courageous, like Ralph Fiennes in *The English Patient*, before the accident.

When it comes to attending 12-step meetings, strategic positioning is of the essence, and all the more so for the seasoned. The key is to get there early (but not too early, which can seem sad) and casually settle into the perfect seat, not too close to the front (teacher's pet-ish) but not all the way in the back either (arrogant or indigent).  When it comes to announcing sober anniversaries (as they are called in New York) or birthdays (as they are called in the South, whatever), things can get tricky, however.  Not all meetings call for the celebratory show of hands at the same time.  And if you miss that window then the only other chance is after the speaker or topic discussion is finished, by raising your hand and maybe or maybe not getting called on to share (which even if you do tends to comes across as bragging when you have as much time as I do).  Fortunately, on this day such risky maneuvers—which are decidedly not my style—were not at issue.  I'd attended the Mid-Day Meeting regularly upon moving to New Orleans, so I knew that anniversaries were announced at the beginning.  And after considering but sagely rejecting the inclusion of a red paisley neckerchief in my ensemble I rushed out into the noon-day heat, assuring myself that a few beads of sweat on my brow would only enhance the desired effect and paying no heed to a not-so-distant crack of thunder.

Expecting to be initially sighted by the usual group of smokers huddled out front until the bitter end, I plowed across Elysian Fields and tracked the iron fence of the block-sized parking lot to Frenchmen.  When I rounded the corner, however, the sidewalk was empty.  And when I stepped inside the building the L-shaped common room was similarly deserted.

Even more alarmingly, the door to the meeting room was shut.

I crossed the foyer and stopped in front of the sheet of paper taped to the door:

### Shhh…Noon Meeting in Progress!!!

At which point I remembered, there's no such thing as a Mid-Day Meeting, at least not here.

Somebody tapped my shoulder.

A deeply tanned man with a wreath of well-tended hair and a frayed Big Book had slipped up on me.

He nodded toward the door. "You going in, Baby?"

"Oh…um…" I bartered for time with a timid smile.

He lifted an eyebrow.

Then a wave of misunderstanding washed over him. "Ohhh…" he cooed with equal parts reverence and delight. "First meeting?"

I hesitated, then confirmed.

He nodded solemnly. "Welcome."

I squinched up my face, which was beginning to burn.

"Is there a bathroom here?" I inquired, knowing full well there was.

He pointed across the lobby. "Sure, Baby. Right back there."

I'm not sure how long I stood in front of the urinal to which I had nothing to contribute, looking at the caramel-colored grout between the tiles and wondering how long the man would wait before abandoning the "newcomer" and going on in, but by the time I came out he was gone. Alone in the lobby next to the institutional coffee pot, I counted the cups hanging above the serving table, some of them personalized with first names, trying to talk myself into attending the meeting anyway. So what if I'd just been less than rigorously honest? So what if the anniversaries had already been announced? So what if it seemed like I was bragging? "Progress, not perfection," my Rumpelstiltskin-like sponsor had pounded into me during those first few months of sobriety so many years ago, along with such other rules of the road as "what other people think of you is none of your business." But as I stood there counting those cups I knew that, for me at least, it most certainly still was. And just as none of those cups belonged to me, neither did I belong among the people inside that room, who unlike me had shown up not only to not be alone, but because they wanted to get better. At least that's how it felt to me, the would-be prodigal son. And so instead of claiming my hard-earned place in that room, I tiptoed across the common area and back outside, where about halfway home, in one of life's rare instances of perfect timing, the thunderstorm swept over me full force.

So there you have it, my last AA "meeting" in the Big Easy. For it was then that I decided I'd piggybacked long enough on the truly committed, and that, for better or worse, it was time to hit that Broad Highway of sobriety on my own steam. Because whatever experience, strength, and hope I might have cobbled together during those eight years, I was still me.

Now, as I sit here in this place I've just obliterated in torrid violation of more than one 12-step precept something else comes to mind: that despite its failure to align with my idea of what a coffee shop should be in terms of wall treatments and ASPCA objectives, I like it here.

A lot.

The cozy maximum capacity of seven tiny tables, two of

which are inhabited by additional patrons who have yet to so much as glance my way.

The way the stork lady ignores me.

The near certitude that no one I know will happen in (compounded by the advent of a light summer squall).

And yes, even the décor, whose eye-popping audacity ups even further the odds that B. Sammy Singleton shall go unnoticed and unmolested.

That second "A" perfectly realized, in other words.

Hm. I wonder if this place serves food.

# These Old Hands

## Sunday, August 21, 2005 – 7:18 p.m.

A productive weekend, even though it didn't start out that way. Friday afternoon post Zotz, I retreated to my apartment and overindulged in a Verti Marte smorgasbord of hot foods and Häagen Dazs, then promptly passed out on my living room sofa. My apartment is, by the way, conducive to that, since despite the crooked doors and floorboard gaps that come with any house this old, there's something womb-like about my three rooms plus bath, kept toasty in the winter by antique gas floor heaters with patterned ceramic grates that shimmer orange and blue, and cool in the summer by the disco-era but still ultra effective Friedrich AC framed into my bedroom wall, which at times seems to be breathing on my behalf, cycling up and down every so often. Nevertheless, I did not feel revitalized by the time I came to on Friday. And as I lay there listening to the rain pattering down outside I was taken back to another drizzly evening chez moi.

I'd been living in New Orleans less than six months, and in that short span Catfish and I had become thick as thieves, with a weekly routine that included getting together two or three times a week at CC's, on top of the endless hours spent hanging out in his Chartres Street shop. We'd also have a movie night at least once a weekend, and on that evening he was sprawled across the sofa waiting for the show to begin. Because the conversation was sprightly and another *Roots* marathon wasn't high on my list, however, I'd been putting off making the popcorn for over an hour. I therefore had no one to blame but myself when, following a regrettable digression into college days themes, I found myself, at Catfish's behest, in the center of the room behind an imaginary podium, holding a college notebook full of Chianti-inspired scribbles.

"Gray," I grumbled.

Catfish beamed his encouragement from the sofa, now fully alert and upright.

I rolled my eyes. Then, reciting quickly:

> *The sky is gray*
> *beyond my pane*
> *and in my heart*
> *the mist rolls in.*
>
> *Tomorrow may bring*
> *blue sky outside*
> *the sun may shine,*
> *but not within.*

Catfish shook his head. "Uh-uh. Slower."

"Oh come *on*."

He crossed his arms.

I grimly obliged, then waited, prepared to accept the obligatory "it's good!" and welcome Kunta Kinte with open arms. Without saying a word, however, Catfish rose and crossed to the

French door and swept back the curtain. Outside, a light rain advanced the slow disintegration of Georgia's courtyard bricks.

"Whadja think?" I finally said when he continued to face away, not because I craved commentary but because the silence was brutal.

He turned and started to say something but stopped, as if he'd just witnessed an event bigger than words, like a flock of green parrots against my dismal gray sky.

"What?"

"It's beautiful."

"It's depressing."

"No it's not. It's…real."

"I certainly hope not."

"It is. It's…"

He held my eyes a moment, then turned abruptly back toward the door.

"What?"

He shook his head, shrugged.

Mist-muffled church bells started to clang. I'd counted seven when he spun back around, his cheeks rigid and pale. "Damn!" he muttered.

"What is it?"

He snatched his jacket off the sofa and headed for the door. "I forgot something."

"What?"

"A Foundation thing," he called over his shoulder. "I'm sorry, B. Catch you later?"

## Chapter 4

Well, enough of *that.* I hauled myself up off the couch and carted a small landfill of Verti Marte styrofoam into the kitchen and, after salvaging a few scraps, dumped it in the trash. On the wall over the can was a vintage wall phone complete with rotary dial, and on the woodwork next to that an asymmetrical Post-It quilt of cell phone numbers, all belonging to Catfish. Unlike myself, he's one of the billions worldwide who have no reservations about spiral cell cancer of the jaw, although in keeping with his manic penchant he's far more on-again/off-again in terms of mobile phone usage than most. One week, he'll have one of the things glued to his cheek, while the next he'll neither know nor give a rip where he put it down. Not that I'm in a position to throw stones. At the opposite end of the extreme, I have a principled aversion to phones, which I feel should be used only when all other modes of communication, including smoke signals and séances and messages in bottles, have been exhausted. For purposes of Internet access I do at least have a land line, however, whereas Catfish has not had a real phone since he closed down his shop on Decatur a couple months back. Regardless, between his quirks and mine, the way we've most often connected during our tenure as friends has been by his showing up either at CC's, where he can be reasonably sure to find me mid-morning, or at my apartment, to which he has his own key. Nevertheless, coinciding with the death in mid-March of his grandfather, Constantine Beaucoeur, Catfish got a new cell phone and gave me the number. And following a complex process of elimination it was this number that I called, several times, only to be tossed directly into voice mail with each attempt. So I dialed all of his old cell phone numbers as well. Also straight to voice mail, or no longer in service. Leaving me with only one other rotary dial option.

For as long as I've known him, Catfish has been living in the Faubourg Tremé, in one of the approximately dozen derelict homes he inherited from his father, Frederick Beaucoeur. Upon Frederick's sudden death in 1992, Catfish also came into a pile of cash with which he formed the Beaucoeur Foundation, whose initiatives included the restoration of said houses into low-income housing for African-American families, with Catfish overseeing the renovations and Infinity handling the legal and administrative logistics. The exception is the two-story Greek Revival Catfish kept for himself, which he has yet to fix up beyond a few vital repairs. As a result, during those times when he's been shopless or cell phone impaired, I've on occasion been able to connect with him by dialing the pay phone on the corner of his block, which can be heard ringing from inside the house thanks to a few missing pieces of siding. When I tried Friday night, however, nobody answered, not even one of the neighborhood urchins who has picked up in the past. Instead, the phone just kept on ringing and ringing. And as it did I imagined Catfish in the celestial blackness of some distant planet, sitting on the cold ground next to the phone, hearing it ringing and knowing it's me but for some reason choosing to not respond.

Which was ridiculous.

Far more likely was that the phone was out of order, or not there anymore.

Nevertheless, for the better part of an hour I kept trying with no better luck, the extra long phone cord looping from kitchen to living room to bedroom before reeling me back. The next logical step, it occurred to me, was to go by the house to see if Catfish was holed up there. It wouldn't be the first time, nor would it be unlikely given what he'd recently been through. And I wasn't just talking about a few nights in jail either. In choosing to call Tess he'd once again—and this was what really irked me—set himself up to be let down by his mother, with whom he'd had no contact (as far as I knew) since shortly after Constantine's funeral. In commemoration, there had been a Mass for the senior Beaucoeur at St. Louis Cathedral followed by a reception at Gallatoire's, during which Tess and Catfish had (to the shock of many including yours truly) appeared almost chummy, and a few days after that there had been an equally uncharacteristic mother and son lunch. With no warning to me or anyone else, however, Catfish had then dropped out of sight for almost a week, not even bothering to get anyone to cover for him at the shop. Prior to that lunch date, Catfish had been at his most feisty and upbeat, while immediately thereafter he'd be as upset (and as drunk) as I'd ever seen him. It wasn't hard to put two and two together, in other words. But when I attempted to connect those dots during a tense pay phone call he cut me off. What's more, while Tess had never been a topic he cared to dwell on, in this case he didn't just dodge the issue as he usually did. Instead, with an imperiousness I'd witnessed many times but never before full frontal, he'd slammed the door on the subject.

Now, as I stood there finding no cheer in the kitchen phone's classic black case, it killed me to think of him all alone in that decrepit old house of his. Nevertheless, I was still a few stops short of going over there, since the Faubourg Tremé is not a place in which pasty white-skinned persons like myself tend to feel welcome. As a matter of fact, I couldn't recall ever venturing into that neck of the woods without Catfish, who though even paler than I seems to be on a first-name basis with everyone between St. Claude and Claiborne.

Still standing in front of the telephone, I put the thought on hold and released the receiver cradle, then dialed the only number I knew by heart.

Several rings, then a mildly garbled hello.

"Mary Agnes?"

"Sammy? Is that you? I was just thinking about you!"

"Really?" I resumed pacing, drifting into the living room en route to the bedroom.

"Uh-huh. While I was gargling. That's why it took me so long to get to the phone. How are you?"

"I'm fine, Mom. How are you?"

Tiny pause. "Okay."

"What's wrong?"

"Oh, nothing."

"Mother..."

"I don't want to worry you, Hon."

"What's the matter?"

"Nothing's the *matter*. It's just that, well...I have this place on my head."

I reached the end of the cord. "A place?"

"Uh-huh."

"What kind of place?"

"I'm not sure what to call it. A scab, I guess."

"Oh. Does it hurt?"

"Not really. But it's pretty big."

"How big?"

"I don't know. It's in the darnedest place. Right on the back of my head. So I can't actually see it. But it sure *feels* big."

"*How* big?"

"Hold on. Um…about the size of a quarter? No, wait…maybe only a nickel."

"You should have that looked at."

"That's what Barbara said."

"Who's Barbara?"

"The woman who does my hair. She has such a hard time. Her husband's in a wheelchair. Anyway, I was there yesterday and she was worried about the chemicals. I had to practically beg her to put a little color on."

I shuffled back toward the kitchen. "Well, it's probably nothing but you should definitely make an appointment."

Sigh.

"What?"

"I hate to bother Dr. Crumly. He's always so busy."

"*Mother*. He's not doing you a favor. He's your doctor. And you're 77."

"I know but the last time I was there he snapped at me."

"What do you mean he snapped at you?"

"I don't know. He just got sort of…impatient."

"About what?"

"I don't remember. Oh! Yes I do. Right as he was about to walk out—and let me tell you he hadn't been there five minutes—I brought up the pains."

"The chest pains? You're still having those?"

"There you go."

"Are you?"

"Rarely."

I slid down onto a kitchen chair. "What did he say?"

"Who? Oh. Not much. You know, I really don't think he knows."

"Do you want me to call him?"

"Oh no. Please, Sammy. Not again. Remember what happened last time?"

"Yeah. They got you in right away."

"Yes, but they weren't happy about it. Let's not talk about this anymore."

"Okay. But promise me you'll get it looked at?"

"Okay."

"Soon?"

"Alright. But for goodness sakes, how are *you*?"

"Good."

"What's wrong?"

"Nothing."

"Are you sure?"

"Yes. Everything's fine."

"Are you still working on that book or whatever it is?"

I wound my finger into the cord. "Uh-huh."

"Not too hard, I hope."

"No…it's coming along."

"That's wonderful. How's Bobcat?"

"Catfish."

"Yes. How is he?"

"Fine."

"You're still friends, aren't you?"

"Of course."

"Well that's good.  You know I really do like him.  He's so well mannered.  And that meal he treated us to was just out of this world.  What was the name of that place?  The Queen's something?"

"The Palace Café."  Something roared in the background.  "Mom?"

"I'm here.  Have you spoken to your father lately?"  Since the divorce in mid-1998, the question had become standard issue.

"Um…not really."

"Well you should call him."

"I will."

"I mean it, Sam.  He's your father."

"I know.  I will."

Another roar on her end, this one even louder than before.

I sprang up from the chair.  "What was that?"

"What was what?"

"That noise."

"Oh.  Just the television.  There's a game coming on.  But I can still talk."

"That's okay.  I need to get going anyway.  Basketball?  Mom?"

"What?  No, baseball.  Basketball's a winter game.  You should know that, Son."  Another roar from the tube.

"Mom?  *Hello*?"

"What?"

"I have to go.  I'll call again soon."

"Huh? Oh. Well I just hate that. Well…alright."

"Love you, Mom."

"Love you too."


Saturday didn't dawn any brighter. To the contrary, in direct violation of an earlier resolution I woke up with one of the worst eBay hangovers I'd had in some time. I know, scouting out wee-hour auctions and swooping in with a few bids at the last minute with no aim other than to drive up the price is not a very sober thing to do. It's also something I thought I'd weaned myself off, and not just on ethical grounds. Like accepting phone calls from the DNC, eBay is a budgetary minefield. Look no further than all the stuff around here I don't need or even like that much, such as an extensive collection of aluminum coasters with matching tumblers, not to mention all this damn Tupperware. As penance, I dragged myself out of bed well before noon, hell-bent on buckling down on the book. According to the Post-It on my fridge, the deadline clock was ticking, and a well-chosen change in venue promised to prod things along.

The newest trendy coffee-drinking establishment in the French Quarter—about which I took copious notes for over an hour—is Café Envie, which is located at the intersection of Barracks and Decatur, at the beginning of the Decatur Street antiques strip. Occupying the ground floor of a corner townhouse renovated recently at enormous expense, Envie's layout is similar to that of the Royal Street CC's. However, vis-à-vis most other coffee shops a key differentiator here is a liquor license, which makes it possible for patrons to get, in true New Orleans style, both revved up and sloshed in a single sitting. Although the liquor thing would normally be enough to keep me away (not because I'm sober but because I'm a purist who feels that booze in a coffee shop is anachronistic, even though coffee in a bar is fine since it no doubt helps to avert the occasional multi-vehicle pile-up), the décor of Envie is so alluring that I occasionally find myself cheating on CC's. Since Envie is also several blocks closer to home, that defection might happen a good deal more often were it not for one thing: CC's has a no-smoking policy, whereas the general attitude inside Envie seems to be *carpe mortem*, with a token smoking section at the front of the shop that's in no way segregated from the rest of the place (which is not uncommon in New Orleans restaurants and other public places, where smoking is still permitted even though it's common knowledge that second-hand smoke kills old people and infants).

Smoke aside, Envie is a giant step up from what was here before, a divey bodega I sincerely tried to like because it was owned and operated by gender-bending individuals with haphazardly penciled-on eyebrows and nerves of steel, but which I eventually gave up on because it was always woefully understocked and, how shall I put this, trashy as hell. Also, aside from the smoke, the only other thing about Envie that I can think of that isn't optimal is the grunge bunch that started hogging the marble-top bistro tables out front right after the place opened, something I seriously doubt the owner had in mind when he was exhausting his retirement fund but which nevertheless lends a certain air of expectancy since it seems like only a matter of time before he shows up with a baseball bat and the blue hair and nose rings start a flyin'. Not that that's something I'd enjoy seeing, although had it actually occurred around noon yesterday I would have seen it. Because by then I was sitting smack dab in the middle of the smoking section—the only place I could find an outlet for my laptop, whose "long-life" battery is good for maybe an hour.

So there I was, making all these great notes, when the metal garage door to the shop across the street—The Warehouse—clattered up and I saw Armando, its olive-skinned owner, stooped over clutching his lower back. Given the accident he was in a few years ago, during which major sections of his torso were crushed by an eighteen-wheeler, followed by any number of botched reconstructive surgeries, you'd think he'd know better. But never underestimate the power of Vicodin, and as far as Armando goes there's been no shortage of that. Correspondingly, by late afternoon there are always a few people milling about the place "helping out," looking extremely relaxed and practically giving things away. I've even seen John Waters nodding off in one of the plantation rockers or fifties garden gliders on the sidewalk out front, amidst the various "sale items" dreamily dragged out during the course of the day. Aside from a junktique jumble consisting of everything from paint-by-numbers artwork to exquisite bronze figurines, about half of the shop is devoted to what Armando calls "vintage clothing," although much of it is suspiciously pristine, as if it just rolled off the line at one of those sweat shops in the Mariana Islands whose operators are, according to Tom DeLay (R-Texas), "a shining light for what is happening to the Republican Party." In addition to the predictable Mardi Gras slant of old costumes and masks and headdresses and such, there's also a distinct military flair to much of the apparel—army helmets and soldier uniforms and billy clubs and so forth—reflecting a certain predilection not uncommon among people who, like Armando, put down roots in the Bywater.

During the past year I've had time to observe, because up

until two months ago Catfish's shop was right next door. Almost immediately after closing down on Chartres in mid-2003, he began to regret it, because that was also when his Foundation activities (and funding) began to wind down. When Catfish opened up next door to The Warehouse last summer, Armando was barely mobile due to multiple classifications of neurological mayhem. As a result, Catfish and I both did our best to help take his mind off things by popping over to chat as he lay there at the edge of the sidewalk, on the Louis Quinze daybed that was the locus of his recovery. "Tell me about it," he'd mumble at appropriate intervals, borderline comatose but still focused enough to avoid using words with an "s" in them around cuties, since when he does they come out sibilantly and he says he's a top. And while this didn't mean we were exactly friends, it was certainly possible that Catfish might have happened by during the past few days, or that the Decatur Street grapevine might have otherwise picked up on him.

Those were, at least, the assumptions under which I was operating when I stumbled out of Envie gasping for oxygen, although the air wasn't much better outside. It was one of those mid-August New Orleans days in which the atmosphere seems to have jelled, making walking feel like underwater labor as I crossed the street, the breathy calliope notes of the Creole Queen darting about me like colored fish.

The Warehouse is a cavernous place that really did used to be a warehouse, with girders and grimy skylights overhead, and as I entered Armando was about halfway back in the place. I spouted a greeting, then paused to inspect the latest apparel shipment, a tableful of white sailor pants sporting large and practical-looking flaps. Receiving no response, I repeated the salutation and penetrated deeper.

Still, Armando didn't look up, even though this time I knew he had to have heard me since we were the only ones there and he had yet to start playing that damn Gal Costa CD. I stopped next to where he was standing and waited for him to finish gnawing the price tag off something he'd changed his mind about.

"Hey," he mumbled, "What's up?"

"Not a lot. How you doing?"

"Fine."

"You look good."

He squinted. "I do?"

"Yes. Well, all things considered."

"The goddamn pins are killing me."

"I bet. Have you seen Catfish?"

"I thought he was in jail."

"No. He got out. On Monday."

"Are you sure?"

"Pretty sure. I picked him up."

"Well, I haven't seen him in like a really really really long time. Not since he closed down next door."

"Yes you have. Two weeks ago? When we were packing up the shop?"

"Oh. That's true. I can't believe it took him that long to empty the place out. Do you know how much the rent is over there?"

I shrugged.

"A butt-load. Oh! That reminds me, is he still having the auction?"

"Uh…I have no idea."

"Because if he ends up going to prison it would be a shame for all that cool stuff to just…"

"He's not going to prison."

"Oh. Okay."

"Why would he?"

"I don't know. Look what happened to Patout."

"This is nothing like that."

"Well, it sort of is. I mean, they did find those things at his warehouse."

"Yes but he had no idea they were there."

"Yeah, but…" he smugly trailed off.

"What?"

He shrugged. "Rich people are different."

"Oh. So you think Catfish is a criminal."

"I'm not saying that."

"Good luck with the pins."

"Wait…"

But I was out of there.

And lucky for him, too. Because fiberglass vertebrae or no, that kind of talk was unforgivable. Especially after all Catfish had done for Armando, including paying *his* rent for more months than Catfish would cop to.

Of course, I'd never really trusted the man anyway, at least not since I spotted him holding that Swift Boat book. But given the content of the innumerable chit-chats he and Catfish and I had had since Catfish was first implicated, there was no way to conclude that Catfish was anything other than innocent. First of all, he said he was, which was good enough for me and should have been for Armando. But there was also "the evidence"—which even *The Times-Picayune* had taken to putting air quotes around. True, they'd found a few broken funerary artifacts behind Catfish's Bywater warehouse. But it was also true that Pinelli—one of a number of petty crooks who'd done minimal time in exchange for their testimony against Patout—had been the one to lead the police there after having himself been arrested with a truckload of far more desirable loot. And alright, perhaps Catfish had been foolish to give the ex-con a second chance. But anyone who knew Catfish also knew that it was perfectly in character for him to help out somebody like Pinelli, who when other kids had been in high school had been in Angola, where he'd survived as "Nelly Pinelli" even though he wasn't gay. In other words, like my good buddy Carla, Pinelli didn't have a whole lot to smile about. So when, after completing a jail term last year for some relatively minor infraction, nobody would hire him, Catfish had.

In need of a friendly face, I ambled over to Big Easy Collectibles, which is on the other side of Catfish's old shop and owned by a guy named Dean, the dealer on the block with whom I enjoy the best rapport (which I like to think is because he's such a nice guy but which I cannot completely disassociate from the musty pile of vintage physique booklets he let me have for a song a few years back). A long-time anchor of the Decatur Street strip, Dean's shop comprises two high-ceilinged rooms of Depression glassware and "smalls," with not a postage stamp's worth of empty wall or shelf space. He also specializes in antique lighting, so the place is always lit up like a sound stage thanks to the blizzard of chandeliers obscuring the pressed-tin ceiling. Despite his girth, Dean is capable of navigating through the shop's aisles with Peggy Fleming-like grace, his pale orb of a face usually aglow with a grin.  Most of the time, however, he can be found behind the wraparound checkout counter toward the back, inspecting new arrivals with a jeweler's monocle, which was the case as I tapped the service bell.

"Sammy!" he enthused.  "Howya doing?"

"Good.  You?"

He rolled his head dizzily, the bleached blonde pick-up stix of his thinning hair maintaining the illusion they'd been inattentively tossed.  "Oh, you know.  Just look at all this shit."

"Those rhinestones are gorgeous."

He lifted an earring to a lobe and inclined his head to one side.  "Aren't they?"

"Hey, have you seen Catfish?"

"No, but this latest bit is pretty wild, huh?"

"It was a mistake.  He's out, you know."

He let the monocle drop.  "Not *that*.  Infinity.  Can you *believe* that woman?"

"What?"

"You haven't heard?"

"Heard what?"

He rubbed his hands together.  "Oh my God!  It's so good!"

"*What?*"

He leaned over and fished out yesterday's paper and slapped it onto the ledge, then bounced up and put a finger down:

**BEAUCOEUR ATTORNEY ACCUSES D.A.'S OFFICE
OF ANTI-GAY DISCRIMINATION, RACISM**

I gasped, doing my best to digest the article as Dean narrated:

New Orleans, Friday, August 21:  At 10 a.m. yesterday afternoon during a well-attended press conference in her office suite atop the World Trade Center, local real estate and civil rights attorney Infinity Feingold accused the New Orleans District Attorney's office of possible civil right violations. Most of the claims are aimed squarely at Assistant D.A. Eugene Tucker.  But according to legal experts, the full array of allegations implies that broader action may be taken against the City of New Orleans if the charges against Feingold's client—Charles ("Catfish") Beaucoeur—are not withdrawn. Last October, Beaucoeur, 44, heir to the Beaucoeur sugarcane fortune, was thrust into the spotlight following a leak believed to have originated with Tucker's office.  Beaucoeur was questioned as part of an ongoing investigation involving stolen cemetery artifacts, following the discovery of a number of objects at his storage warehouse on Burgundy Street near Franklin Avenue.  On Friday of last week,  Beaucoeur was charged with possession of stolen property and incarcerated in Central Lockup.  Released on his own recognizance, he was seen entering the courthouse on Monday morning with Feingold, where the two attended a closed-door meeting with New Orleans District Attorney Arthur Bland.   During yesterday's press briefing Feingold stated that if the charges against her client were not dropped within 24 hours, additional information about Tucker's background would be made public.  "Mr. Tucker's deplorable past speaks for itself," Feingold stated. "Given his history, every action he has taken in this absurd witch hunt must be questioned as part of a self-serving vendetta."  The District Attorney's office refused requests for comment.

"Oh my *God*!" I squeaked, too keyed up to do anything more than scan the rest of the article, which provided additional background on Infinity and Catfish.

Dean beamed. "Ain't life grand? I knew something like this was going to happen. This whole thing is a sham."

"I know, but...do you think she really has anything?"

"I know she does."

"How?"

"Because it's already out."

"What?"

He leaned forward. "Well. You know about Tess's David Duke fundraisers, right?"

Who didn't? During 1991, David Duke, a former Grand Wizard of the Knights of the Ku Klux Klan, had come in second in the Louisiana governor's race.

"Guess who was one of the biggest donors?"

"Tucker," I obliged.

"His wife. Apparently she and Tess go way back."

"No."

"Wait. There's more. You know how Tucker likes to go off every chance he gets on how affirmative action is reverse discrimination? Well apparently that's just the tip of the iceberg. Because get this. Before he became a lawyer he was Justice of the Peace in Tangipahoa Parish. And guess what he did while he was?"

"What?"

"Refused to marry interracial couples. Several."

"You've got to be kidding."

Dean snorted. "You can't make this stuff up. But wait, it gets better."

"It can't."

"Believe me, it does. It just so happens that the Tuckers have a son they haven't spoken to in years. Guess where he lives."

"San Francisco?"

"Atlanta. Midtown."

"No!"

Dean nodded. "A big girlfriend. And she's speaking out."


A half hour later I was still there, loitering in front of the counter and savoring the moment, when something bumped me.

Someone, actually.

"Coming through!" she honked.

It was Dean's shop assistant, an old black woman people call Mother who spends her mornings trolling through yard sales in marginal neighborhoods in a Toyota truck "on loan" from Catfish. With her mammy doll act and closet passion for Faulkner, she was a fixture on Decatur Street long before Dean. After losing toes to diabetes a few years back, however, she closed down her shop and moved into a Foundation home with her son Jerry, a Gulf War veteran incapacitated by a condition that doesn't qualify for V.A. assistance.

I squeezed up against the counter and let her pass.

Dean rolled over in his chair and lifted up the hinged counter section.

"Hey, Darlin'," he said. "Whatcha got there?"

Mother grunted and handed through several wrinkled Schwegman's bags, then slipped behind the counter and dropped down into a chair. She pulled a tissue out of her big-pocketed dress and dabbed at her forehead.

Dean peered inside one of the bags and whistled, then dumped its contents—a treasure trove of vintage glass Mardi Gras beads with the little "Made in Czechoslovakia" tags still on them—out on the counter. "Wow! You hit the jackpot."

Mother fired up a cigarette. "Again."

"You're not supposed to be smoking."

"I'm not supposed to be doing a lot of things. Like still working at my age."

"Yeah," scoffed Dean. "Because you work so hard."

"Hey, Mother," I chimed in. "You haven't seen Catfish have you?"

"Not since this morning."

"Oh. You saw him today? Where?"

"Up the street. At his house."

"Are you sure it was him?"

"'Cause of all the other red Jeep Cherokees on our block?"

"But I mean, you saw *him*."

"Yes, Child. The eyes still work fine."

"Did he say anything?"

"No. I don't think he saw me. Why?"

"No reason. If you see him again, would you please ask him to call me?"

"You two aren't fighting again, are you?"

"We weren't…"

"'Cause these old hands are already full."

Dean cocked his head. "Dorothy…"

"I'm kidding. Of course I'll tell him."

"Thank you, Mother."

"You're welcome, Samuel."

I put the paper down, then lifted it again.

"Hey, Dean," I said. "Mind if I keep this?"


Back home I devoured the article in its entirety along with the leftover Verti Marte, then watched a little television and slept like a babe. This morning, I was up before ten, and post Frosted Flakes I piloted myself through an action-packed day. First on the list, a heartening supply of staples procured from the Royal Street A&P (which while tiny, not that clean, and much further away, still wins hands down over the slum of a Robert "superstore" on the corner of Elysian Fields and St. Claude). Next, a top-to-bottom apartment cleaning followed by two Lean Cuisines and a nap.

Which brings us to a few hours ago, when I took up my present post at the kitchen table and threw myself into the book, with enviable results. Winnie edicts aside, that a brief historical introduction to New Orleans coffee shop culture is indispensable is all any sane person can conclude, and fueled by a fresh-off-the-rack packet of microwave popcorn, that gem is scoped out.

As for Catfish, I can only imagine that he's as uplifted by this latest turn of events as I am. Because while Infinity does tend to be overly impressed with herself, there's no way she'd pull a stunt like this unless it was a slam dunk. Despite a number of additional fruitless attempts to reach Catfish by phone, it therefore wouldn't surprise me one bit if he came knocking right about now, toting a couple Louisiana Pizza Kitchen pizzas and *A Raisin in the Sun.*

In which case we're all set on Milk Duds and popcorn.

Plus, courtesy of Tower, my own classic film favorite: *Butterflies Are Free.*

Which, come to think of it, I may pop in.

5

Ruined Finery

**Tuesday, August 23, 2005 – 10:22 a.m.**

The Coffee Shops of New Orleans

[Draft Introduction]

New Orleans has always been famous for harboring a deep appreciation for, if not a mule-headed focus upon, life's little pleasures. Thus it should come as no surprise that New Orleanians ingest caffeine at two to three times the national average, nor that the Big Easy is arguably the coffee epicenter of the United States. During the early 1800s New Orleans coffee beans were roasted far longer than in other parts of the country, resulting in dark blends so strong outsiders were often appalled, albeit not nearly so much as they were by the local practice of plying drowsy children with café au lait. During the Civil War, when New Orleans was under a federal blockade and could not import coffee in sufficient quantities, Southerners began adulterating coffee with chicory, a wild perennial herb also known as coffeeweed or cornflower, a practice New Orleanians clung to after the war even when the cost of chicory exceeded that of coffee.

For more than 200 years coffee in New Orleans has also been as much business as pleasure. By the 1840s the Port of New Orleans was a top coffee bean importer, and during World War I the Delta Steamboat Company became known as "The Coffee

Line," going on to become one of the biggest java shippers in the world. Today, New Orleans remains one of the top two coffee ports in the country, second only to New York, and accounting for one-quarter of the beans that make their way to these shores. Throughout its history the city has also been home to dozens of roasting companies and brands, including French Market and Luzianne. Nor has there been a shortage of retail coffee establishments, with over 500 coffee "exchanges," which doubled as taverns, appearing in the 1850 City Directory.

Sadly, that coffee heyday was well before my time, with only a handful of ventures remaining as of the 1980s. And it was not until Starbucks came to town in the early 1990s that the local coffee shop scene started to percolate anew. Don't get me wrong. I am not one of those cultish Starbucks loyalists, and far be it from me to judge or discriminate on the basis of brand image or geographical origin. But you've got to hand it to Howard Schultz—a guy raised in a Brooklyn housing project—for having taken a simple concept and run with it. From its roots as a single shop in Seattle, Starbucks sprouted into a global empire of 13,000 stores in 40 countries, a true testament to the power of caffeine.

Like I said, though, I am not one of those wide-eyed Starbucks loyalists. Despite my love of virtually all things European I refuse to refer to Starbucks coffee shops as coffee*houses* (a transatlantic expression that fails to pay homage to this uniquely American spin of grab-and-go/leave-me-the-H-alone genius, while somehow also calling to mind smoky basements and endless acoustic guitar loops of "Blowin' in the Wind"); or to refer to entry-level coffee shop workers as *baristas*; or to use the term *tall* to refer to Starbucks' smallest size cup (although *grande* for a large totally works for me). Still, I personally put Starbucks up there with Martha Stewart as one of the most important positive influencers of modern American culture, with both parties having made our collective American life immeasurably better. Indeed, it may be said, I do believe, that Starbucks has done for over-priced-tiny-apartment dwellers and alcoholics in recovery every-where what Martha has done for gay men and yearning house-wives from coast to coast: creating an orderly, attractive, escapist haven that is both easily attainable and completely removed from reality.

But I digress...

So I'm not a Starbucks loyalist—although I have to admit I do get rankled when I hear pseudo-sensitive, anti-establishment, drank-the-Kool-Aid liberals gratuitously trashing the place, complaining en masse about the corporate "ubiquity" of Star-bucks as if this were somehow a fresh perspective, rotely alleging that the chain is "homogenizing" the U.S. coffee shop scene and putting mom-and-pops out of business right and left. Excuse me, but outside urban centers and college towns, just what "coffee shop scene" might that have been? If anything, Starbucks single-handedly made the U.S. coffee shop industry viable for *more* operators, throwing open the door for new businesses and forcing old ones to shine up their counters, dust off their espresso ma-chines, and, for God's sake, clean up their bathrooms. Let's face it, without Starbucks and its galvanizing effect on the U.S. econ-omy—coffee aside, consider all the paper cups, plastic straws, corrugated cardboard cupholders (did those even exist before Starbucks?), milked cows, sweet baked goods made by local bakeries, tea, sugar, NutraSweet, Sweet & Low, Equal, candy, gum, ceramic coffee cups, coffee makers and accessories, greet-ing cards, napkins (did I already say that?), paper towels, toilet paper, rental income for landlords, add-on revenues for merchants located near Starbucks, billions in salaries to employees and premiums to healthcare providers—if not for all that, the inevitable transition of this already foundering capitalist oligarchy we choose to call a democracy into a more sustainable model would be at least a generation closer.

Like I said though, I am not a Starbucks loyalist. I just know a good thing when I see one. And as dear old Martha herself might say, as far as pumping up the economy and boosting consumer morale by providing an affordable luxury and a comforting left-leaning retreat during these rabidly right-wing record-deficit war-mongering times, Starbucks has been and continues to be a very good thing, including for the locally owned coffee shops of New Orleans.

Perhaps the best known of these is PJ's, part of a New Orleans-born franchise founded by Phyllis Jordan, who opened her first shop in 1978. PJ's has several stores about town (I just cracked the phone book and counted seven), including a high-traffic spot at New Orleans International Airport in Kenner and a corner in New Orleans' D-Day museum on Magazine Street, in addition to its flagship location on Maple Street. However, for B. Sammy Singleton as for most Americans, convenience is king. So you can pretty much just cross off the list anything that involves crossing Canal Street or, God forbid, slogging to Metairie or Kenner (the latter of which is, BTW, named after one of the biggest slaveholding families of the antebellum South). For quite a few years, there was also a PJ's on Frenchmen Street next to Washington Square. But that spot is now home to the Café Rose Nicaud, the first coffee shop in the Marigny that is, in my humble opinion, able to give the Royal Street CC's a run for its money.

In addition to slinging a great cup of joe, the place is named in honor of perhaps the most enterprising figure in New Orleans' highly caffeinated history. A Creole slave who bought her freedom in the early 1800s, Rose began the tradition of coffee stands and "exchanges" in New Orleans by selling her brew from a portable stand in the French Market, a brew described by one of her patrons as "like the benediction that follows after prayer" [USE IN BOOK]. Another local coffee haunt not far from here is Rue de la Course, which has its own story to tell, as does the world-famous Le Café du Monde. Within a few blocks of where I reside in the Marigny, there's also a panoply of a-tad-too-funky-pour-moi neighborhood shops, including Flora, the Sound Café, and "Coffee, Tea, and..." (about which I think the name pretty much says it all, since the only excuse for ellipses in the name of any retail business is a sign painter with Alzheimer's).

Anyway, for once I do *not* digress, since as peripheral as this may seem it's actually all marvelously relevant in terms of the book.

Okay, *GUIDE*book, although I'm sorry but I'm still not buying this stunted *Coffee Shops of New Orleans* vision of Winnie's.

Which is, I'd like to think, the reason I'm having a hard time staying on track.

The truth is, however, I'm beginning to get a tad bit annoyed with Catfish, whom I've still not heard from and who I keep thinking will show up here at CC's or my apartment (as was not the case this weekend). True, we made no plans during our little joy ride to City Hall, and I'm sure Infinity's theatrics are keeping him jumping. But to just leave me hanging post prison pick-up? Not that I want or require some unduly protracted thank-you or apology. But a little elaboration would be nice, even if it's only on such follow-up themes as how his meeting with District Attorney Bland went or how Infinity's about to blow Assistant D.A. Tucker out of the water. Or—and not to beat a dead horse here—why in God's name Catfish called Tess instead of Infinity, which seems just plain self-destructive, like trying to cross a bridge that's not only burning but lying in smoldering ashes at the bottom of a rocky ravine, thanks to a *Dynasty*-style knock-down, drag-out that predated by six years my arrival in New Orleans.

Flashback to December 1992 and the following tragic news and turns of events: En route to see his son Charles (aka Catfish) in San Francisco, Frederick Lucien Beaucoeur's Junior Cesna, rerouted due to inclement weather, goes down in the Jean Lafitte swamps, killing all persons aboard: Frederick; professional aviator and co-pilot Mack Guillot; and Ruthie Rush, whose esteemed Rush Antiques chain includes two shops in New Orleans (one on Magazine Street and one in the French Quarter), plus a third shop in Baton Rouge. Tongues wag. Because while Ruthie is identified by *The Times-Picayune* as "a close family friend," her presence on the airplane is, observes Upper Line society columnist Mitzie McClanahan, "hard to explain." Catfish flies in and is met at the airport by Ruthie's daughter Lee Ann, a close childhood friend who, depending on which channel you're watching, is either shattered or stoic.

Within 72 hours the next explosion goes off: 30-plus-year marriage to Contessa Beaucoeur notwithstanding, Frederick has left the bulk of a liquid estate valued at over $12 million to his only child Catfish, along with roughly a dozen run-down properties in the Faubourg Tremé, with Tess receiving a slap-in-the-face one-tenth of that amount. Citing Frederick's "indiscretions" and changes made to the will without their client's knowledge, Tess's lawyers vow to contest the legacy and are swinging into gear when a gaggle of Xavier undergrads show up in front of the Beaucoeur mansion on St. Charles Avenue, pickets in hand, championing the cause of former Beaucoeur plantation slaves and "sullying" the Beaucoeur family name (a term Buddy Lowell, the attorney heading up Tess's team, uses repeatedly in addressing the press, apparently under the impression, Mitzie roundly observes, that his client's David Duke ties had no such effect, nor for that matter a family fortune indeed flowing from a sugar empire built on the backs of slaves). To the surprise of all, as well as to the delight of the students and the liberal media, Catfish wastes no time in earmarking half of the estate toward making reparations to those whose ancestry claims can be substantiated, claims Tess's lawyers make clear they intend to challenge every step of the way.

New wrinkle:

Throughout the grueling search-and-recovery effort, which goes on for more than a week, Catfish has been staying at Lee Ann's Lower Garden District home. But following an abbreviated return to San Francisco he moves back to New Orleans and takes up provisional residence in the French Quarter, in the apartment above Ruthie's temporarily shuttered Chartres Street shop. His attorney, a former big-game hunting buddy of Frederick's who is also executor, holds a brief press conference, making the point that "New Orleans is, and always will be, Mr. Beaucoeur's home" while stressing that his client "has every intention of carrying through with his noble goal." And just when it seems like Catfish cannot yank Tess's chain any harder, he does. Because within two weeks of moving into a building owned by his dead father's late "female companion," reports Mitzie, Catfish "embraces the alternative lifestyle that has come to define our beloved French Quarter" (the last comment made in oblique reference to a speech delivered by Catfish at the first annual Crescent City Gay People of Color AIDS Awareness fundraiser). Adding insult to injury, less than a month later Catfish commits what to Tess's way of thinking may be, posits Mitzie, an even more heinous offense: he descends directly into the masses of working folk by giving Lee Ann a much-needed hand, reopening Ruthie's Chartres Street shop and eventually taking it over altogether (with the full blessing of both Lee Ann and the tax attorney handling Catfish's inheritance).

For the first time, during a televised press briefing, Tess steps up to the mike. Taller than most men, she's nevertheless feminine to the point of seeming almost frail, her pale hair swept back from a visage famously sans cosmetics. The crowd falls silent, as awed by her raw beauty as they are shocked to see the one-time belle of St. Charles struggling to maintain her composure while making a rare public appearance. A charged moment later, Contessa speaks, her breathy voice quavering slightly:

"As many of you already know, my son is not well. Twice when he was a child he tried to take his own life. I believe this was a direct result of his decision to become a homosexual." Her chin quivers. "It is a load no mother should bear. I accept it. With God's help, I carry it every day. And every day I pray for the means to save my dear child. Please join me in that prayer. Please stand for truth in questioning not just the morality, but the judgment, of any person who would shun God's grace. Of any person who would denigrate the heritage of this great country and throw away all hope of redemption. We cannot let that happen. I can't. I won't. It is for this reason that today, regardless of the outcome of these proceedings, I pledge my unqualified support of Deliverance, whose mission is to promote liberation from the sin of homosexuality through the miracle of Jesus Christ. It's been over thirty years since my son made his choice. But I've not given up. And I never will." She swipes back a tear. "My husband is dead. My child is lost. But I, Contessa Beaucoeur, am not alone. God helps those who help themselves. I know that. And I know that with your prayers, and the prayers of all true Americans, God shall prevail."

Tess's attorneys take it from there. In their zeal to dredge up more recent examples of Catfish's alleged instability, they hire a private detective to gouge out every crevice of his life—from the time he moved to France following the second wrist-slashing, through his college years in England, through the past decade in San Francisco. Here, it becomes especially personal and ugly. Because while Catfish's partner of 12 years, a cardiologist named James in the process of exiting Catfish's life, refuses to have any involvement in the case, Tess's team is able to coax unfavorable revelations out of a number of other potential witnesses. "Volatile" and "scary" comments one out-of-breath Noe Valley resident in characterizing Catfish and James' on again/off again relationship, with a former Cambridge classmate calling Catfish "flighty" and "unreliable" while bringing up the college major he changed twice before dropping out. No, huffs a VIP member of New Orleans Midtown Sauna when asked to elaborate, he has not *personally* seen Catfish there, but he knows people who have. Mitzie does her part, too, using her column to remind those questioning Tess's "new-found faith" that "Mrs. Beaucoeur's Christian crusade actually began in the 1970s when, not long after her son's second suicide attempt, she and Anita Bryant became close. It was, in fact, none other than Contessa Beaucoeur who flew to the side of the former Miss America runner-up from the Sunshine State following the unfortunate pie incident in Des Moines." Catfish receives a call from the ACLU, whose director assures him that the group is "monitoring the situation" but declines to get involved in what is "essentially a family matter."

As preposterous as it may seem, Tess's smear campaign appears to be working. For while Catfish may be every iota as stubborn as Tess, he can't begin to compete on mean. Especially distressful are the public revelations about him and James, which Catfish refuses to dignify with a response. Nor is Catfish the kind to counter his mother's mud-slinging with anything even remotely self-congratulatory (such as the fact that, while living in the Bay Area, he completed his degree at Stanford—a B.A. in architecture—and donated most of his time to pro bono work on affordable housing construction in the Greater S.F. area, with the rest of his free hours going to AIDS counseling in the Castro).

There is talk of a settlement.

Enter Infinity Freeman (Catfish's knight in shining armor—if I've heard it once, I've heard it a million times). Petite. New Kenneth Cole briefcase. Smart footwear. About Catfish's age and twice as calm as he is hyper at his most manic. The Chartres Street shop, which is long and not wide enough for its purpose, is still unmistakably Ruthie Rush: country French antiques with a heart-wrenching edge of adoring wear. But Catfish's weakness for local pickers in need of a few quick bucks is already beginning to manifest. To accommodate the cartons of "smalls" pedaled by on a daily basis, new pine display shelves now encase the inner brick wall while a clutter of rustic items stands united inside the front door like strangers who have discovered much in common while waiting for a downpour to stop: a coat rack fashioned from saplings partially covered with bark, a ceramic-topped wash stand with a wobbly iron base, several rusty farm implements with warped wooden handles, two or three crooked chairs with frayed cane seats.

Catfish's head emerges through the flap of a cubbyhole behind the counter at the rear of the store.

"Good morning!"

"Hello."

"Let me know if you have questions."

"Thank you."

The customer proceeds to examine the merchandise on the shelves. A clay pipe. The imprecise curl of a rusty shutter hinge. A doll with a gingham dress and a faded black cotton head with yarn hair and stitch eyes, which holds enough appeal for the woman to caress its cheek. A budding collection of second-hand local interest books. On down the row to where the shelving stops and a peg rack of quilts completes the run to the check-out counter.

Catfish re-emerges.

"May I help you?"

The woman turns, the orange and yellow rays of a sunburst quilt tinting her complexion a toasted ginger. "I was just about to ask you that same question," she smiles. The words are as soft and unambiguous as vintage velvet. She elaborates.

Catfish is sold. Who wouldn't be? A black girl growing up in Texas in the '60s. A single mother and extended family of women who saw to it that Kim Baker had every opportunity. A father Kim never knew—a man named John Freeman—killed during a race riot in Alabama.  From North Dallas High to Xavier to Harvard Law (where the name change took place).  And from there, not up the corporate ladder but to New Orleans and her own civil rights practice on St. Claude Avenue.  Lots of pro bono.  No lost cases.  And no compunction whatsoever about using all that to "jazz things up" in the case of *Beaucoeur Slave Descendants v. Beaucoeur.*

Infinity Freeman takes charge.

The media laps it up.

The case turns in Catfish's favor.

Now it's Infinity's personal life that Tess goes after.  And it's a sure bet the "conflict of interest" issue would have originated from Tess's camp.  Before her people can uncover and exploit that angle, however, Infinity makes the move.

"Ladies and gentleman," she announces from atop a Brown's Dairy milk crate on the sidewalk in front of the Beaucoeur mansion, where Catfish has joined her.  "I have just returned from a trip to see my family in Dallas.  Literally."  She nods at the carry-on next to the crate.  The crowd chuckles.

"Cornelia, my mother, says 'howdy'."

A few more titters.

"But of course that is not why we're here today.  We're here because I have new information relevant to the case of *Beaucoeur Slave Descendants v. Beaucoeur.*  Information my mother chose—for reasons I'm sure you will understand—not to reveal to me until this weekend."

Drum roll of silence.

"*I* am the descendant of a Beaucoeur slave."  [CONSIDER NOVEL.  (BUT IF SO, *TONE DOWN SOUTHERN GOTHIC.*)]

The crowd goes wild.

Infinity holds up her hands.

"Please, let me continue…"

And continue she does. After working as slaves and hired servants for the Beaucoeur family for nearly two centuries, Infinity recounts, her entire family was "exiled" by none other than Contessa Beaucoeur, who belatedly blamed the maid—Infinity's great aunt Sara—for the drowning death of Tess's toddler daughter prior to Catfish's birth, even though Frederick had taken full responsibility. Unable to find work, the entire family—Sara, her sister Margaret, Margaret's daughter Cornelia, and little Kim—was forced to relocate in order to put bread on the table, which is how they'd ended up living in Texas.

"And yet…" Infinity goes on following a heavy pause, "here I am. Standing before you today. A Harvard-educated attorney. A success, you might say. She beat the odds! Ain't America great! Isn't it wonderful what hard work and determination can do! Yes. It is. But that's not the whole story. Because as blessed as I am to have a mother like Cornelia and a grandmother like Margaret and my two wonderful aunts—as extraordinary as all of those women are—I doubt I'd be standing here were it not for…a white man. A white man by the name of Constantine Beaucoeur. My client, Charles Beaucoeur's, paternal grandfather."

Murmurs of puzzlement as the lawyer steps down.

Catfish steps up. A few people applaud. He shakes his head. "In a family like mine there's not much to be proud of. So when Infinity told me what my grandfather did when he found out about the unconscionable actions of my mother, I cried. By establishing a trust fund for the Baker family, a family that served our family for generations, he provided an opportunity. I don't know why he did that. To appease a guilty conscience? Because he genuinely cared? I don't know. We're not close. I just know he did. I can't undo the past. None of us can. But my hope is that…" he glances down at Infinity, who reaches up and takes his hand, "…my hope is that together we can do better. Starting now."

Infinity and Catfish trade places. To avoid any suggestion of conflict of interest, the attorney concludes, she will not only not be listing herself as a plaintiff in the case, she will be proceeding on a pro bono basis.

Too stunned to respond, the crowd remains silent as Infinity steps down, then crackles into light applause, a stray tear trickling down more than one cheek. Even the press is moved. "Heartfelt and highly effective!" enthuses one of WDSU's twin Mackel brother reporters.

But is it? At least one media voice begs to differ. "The only thing missing was Pavarotti," snipes Mitzie in her weekly column. Nor can Tess let it go, targeting not only Infinity but the lawyer's family in an interview with Richard Angelico. "That that…woman would defile my daughter's memory after what her aunt did? I think that says it all." The next day, in an unprecedented Upper Line Special Edition, Mitzie unloads, briefly siding with Tess in calling Infinity's reference to the deceased child "tasteless" but then digging in further, reprinting the full account of the 1958 drowning death and taking Tess to task for implying that Sara Baker had any part in the tragedy. "Poor Mitzie," sighs Tess during a follow-up interview. She leans into the camera and shields her mouth. "You see, her mother McKinsey had plans for

Mitzie and Frederick."

Given this Uptown in-fighting and the racial composition of the jury pool, things are looking good for Catfish at the local level. But the national scene is another matter. Although there's plenty of sympathy in the media, the right-wing legal pundits are apoplectic, with Rhett Buchanan telling Dan Rather that a victory by the plaintiffs would "open a can of worms for anyone whose ancestors had even *thought* about owning a slave." Tess's attorneys, meanwhile, have laid the groundwork for appeals at the state and federal levels while Tess has taken over the PR side. "God works in mysterious ways," the coy media darling confides to a Baton Rouge reporter following tea with the wife of a former State Representative. "The last time I checked, this was not a socialist country," she icily quips when buttonholed by a skeptical *Gambit* reporter at the airport while en route to Florida for a Deliverance board meeting.

Well aware that their chances of winning are far slimmer outside New Orleans than in, Infinity is debriefing Catfish when the familiar face shows up at her office at One Shell Square, where she has recently relocated because she "needs more light" (per the same *Gambit* reporter). Ushered in by one of a few paralegals humming about, the stranger needs no introduction. Even bigger and bolder than in his commercials, he is personal injury legal legend Morton J. Feingold Esq. ("Be Bold. Feingold!"), whose ski-mask tan began showing up on billboards long before Morris ("One Call. That's All") Bart began to horn in. He takes off his hat and smoothes back his hair, a fragrant brown meadow ribboned with white.

"Sorry to intrude."

Infinity and Catfish stand up. "Not at all," Infinity smiles.

"Mr. Feingold.  Charles Beaucoeur."

The men exchange pleased-to-meet-yous, shake hands.

"How can I help you?" Infinity asks.

"By allowing me to be unforgivably presumptuous."

"I beg your pardon?"

"I'd like to offer you some unsolicited advice."

"Pro bono?"

Feingold smiles.  Infinity glances at Catfish, who shrugs. "Be my guest," she says.

"Thank you.  I promise not to take up too much of your time."  Feingold picks a speck of lint off his hat, then jumps in. "I make it my business to not judge anyone.  And I consider myself to be good at it.  After all, you never know who your next client may be.  But in my thirty-some-odd years of practicing law in New Orleans I've occasionally failed in that not purely noble pursuit.  One of those occasions is Tess Beaucoeur."  He turns to Catfish.  "Mr. Beaucoeur, my condolences on the loss of your father.  He was a good man.  But Contessa Beaucoeur..." he shakes his head, then releases a heavy sigh and forges ahead. "For too long have I sat back while she spewed her venom about blacks, Jews, gays, you name it—and got away with it.  Patted on the back, even.  I wouldn't blame you if you asked me to step outside."  He pauses a beat.  No reaction from Catfish.  Feingold redirects to Infinity.  "Or told me to get the hell out.  But this time, well, I couldn't sit back."

Infinity circles her desk.  "We appreciate that Mr. Feingold, but...?"

"I'm advising you to settle."

"That's out of the question."  Infinity's response is automatic.

"There's no precedent," Feingold counters.

"Exactly."

"Not to mention the statutes of limitations."

"We're prepared to fight."

"Are you prepared to lose?"

"The opposite, actually."

Feingold smiles. "I admire what you're doing, Ms. Freeman. Truly. But there are battles that can't be won." He turns to Catfish. "Aren't there, Son?"

Catfish is caught off guard. "I…"

Infinity cuts in. "Mr. Feingold…"

"You'll win here," Feingold continues. "How could you not? But in the end, you'll lose. The money. Your career. Yourself maybe."

Infinity shakes her head. "I sincerely doubt that."

"You think she's after the dough? Sure. But that's the least of it. The woman's a soul stealer. And she's already got one foot in the door. Your door. The doors of all the good people paying for this nice view of Lafayette Park. She's been scratching at my door for years."

"I'm sorry Mr. Feingold…"

He lifts a hand. "You're right. It's none of my business. But I've been around a long time and people of my age and persuasion, we know people, people who hear things. As a matter of fact, I just got back from D.C."

Infinity crosses her arms. "And?"

"Word on the street is that Tess Beaucoeur is going to hit a grand slam."

"Do we look worried?"

"There was another woman on the flight. The will was changed."

Infinity moves to the door. "We appreciate your time."

Feingold turns to go, stops.

"I'd offer her half," he counsels, face to face with Infinity. "She may not take it, but then again, she might. You can do what you want with the rest. It'll be a triumph."

A little bow and he's gone.

On the wall next to the door is a bubble-glass portrait of a just-married Creole couple smiling over a cake, an office-warming present from Catfish, who's not missing a trick. Infinity metronomes over and inspects her reflection.

Catfish waits for her to return to her desk, then sits down and jerks his head toward the picture. "What was that?"

"What was what? Oh, please. He's got to be at least a hundred years old. Where were we?"

"He's right, you know."

"About?"

"Tess. She won't stop."

"This is news?"

"Ever."

"And?"

He shrugs.

The lawyer shuffles some papers. "You're the client."

Catfish turns toward the window, which runs the length of one wall. It has begun to rain. The square of Lafayette Park is dotted with watery green buds.

The view really is nice.

He sighs.

Feingold is right.

Flash forward three days, post a long Easter weekend Infinity has spent with her family in Texas. Within a year Catfish will move into one of his Tremé houses, having packed Ruthie's apartment full of picker junk. But for now he's still living above the Chartres Street shop. The phone rings next to the bed there and he picks up. Listens. Agrees.

The evening news carries the clincher: Tess Beaucoeur has agreed to settle for one-quarter of her husband's estate. Half of the balance is going into a trust for descendants of Beaucoeur slaves, to be doled out on a first-come basis as the genealogical investigations are completed. Infinity Freeman is hailed as a miracle worker. Catfish—"The Last Beaucoeur"—is a hero in the African-American community. The would-be class-action plaintiffs are happy. The Xavier students are happy. Even Infinity is satisfied since despite the settlement the case is viewed as a landmark.

What the frick just happened?

Don't ask me. All I know is that by the time I landed in NOLA in 1998 the Beaucoeur Foundation had been expanded to include Catfish's Tremé properties, half of which had been converted into modified Section 8 homes supervised by Infinity. For his part, Catfish had not just provided the architectural know-how but taken a hands-on approach to the actual renovations, to such a degree that the Chartres Street shop—now under lease to Catfish from Lee Ann, and operating under the name Creole Heart—was closed more than it was open. It was also during that period that

Catfish made the acquaintance of another San Francisco expat, Georgia Moore, in whose Faubourg Marigny "River House" Catfish periodically stayed while assisting with the resurrection of that property as well. On the other hand, it was not until I'd been living in New Orleans a few years, shortly after 9-11, that Catfish took up with a meticulously groomed third-generation Senegalese-American we shall call Joseph.

Hm.

Truth be told, I never liked him. A low-hipped man with a tiny waist and powerful upper body, he came across as the perfect little boy: well-scrubbed and polite, precise diction, quick to laugh at even the lamest attempt at humor. Underneath it all, however, there was an agenda, I maintain to this day (not to mention a wife and kids in New Orleans East). At the same time, tightly packed into an aggressively white T-shirt and starched jeans, Joseph was undeniably in possession of a certain fierce eroticism. And while it was clear to me that Catfish was not in love with him, it was equally clear that he valued something Joseph was good at providing. So, loyal friend that I was, I promised myself I would keep my mouth shut. Which I managed to do (sort of) for almost two years.

Nevertheless, even B. Sammy Singleton has his limits, such that this past August things finally came to a head, pursuant to a late lunch at Catfish's Tremé house. It was one of those soupy New Orleans afternoons that seems like it won't ever end, when it's so breathlessly hot all you want to do is sit around on the balcony drinking mint juleps, draped in ruined finery, thanking your lucky stars for the least tickle of a breeze, which was precisely what the three of us had been doing all afternoon. Except that the balcony of that house had long since collapsed onto the sidewalk; and the mint juleps were out, since Catfish was a teeto-taler and I was sober and Joseph said he didn't drink; and the ruined finery was all in my mind. Okay, no breeze either. Which I guess pretty much just leaves us with the damn afternoon heat, of which there was plenty, including inside the house, since the provisional repair of the circa 1980s central air unit had rendered the system capable of making cobwebs flutter but not a whole lot more.

In any case, with the Chartres shop closed as of the previous summer and renovations to his Foundation homes all but complete, Catfish had begun to grow restless. So when over lunch he mentioned for the first time that he'd written poetry in high school and that he'd recently resumed that diversion, yes, I was surprised, but no, I wasn't opposed. Anything was better than the Internet thing he sometimes did now that he had too much time on his hands, spending hours on end draped across one of the sweat-stained leather club chairs at the back of CC's lost in his laptop, unable to tear himself away from websites like The Huffington Post even when I rose and announced that Handy Stats spreadsheets called. For while there may be happy news to be had online, it was not to such reports that Catfish was drawn. Rather, it was into the ickiest patches of that electronic sea that he chose to cast his net, his face growing paler and paler as his irises swept the screen until his left eye started to twitch and his neck vein to throb, no matter how often or indiscreetly I implied by way of putting the brakes on that there really *wasn't* much one could do, for example, to make the good people of South Carolina understand that things like Confederate flags and segregated proms (yes, still) send unambiguous signals.

This was all the more alarming in that the man normally

couldn't sit still for more than five minutes. But on this August afternoon he was his old charmingly hyper self, making a little too much over how "the chef" (i.e., Joseph) had "done it again" (i.e., jambalaya, again), then hopping up from the table and transporting the chipped but still glorious Old Paris china he'd indirectly inherited (and I openly coveted) over to the gruesome stainless steel sink (which if I had my way would be the first thing to go if this final renovation ever got underway). As usual, Joseph had then clambered up after him and insisted on doing the dishes while Catfish protested, resulting in a patter of good-natured bickering until Catfish was whipped on the rump with a dish towel and dismissed. Still grinning, Catfish then made a quick run upstairs for his poetry pad while I helped myself to some iced coffee and retired to my customary post-lunch station on the ancient divan opposite the kitchenette.

A minute or so later, Catfish returned and began pacing up and down the expanse of the vast double parlor, pencil poised above mini legal pad. And as he immersed himself in verse and I waited for Joseph to finish and scram, I watched out of the corner of my eye as Joseph put on his usual dish-washing pre-show. It went like this: First, he'd unfasten his pants and pull them down much lower than necessary, in the process of restoring his T-shirt to the perfectly tucked-in state he maintained at all times. Then, assuming the look of a man heading off into battle, he'd roll up a pair of imaginary cuffs and install himself Terminator-like in front of the sink. Finally, with over-the-top Marine Corps rigor, he'd start actually washing and drying the dishes while exercising yet another of his annoying habits: humming show tunes while other people are trying to think.

Meanwhile, Catfish continued his pacing, back and forth,

from the kitchenette at the rear of the space to the decrepit grand piano up front, over six feet tall and thin as a reed, sidestepping iffy boards in what was once a gorgeous, ochre-colored pine floor, practically floating I believe it would be fair to say, back and forth, like a willow frond caressing a sleepy pond. Wavy to the point of the occasional curl, his reddish blonde hair was, as usual, magnificently defiant, sticking out from his head with a savagery that suggested it would be capable if necessary of capturing and devouring a small bird, or, far more likely, becoming its nest.

"There's a river of blood running under this land...," he muttered as he drifted past, attempting to get his mind around an elusive but essential iambic flourish. And fully empathizing with his need for unconditional concentration I was just about to request that Joseph cease and desist with the soundtrack when a plate slipped out of his hand and exploded on the floor.

"Good Lord!" I cried, shooting up from the divan like a spring through a cushion, more or less launching myself in Joseph's direction.

Joseph turned.

In the center of the front room, Catfish stopped pacing, not quite back from the land o' cotton.

"Hey, Babe," Joseph said as I stormed the kitchenette, smiling to reveal teeth as white as his Calvin Klein. "Chill out. It's just a little ol' plate."

"That's not the point," I said, dropping down onto my knees and snatching at shards of broken china.

He knelt next to me, attempting to hijack my clean-up effort. "Oh? And what *is* the point?"

"Just forget it."

He touched my arm. "No," he said. "I'd like to know."

At which point, caught off guard by this aggression, I cut myself, pretty badly, spewing blood onto his T-shirt.

"Ow!" I cried.

"Joey!" Catfish bellowed.

Thinking on his knees, Joseph snatched a dish towel and swiveled back. "You're fine, Babe," he said. "Just stay where you are." And before I could utter another word he was wrapping my hand, his actual Army Reserve training kicking right in. And because I was already beginning to feel light-headed, I allowed him to, watching the clean cloth from the load of laundry he'd picked up for Catfish that morning go round and round and round until it was time for his slender fingers to tuck in the ends. "How's that?" he said following a final tug. And whatever else may have resided behind those almond-shaped eyes, in this instant when I met them nothing but care came through. And I wanted to thank him. But then the first black-felt-backed stars burst and Catfish's Cole Haan arrived next to my knee and I felt so silly I instead made a lame attempt at humor I still wish I hadn't.

"The point is..." I said as Catfish knelt down beside us, "It's so hard to find good help these days."

Then I passed out.

When I came to on the way to the hospital, my hand still beautifully bundled, I was staring at the underside of Catfish's chin. With Joseph at the wheel, Catfish and I were in the back seat of the Cherokee, my head in his lap. Through slatted eyes I looked up at him, completely ashamed, my true hateful nature having at last been exposed. From its animated state during lunch his face had lapsed into a bony rack for his skin, confirming what I already knew: I'd crossed the line. And yet maybe, just maybe, all was not lost. For I knew just as well that all I had to do was utter those two little words—I'm sorry—and I'd be forgiven, or at least headed in that direction. The only thing was, and I'm not proud of this, part of me wasn't sorry, not in the least. And so instead of saying those words I squeezed my eyes shut and waited for Catfish to be gone.

Later, my hand splinted and bandaged, I saw wavering slices of Joseph and Catfish through a ripple of curtain as a nurse filled them in: Quite a little web gash there...no wonder they had trouble getting the bleeding stopped. Fortunately, no damage to the radial nerve between thumb and forefinger. The fainting? Not abnormal given the sudden drop in blood pressure, but probably worth mentioning during my next physical.

Then the curtain rings jingled, announcing another prime-time opportunity to make amends as Catfish came in to check on me. But, I suppose because our better instincts are seldom a match for the others, I did not. Instead, before he could ascertain that I was not really dozing, I snapped my eyes shut and waited.

And waited, extending the thick silence of the ride home from the hospital (this time with Catfish in the passenger seat) into one month, then going on two, bullet-proofing my justification day by day. For as long as I'd known Catfish there'd been a line of moochers at his door, ready to take advantage of his overly generous nature and too often successful in that pursuit. And while Joseph may have been close to the top of the list, don't even get me started on Infinity. Because no matter how many times Catfish used the word "pivotal" to describe her role in his life—and no matter how much assistance she still provided in handling the day-to-days of whatever was left of the Beaucoeur Foundation—it wasn't like the woman hadn't made out like a bandit herself. Riding the wave of *Beaucoeur Slave Descendants v. Beaucoeur*, which culminated with her finally (i.e., after being bumped twice) getting five minutes on *Larry King Live*, Infinity had branched out from her civil rights roots with a legal practice now focused on "urban redevelopment," while also forming her own property management and construction companies created under the aegis of the Beaucoeur Foundation. In the intervening years these two ancillary businesses had thrived, purchasing low-rent properties all over New Orleans, bringing them up to technically habitable levels, and renting them out under Section 8 provisions reserved for Foundation properties—activities that had raised questions at the City Planning Commission and cast an unsavory shadow over Catfish's legacy. Two or three years back the situation had reached a head with a front-page investigative report in *The Gambit* headlined "Infinity Feingold: Slumlord or Saint?" In the stark cover photo, the lawyer was shot at a dramatic angle, arms crossed in front of one of her apartment complexes in the Bywater—a three-story, that-paint-must-have-been-on-sale affair without proper zoning or fire escapes, whose first floor functioned as a storage facility for her construction company and was chock full of combustibles. On the other hand, entire low-income stretches of the city routinely implored her to run for mayor despite her affiliations with Big Business, for which she brokered the intermittent high-profile deal advancing the very kind of gentrification her own properties were accused of hampering under their trademarked guise of "Total Electric Living."

And yet my personal dislike for the woman ran even deeper than that, stemming primarily from the way she condescended to Catfish, as if she'd be in any position to do so were it not for the opportunities he and his grandfather had provided (although becoming Mrs. Morton J. Feingold six months after the Beaucoeur settlement hadn't hurt either). And yet still, like Joseph or any number of other hangers-on, in Catfish's eyes Infinity could apparently do no wrong. Whereas—and maybe this was just me—my own standing with Catfish had always felt more like "one strike and you're out."

Nevertheless, it was the Josephs and Infinitys and Lydias that Catfish seemed to not only attract but to welcome indiscriminately into his life. And since this was a dynamic he had no desire to discuss, much less alter, what could I do? Ignore it? Enable him? Is that what "friends" did? No. Of course not. Some tough love was in order, I concluded promptly after the fiasco. A couple weeks in, my resolve was strengthened by the news (courtesy of Dean) that Catfish and Joseph were, for whatever reason, no more. And a week or so after that, upon learning that Catfish had opened a new shop on Decatur, I rigorously boycotted, taking Chartres instead. In my righteous fantasy that he'd bottom out on being exploited and thank me one day, I was even encouraged by the rumor that his finances were dwindling. The new shop was a long way from breaking even, and word had it that Catfish was living off a trust fund set up by an aunt in England, a woman named Cleo, with whom he'd spent his holidays while at Cambridge.

Nevertheless, with almost two months gone by, I'd forgiven him for not having forgiven me. And besides, maybe he had, in some less than obvious manner that might become apparent were

I to tap more heartily into the Decatur Street grapevine on the not-infrequent days Catfish's shop failed to open. Which I did. And while there was nothing to be gleaned on the personal front, on the fiduciary front the vine was ripe. In addition to the Aunt Cleo update, word had it that other Beaucoeur relations were watching Catfish's every move, well aware that his grandfather's days were numbered and determined to stake a claim should the opportunity arise. To this end palms were being greased and backs scratched (including Infinity's, I'd even heard), or so the talk went. Thus it was almost impossible not to feel sorry for the unsuspecting "Charles," as some of the dealers had (rather presumptuously if you ask me) reverted to calling him. And I was just beginning to wonder how long I intended to persist with the stonewalling when the ultimate opportunity for no-fault reconciliation presented itself:

*Beaucoeur Heir Named in Cemetery Theft Investigation*, declared the October 8, 2004 *Times-Picayune* headline.

Not even bothering to finish my double cap, I was up like a shot, short-cutting from CC's to Catfish's shop, hoping he was there. And there he was, in the middle of that musty brick space, standing up reading the paper, wearing the same Cole Haans and surrounded by objects from antebellum to 80s.

I inventoried him from the threshold of the propped-open door, then rapped on the glass.

He tilted the paper forward.

"I'm busted," he said.

"It's about time," I replied.

I stepped in and scanned. The shop was wide but low-ceilinged enough to make him look twice as tall as he was and me to feel twice as dumpy as I am. Off to one side was a vinyl recliner with my name on it.

"Mexico, here I come," he sighed.

"I hear it's nice this time of year."

"Wanna go?"

I moseyed over to the chair and dusted the seat off, then kicked back. "That depends."

"On?"

"Will Joseph be coming?"

Immediately I wished I hadn't said that. But the flicker across Catfish's face was faint and the recovery swift.

"I'm serious, B," he said. "Let's you and me go somewhere." Then, "Want a latte?"

Need he ask?

I was completely in my element, lording over the subjectless kingdom from my recliner while mentally reenacting Catfish's and my flawless no-fault reconciliation when I heard something thumping around in back. A moment later, Mother appeared in the doorway to the rear storage area, mallet in hand.

"Well," she intoned. "Look what the cat finally dragged in."

"Hey, Mother. What're you doing back there?"

She put down the hammer and pulled out a Pall Mall. "Picking up the slack. Now that Joseph's gone, somebody's got to."

Determined to let that one go by, I nodded hospitably to a young couple who'd paused outside the shop's door, despite the guy's sock/sandal combo and the girl's machine-embroidered peasant blouse.

Mother wasn't having it. She shuffled over and helped herself to the vinyl sofa that went with my recliner.

The young couple opted out.

Mother squinted at me through a cloud of smoke. "Now that you two are making travel plans together, may we assume you're back to stay?"

"Everything's fine," I shrugged.

Her dark-circled eyes pinned me like a butterfly. "He hasn't been himself, you know."

I saw to it that the loose corner of the price sticker on the arm of my chair was firmly pressed down.

"He'll be fine," I said.


It hadn't even occurred to me to take either Catfish's invitation or Mother's dig seriously. But less than two weeks later Catfish and I were indeed winging our way abroad, not to Mexico (drug wars) but to Tortola, in the British Virgin Islands (as long as it was outside the U.S. and on the beach, Catfish was happy to leave the locale up to me). It was the first vacation either of us had had in years, as well as our first and only trip together. And in a rare show of extravagance involving his own comfort, Catfish had rented a bungalow at an upscale resort recommended by Infinity. "Go!" she'd cajoled after assuring him that the appearance of his name in the newspaper article was nothing more than "pure politics" and possibly libel. And Long Beach had more than lived up to the lawyer's recommendation, from the inspirational sunsets and casual dinners on white tablecloths to the baby sea gulls pecking around outside our door.

And of course, no Joseph.

It had been wonderful.

*Could it have been more?*

No, it could not have been!

Why am I even dredging all of this up anyway?

*Because Catfish* wasn't *fine?*

And really, is there any point in attempting to explain how easily that picture postcard could have been ruined, how one false move could have blurred that sun-drenched image into an absolute mess? Or in trying to explain that within hours of stepping off the ferry onto that quaint Road Town wharf I finally comprehended that I'd kicked a strut out from under my friend that I couldn't replace? Or in trying to justify how greedily I'd gobbled up that all-expenses-paid week of not the slightest demand, which had been as uncomplicated and affectionate as a brotherly hug, a Caribbean adventure (ah, the boulders of Virgin Gorda!) about which I'd not alter a thing?

*Really?*

To all of the above, no, there is not.

And again, post Joseph, *Catfish was fine.*

At least as fine as could be expected given the slanderous cemetery theft business and the usual holiday doldrums and the death of his grandfather and his subsequent dealings with Tess.

And, in the long run, much better off without Joseph, no doubt.

Plus, nobody could say *I* wasn't there for him.

Because just like now, as I sit here in CC's playing the waiting game nine months later, I couldn't possibly be *more* available.

## Chapter 5

Unlike some people who haven't even bothered to check in with me in, hm, let's see now, what's today?

Wonderful World

**Wednesday, August 24, 2005 – 8:30 a.m.**

What a difference a day makes. Following a committed nap yesterday afternoon I resolved to knock out the first few coffee shop odes, even if that meant staying up all night. Imagine my surprise when I reviewed the fine print only to find that the first draft was due not next Wednesday but *this* Wednesday. As in today.

Not exactly the first time I've miscalculated a deadline, this little contretemps did not, I must confess, come as a full-blown surprise, nor was it altogether unpleasant. What's more, after the initial alarm subsided I found myself uplifted by a mildly jubilant sense of relief since, steely under pressure though I am, there was no way I could pull off two dozen reviews in a night. Five, no problem. Ten, assuming ample Internet cooperation, maybe. But any more than that, well, a masochist I'm not. And besides, what really was the point of writing even one if I was already toast? Wasn't the only sound course of action to put the writing on hold until such nitpicky details as preliminary deadlines could be resolved?

Since our first and only face-to-face, I'd communicated with Winnie only by email, bouncing the occasional query off her to let her know that, irrespective of her own limited vision, shrewd literary choices were in fact being made. And based on her swift no-nonsense replies I concluded that an economical electronic missive was again in order, a few well-chosen words assembled in my medium of choice that would leave a slightly dazed Winnie brimming with comprehension: *So what if he's a little absent-minded? That man is at the top of his game.*

Or not.

"Go see her!" the choirboy piped, insensitive to my position that such encounters fall squarely under To Be Avoided At All Costs.

I nuked a Lean Cuisine and hit the couch, unable to summarily dismiss the notion that an in-person appearance might have PR value.

I snatched up the remote and snapped on the TV, then levered upright.

Courtesy of a listless channel surf, a wholly unexpected programming bonanza—a PBS marathon of *Brideshead Revisited*—had just taken priority.


Thus now I sit bleary-eyed at Le Café du Monde, waiting for two things: 1) Winnie to report to her pitiless place of commerce, which is right up the street, and 2) the snail-like Gretnan who took my order to reappear with my breakfast. In the meantime, I'm making notes just in case, since this place's prominence in the guidebook is of course a given. Besides being the oldest continuously operating coffee stand in the country, established in 1862, Le Café du Monde is the only coffee establishment in the world where you can get an authentic beignet. Located at the north edge of the French Market, which runs alongside the river from Jackson Square to Esplanade Avenue, it also bears the distinction of never closing except, as the menu decal on the napkin dispenser informs, "on Christmas Day and on the day an occasional Hurricane passes too close to New Orleans." It's also...

Wait...

Oh boy, here it comes.

Ah. Heaven, if it existed, would surely be something like this, a trivial-at-most variation on the theme of coffee, confectioners sugar, and deep-fried dough. And as I tear off a chunk of beignet, pack it full of powder with the back of my spoon, dunk it in my chicory-laced café au lait, and pop the coffee-logged morsel into my mouth, I find it indecent that I don't come here more often. I'd forgotten how much I used to love this place during my first years in New Orleans, hardly able to believe that it was both open 24 hours and within an easy walk. What more could a chronic insomniac ask for? Not that large quantities of sugar and coffee are conducive to sleep. But I was, after all, still operating under the illusion that time was on my side, a misperception no doubt abetted by early sobriety.

Calling to mind an AA saying I can't quite remember but which has something to do with a broken shoestring, the idea being that it doesn't take much to make a recovering drunk pick up a drink. In the case of my 1998 decision to pick up and leave the Big Apple following a 16-year love-hate relationship, my shoestring was an early morning ambulance shrieking down Lexington Avenue as I stood outside Bloomingdale's ("outside" being the operative word, as I couldn't even afford to window shop there), fingers plunged into ears so forcefully it's a miracle no damage occurred. In that moment, I knew that the Big If-You-

Can-Make-It-There-You'll-Make-It-Anywhere Apple was never going to be my apple, forcing me to join the ignoble ranks of those obliged to wonder: Does *not* being able to make it there mean you won't make it anywhere, or just dramatically lower the odds?

Whatever the case, my settling on New Orleans for my great escape was based on a few factors, including location (warmer), lower cost of living (my days of paying two-thirds of my salary for a matchbox were over), and streetcars (having never owned an automobile and harboring no desire to). Also appealing was the history angle since I'd majored in French and spent my Junior year abroad. Nevertheless, the intensity with which this otherwise unlikely place sprang to mind as the ideal locale for a restorative sojourn on my way to some place more practical has always struck me as more fortuitous than planned, since my sole previous visit to New Orleans took place in 1973, exactly a quarter century before I made the semi-deliberate leap.

The occasion in that eons-ago circumstance was one of the regional Baptist conventions that in Daddy's mind did double duty as a family vacation, fooling no one but in this case generating a good deal more excitement than usual chez nous. And truly, with the exception of Becky, who remained her usual unimpressed big sister self, the rest of us had been preparing as if it really was going to be fun. In her efforts to rally the troops, Mom had not only checked a pile of history books out of the library but purchased a guidebook, which between her and me had been consumed and regurgitated to my father and my big brother Noah every chance we got, like mother birds preparing their chicks for flight. Between those books and the household set of *World Book Year Books*, I for one felt well-prepped. I'd also formed a number of rather titillating impressions that placed this destination in a whole other category from our usual excursions to places like Union City, Tennessee. On the one hand, there was the recreational side of New Orleans that the guidebook sought to emphasize using terms like "historic" and "celebratory" and, a good deal more intriguing, "revelry" and "debauchery." Then there were the crisper, no-nonsense *World Book* recaps of a city still recovering from "Billion-Dollar-Betsy," the costliest hurricane in U.S. history, with colossal economic initiatives designed to hasten recovery including the new 33-story International Trade Mart Tower (subsequently renamed the World Trade Center) overlooking the Mississippi River, the $13.5 million Rivergate Convention and Exhibition facility (in which my father's meetings were held), a $35 million domed stadium for use by New Orleans' new major league football team (whose name for some reason caused my father to shake his head), expansion to NASA's Michoud rocket booster assembly plant on the outskirts of the city, and a second 24-mile-long "causeway" bridge across the lake to the North. Despite this aggressively pro-development phase, New Orleans was also the home of preservationists impassioned enough to have quashed the U.S. Bureau of Public Roads' proposed six-lane Vieux Carré Expressway through the heart of the French Quarter, where in 1968 much of the city's 250th anniversary celebration took place, with torchlit parades and Mardi Gras floats on the river and a weeklong jazz celebration featuring Duke Ellington, Dave Brubeck, and Louis Armstrong—all of whom just so happened to also strut their stuff on one of the sampler albums that had come with the Sears stereo system Daddy had surprised us with a few Christmases back. As if all that weren't enough, there was also the intriguingly Big City side of New Orleans—what the

*World Books* referred to as "racial unrest," embodied by things like Black Panther arrests and fire bombings, with the city's "Negro" population having soared 15 percent during the 1960s while the total population fell 5 percent; corruption spotlighted by the "perverse turn" in the political fortune of District Attorney Jim Garrison, who following national acclaim for his investigations into the assassination of JFK had been arrested with nine other men on charges including interstate transportation of pinball machines for gambling; and the "monumental nightmare" (according to then Police Superintendent Joseph Giarrusso) of "roving young toughs" attacking Mardi Gras visitors in the French Quarter and hitting Al Hirt in the mouth with a chunk of concrete during a parade.

In short, as a hyper-inquisitive kid from Paducah, Kentucky, I was raring to go, although in advance of that voyage I never imagined that Noah and I would do what we did. And yet with Daddy at the convention center and Mom taking a nap and Becky off sulking about something or other, there Noah and I were, in the lobby of the church dormitory on Rampart Street, staring out the squat picture window and jokingly daring one another in forbidden directions when a spark of rebellion flared and we found ourselves waiting for the old lady concierge to turn her back. Well aware that by venturing off church grounds we were in flagrant violation of one of those Reverend Singleton edicts Not To Be Questioned much less disobeyed, it was, needless to say, not without apprehension that we took the plunge. And we'd gone no more than a block when my outlaw resolve started to get wobbly knees, with formerly abstract descriptors like "seedy" and "high crime" assuming vivid proportions as a face heavy with makeup yet not persuasively female floated alongside us staring but saying nothing as we navigated our way around a man snoring into a puddle of puke beside an overturned trash can. And as the face finally lurched away, my fingers darted out and latched onto the hand of my older brother, who'd been plowing single-mindedly forward. And even more than afraid I all at once felt ashamed, because at age thirteen and fifteen we were too old for that. And so I was reluctantly loosening my grip when with a flip of his wrist Noah secured my hand in his and the dinginess began to recede, as if we'd been blessed with a second sunrise or detoured into Disney World (which had opened the year before and was high on my list) or some other world where things didn't just shine but *glowed*, from the Gingerbread houses to the cobblestoned streets. And as we proceeded deeper and deeper into the Quarter, hand in hand, I felt privy to something at once everlasting and fleeting, an impression encapsulated in a single moment silent but for the shrill chorus of scores of invisible birds, which as Noah and I burst out onto Jackson Square lifted up from inside a great magnolia, the dark swatches of their powerful featherweight beings swirling and banking in daredevil unison, then exploding like expanding consciousness across the luminous morning sky.

And then, there we were—at Noah's intended destination, I presumed. For after squeezing between a sleepy coffee stand (yes) and a concrete floodwall and chugging up the levee he'd come to a stop, standing stock-still and gazing out at that roiling ribbon of life. And boy oh boy, even at that early morning hour fully alive the Mississippi was, the flickering tongue of the halfway-up sun flopped all the way out across that great river's silvery width, which was hooting and churning and whistling with every manner of watertight contraption short of a raft sailored by

Huck and Jim, all within what seemed like throwing distance of where *we* were, while a little ways down on our left other vessels creaked against wooden wharves piled high with cargo being heaved about by rough-looking men—homeless, perpetually restless souls with no true desire, my young mind had no trouble imagining, than to shove off again the first chance they got.

How long we hung out there I don't know, only that—as much as part of me wanted to stay all day—it was time enough for me to start worrying about us getting back, along with this silly notion: What if Noah, who tended to get fixated on things, wanted to watch those boats forever?

"Ready?" I nudged, breaking the spell.

And we were on our way, with me taking the lead, heading back the same way we'd come, through the cut-out in the flood-wall and across Jackson Square and up St. Anne. Except that this time at Bourbon Street I peeled off to the right, wanting to underscore that I was no longer afraid by offering a final gulp of that illicit infusion. Conscious all the same of the need to make time, I committed myself to a brisk pace even though Noah seemed to be dragging his feet, and I was about to turn left toward Rampart when I realized he was more than a few steps behind.

"What?" I called out from the corner of St. Philip.

He put a finger to his lips and motioned for me to join him.

Hesitantly, I made my way back to where he lingered, staring into the mouth of an ancient pub as if transfixed.

"Noah…"

"Shhh…"

And then I heard it too—that unmistakable voice—delivering its sacred message straight unto us:

*Wonderful World*

*I see trees of green,*

*red roses too,*

*I see them bloom,*

*for me and you,*

*and I think to myself,*

*What a wonderful world.*

So, bully for me as I stood outside Bloomingdale's, the first and only place that came to mind was New Orleans. Sure, the place has its share of problems (you know a city's corrupt when top school officials embezzle millions from their own pitifully impoverished districts). But just as there's something to be said for living in the City That Never Sleeps, there's something down-right sublime about residing in a town that peddles itself as the City That Care Forgot, where Time does business in pajamas and takes frequent catnaps. And undeniably, New Orleans has made the concept of *laissez-faire* into an art form dating back at least to the Civil War, when it became the first major city of the Deep South to be occupied by Union forces, which remained through-out the last three years of the war. The alternative, I suppose, would have been for the citizens of The Paris of the South to fight back. But as the ships of General Farragut came up the Missis-sippi in 1862, the closest the people of New Orleans came to taking up arms was to stand alongside the levee brandishing their parasols and shaking their fists.

Nevertheless, when at just over three years sober I an-nounced to my home group that I was moving down here, a collective gasp filled the room. Although those who shared subsequently refrained from commenting, after the meeting one well-meaning recovering alcoholic after another tried to talk me out of "pulling a geographic," each proffering some tale of rapid and absolute moral decline in the Big Easy. The exception was a frisky old gentleman named Elmer G., one of those alcoholics who has smoked so hard and so long that the skin has begun to flake off from the collar bone up, through whom I came into possession of a coffee-stained napkin inscribed with the phone number of a one Louella Arceneaux.

As it turned out, Elmer apparently cared more about scoring points with his former lady friend by helping her rent out her dependency apartment than he did about the destiny of a fellow 12-Stepper, since what Louella considered a "bachelor pad" I placed in the category of crimes against humanity. After checking into the Days Inn on Canal Street, I'd gone straight to Louella's Royal Street gallery (where an entire wall of Nagel prints should have tipped me off), then been led through a perfectly charming courtyard up a perfectly charming set of wooden stairs and onto the perfectly charming gallery of a slave quarter dependency—then back into a dank hovel that hadn't been redecorated since the 1970s...*if* you could envisage what was there as "décor," as I endeavored to do as I held my breath and nodded while Cruella informed me that the place came furnished. Far easier was to imagine a long line of hunched-over NYC expats drinking themselves to death out of jelly jars not destined for eBay bidding wars at the knotty pine table that took up most of the living room—that is, when they were not passed out behind the threadbare sheet Cruella referred to as "drapery" as she regally yanked it aside to reveal a toffee-colored mattress inside the wall indentation she called a bedroom. Why, it was exactly like being in New York City! Except for one thing: It wasn't NYC, where while living in squalor you at least still get to tell people you live "in The City," automatically implying that your life is interesting and teleological, and sometimes even buying into the illusion yourself. But this was New Orleans. Louisiana. Yankee Doodle Doo. And even if that apartment was only three hundred and fifty dollars a month, it would never be a place I could live (at least not without Mr. Hennessy), not even if all of its furniture and curtains and wallpaper and plastic eating utensils with tooth marks in them and everything else not nailed down were catapulted into the courtyard for a bonfire I could rumba naked around. So, in one of the rare and merciful instances of my being able to not "people please" (as they also say in AA), I looked Cruella in the false eyelash and told two bald-faced lies:

"This is *fabulous*!"

and

"There's just one other place I need to check out!"

"Not a prob!" she croaked through lipstick-encrusted dentures.

Nevertheless, it was clearly at that point that she began to wise up because that's when she introduced me to her framer. "Hey! Christopher!" she said, snapping the filter off a More, "why don't you show Sammy here around!"—perhaps thinking his doe-eyed sweetness would sway me her way. And indeed, to give credit where credit is due, from the get-go it wasn't hard to imagine Christopher and I sipping chicory coffee at the cast-iron table beneath the fruit-laden banana trees in the gallery courtyard, crisp curtains fluttering from my in-the-process-of-being-reinvented (*might* that wall come down?) Crescent City nest, where we tended to sleep quite late. Also in all fairness, it's to

*The Coffee Shop Chronicles of New Orleans*

Christopher that I owe at least a smidgeon of my fondness for Le Café du Monde, since on that first day almost seven years ago it was he who instructed me in the dying art of dignified beignet-eating in breezy weather. And not just that, for his passion for those hot, sugar-topped delicacies was a privilege to behold, like an orthodox ritual, with him not hurrying the precious cargo to his mouth but pausing beforehand to ingest its aroma, eyes closed, knees pressed together and skewed to one side, head cocked to the other, as if preparing to accept a wafer ensuring life everlasting. A few months later Christopher died from AIDs complications, although I didn't receive that news for more than a year, long after my zany impulse to call him up and ask him out had puffed by like powdered sugar in the wind.

Beignets aside, after I'd thanked Christopher and bid him farewell it dawned on me that I was going to have to find an apartment, quickly, since no matter how much I adored the concepts of maid service and complimentary continental breakfasts, the Days Inn wasn't a long-term fiscal option. Until then I'd been entertaining the possibility that there was something providential about my choice of New Orleans, the rainbow being Elmer G.'s apartment referral. Now that I'd seen the place, however, the destiny angle had been dashed asunder, forcing me to put a checkmark into the "No" column of my never-ending spiritual debate as I faced the prospect of having to tramp around New Orleans looking for a place to live. Which is when I came up with an idea so practical it still concerns me: Pick up the paper and check the Classifieds.

Ten minutes later I was in Jackson Square, seated on a park bench facing St. Louis Cathedral, *Times-Picayune* spread out on my lap, Bic poised, bracing myself for the disappointment of taking days if not weeks to find something decent. And yet as I sat there drawing circles around unreliable clusters of words I found it difficult to muster an appropriate level of dread as the square filled up with people plying their trades—artists and tarot card readers and face painters and musicians—mixing and mingling with tourists and residents alike. It was one of those sunny, low-humidity November days when the weather's so good you wonder why everybody doesn't live in New Orleans. And with my tummy still warm with café au lait and beignets I found myself defiantly lazing there, wondering about the statue in the center of the park (General Jackson, I presumed?), fantasizing about landing one of the grand apartments overlooking the square (commissioned by the Baroness Micaela Almonester de Pontalba, I'd later learn, whose rapacious father-in-law shot two of her fingers off before killing himself with the same pistol), distracted by the diffuse aroma of what I'd come to recognize as boiled crawfish (from the restaurant on the corner I'd come to identify with its treacherously lardy sidewalk). At the same time, I became aware of my attention returning again and again to the soaring facade of the church itself, my eyeballs docey-doe-ing between its two towers before landing on the panel doors at ground level, through which citizens of the world every bit as unhurried and aimless as I kept going in and coming out, like air being breathed. At no time, however, did I entertain the notion of going inside. And yet, I did.

While living in France I'd toured many great cathedrals, from Strasbourg to Paris to Aix-en-Provence. So even though the foyer to St. Louis Cathedral was almost large enough to house the little church I'd grown up in—and despite the plaque claiming that it was the oldest Catholic cathedral in America—I wasn't expecting much. Yet the instant I set foot inside that candle-lit cavern I felt at ease in a way I hadn't before. Because unlike those other churches, which tended to be overwhelming and cold, this one was of a scale at once holy and unassuming, with a second-floor gallery that humanized its sky-high columns. And as I stood in the back watching specters of incense rise, in my never-ending tally the God pictured on the frescoed ceiling seemed not just possible but certain, because how else could man have accomplished a feat such as this? And so struck was I by this spontaneous reverence that I didn't realize a mass was in session until a woman stood up and began to sing.

Latin? Italian?

I wasn't sure, but I can tell you this: It was a sound not of this day but of ancient times, of sieges and martyrs and sons and daughters who'd believed and served and died for...all this, I guessed, a sound that would have given Callas a run for her money and one that had me putting a checkmark in the "Yes" column before I even realized I'd picked up the scorecard. Next, a period of chanting I comprehended no more than the words of the hymn, a calling out and responding between priest and parishioners, which, like an abstract painting that can be experienced only through the abandonment of the intellect, exerted an effect on me so subtle I couldn't resist, as if I were both falling and being lifted up.

As the chanting stopped and the congregation settled back into the pews, a bent man appeared from a shadowy alcove and began to shuffle down the center aisle. From where I was standing, it looked as though one of his arms was freakishly long, with a clawlike hand the size of a baseball mitt. But as he moved closer I realized he was holding a stick with a collection basket lashed to it. *Ha!* Clearly Roman Catholic wasn't so different from Baptist after all, I concluded as the old man notched the basket into row after row. At the same time, every so often he jerked his head in my direction as if he was trying to get my attention, an agenda I persisted in doubting until he ended up a few feet away, glowering at me.

For a long moment I tried to ignore him, but he kept on staring. And with his gaze burning into me I finally turned and nodded, thinking he might be a stroke victim and that grimace a smile.

No such luck.

Instead, he kept on glaring in an increasingly hostile way, to such a degree that I felt like I might should skedaddle.

In that instant, however, he hobbled over to the placard behind the last pew and thrust out a knotty finger:

### CHURCH GUIDELINES

*And?* I thought, since I'd already seen the darn sign, which practically slapped you in the face as you entered. On the other hand, it also occurred to me that I'd stopped reading after the first few words, as in immediately following the "WELCOME TO OUR CATHEDRAL!" part.

*Look! Look! Look!* the crooked finger seemed to screech as it sawed back and forth across the bulleted points under the greeting.

*Would you please just leave me alone?* I telepathically implored.

The answer was no.

*The Coffee Shop Chronicles of New Orleans*

Seeing no other remedy, I stepped forward and squinted at the sign:

**PLEASE DO NOT STAND IN BACK OF CHURCH
WHEN SERVICES ARE IN SESSION.**

The man nodded and lowered his hand. And for a moment we hovered in ocular stand-off, Organized Religion v. B. Sammy Singleton. And ordinarily, that would have been it, and I would have been gone.

But there was nothing ordinary about this day now almost seven years past. Because there I was, in that city that had already offered to take me in, no questions asked. Preparing to embark on something new. To set a course toward I had no idea where and yet somehow trusted to be better than where I'd been. And so instead of forsaking that house of God, I tucked my *Times-Picayune* under my arm and pulled out a ten-spot and tossed it in the old geezer's basket, then took my place in the congregation.

Lucky Dog Dollars

## Wednesday, August 24, 2005 – 9:30 p.m.

E ven when the act is at least partially induced by sleep depri-
vation and fanciful images of a taut and wistful young Jere-
my Irons, facing the proverbial music apparently pays. The short
of it is, I've just received a new lease on life thanks to the brave
and beneficent Winnie Hargreaves.

Like I said, Lucky Dog Press is only a few blocks from Le
Café du Monde, and after making the short trek past Jax Brewery
and Tower Records I paused at the football-field-sized French
Quarter parking lot. In the far corner facing the river, Winnie's
building shot up like a middle finger, daring anyone to try to
rezone it or tear it down, even though it looked like it might come
down on its own at any time. During a post-down-payment
thank-you lunch with Lyle at a place of his choosing, I had in fact
wondered aloud how it was possible from a safety and permits
perspective to operate a business on the top floor of a building
that should for all outward appearances be condemned.

"Fire doors," he'd said, winking at a Lucky Cheng's server.

And truer words were never spoken, for it's not hard to imagine that any structural integrity the building may claim hinges
(as it were) on the two-inch-thick steel doors blockading every
exterior and interior doorway and the similarly sturdy-looking

sheets of metal riveted across every window opening. The effect, once inside, is that of a bunker that might easily have resisted bombardment by Farragut's Union navy had it been unleashed. Yet rather than being dark and stuffy inside as one might expect, the building is scrupulously climate-controlled and lighted via an elaborate system of miniature windmills bolted to the roof, reflecting at least one surviving component of Winnie's original business plan.

In any case, by the time I'd cut across the parking lot and stepped into the building's jagged shadow, I'd begun to reconsider my options. There was, after all, a miniscule Starbucks shoehorned into a nook of the Canal Place Shopping Center on the far side of the lot. Helping to compensate for that tease of a coffee shop, there was also an oversized Rue de la Course to my right on South Peter, as well as the venerable Le Café du Monde a few blocks back, each of which presumably came equipped with a phone that could be used to babble some sorry excuse to Winnie. And yet on some relentlessly rational level I knew I owed her a good deal more, having more or less absconded with four thousand Lucky Dog dollars with what the imagination-challenged might consider nothing to show for it. Plus, the slimness of Winnie's chances of seeing any of those sawbucks ever again did imply a certain amount of leverage on the ol' Singleton side.

I sucked it up and circled around to the sole functional entry point and hit the intercom button.

Security equipment whirred.

A red dot blinked.

Then, through the speaker grill, Lyle: "The elevator's busted. You'll have to take the stairs."

"Ha ha. Hey, Lyle. You're kidding, right?"

"Do you hear me laughing?"

Nine flights and twelve fire doors later I staggered up to his desk while wondering if paramedics did multiple stairs.

"Morning!" I panted, willing my chest not to explode.

"Morning," Lyle sighed. And immediately I knew something was up. Because while he was every bit as rumpled and oily as usual, as if he'd just tumbled out of bed fully dressed and inaugurated his morning with a bucket of Popeye's, his natural aura of baseless confidence wasn't quite coming across.

He finished flicking through a short stack of envelopes and slid one forward.

"What's that?" I said.

His horn-rimmed glasses see-sawed atop his teensy nose. "Your next check. Winnie's going to be gone awhile."

*No.* "Oh. Is she okay?"

"She's fine."

He removed the specs and massaged his temples while I flipped open the envelope and peeked inside.

Another four grand. Oh. My. God.

*You wouldn't!* the choirboy gasped.

"Um…listen, Lyle. I'm going to need a little more time."

He vacantly surveyed his desk, which looked like a Mardi Gras parade route the morning after.

"I'm really sorry.

"What? Oh. Fine."

His chin started to tremble.

"Lyle?"

He pushed up off his desk and hurried toward the rear of the loft, wending his way through the cubicles like a lopsided pinball.

"Lyle?" I called out across the wide open space, deserted except for us.

No reply.

I caught up with him inside Winnie's partition, where he stood with his back to me, beside her desk. At the base of his neck was a baby ponytail that was new to me and probably not a good idea.

"Um...Lyle?"

He remained silent a few seconds, then lifted a framed photograph high enough for me to see it over his shoulder. It was the picture from Winnie's desk that I'd observed before, the one of the funny-looking little old man.

"How old do you think he is?"

I shook my head. "Who is it?"

"Jake. He just had another heart attack."

"Oh." I drew the word out in a way that suggested I got it, which I did not. I took a stab. "Winnie's husband?"

Lyle turned to face me. "No, nimwit. Her son. He has progeria."

An icicle started to form in my gut.

"Pro...?"

Lyle studied the picture. "It's a disease. A real motherfucker."

"Oh. Damn."

"He's only 12 years old. Kids with progeria age about seven times faster than normal. Their bodies, that is. Otherwise, they're just regular kids. Except smarter."

"Is he going to be okay?"

He glared at me but let the inanity of the query go. "He's got so many problems. He's had congestive heart failure for years. I've been working here a long time so I've watched him grow…" his voice cracked. "…up."

I gave him a moment, then held out the envelope.

"What?" he said.

"I can't take this. I haven't even…"

"Don't be an idiot. Winnie wouldn't have left it if she didn't want you to have it. She says she thinks you've got a book in you."

"Really?"

"Yes. Really. So go write."


I did.

In fact, aside from an indispensable swing by Bank One, that's pretty much all I've been doing all day long, hunkered down here at my kitchen table, to the point that the old shoulders and eyeballs are beginning to ache, as they should. Because while it's one thing to inconvenience a publishing maven devoid of literary virtue, it's another to place unnecessary stress on the working mother of an afflicted child.

This front and center in mind, the first thing I did upon returning home was put on a pot of French Market and flip open my laptop and settle in for a reality check:

Total number of coffee shop reviews required: 25

Total number of coffee shop reviews written: 0

Pithy historical introduction: 1

Was that a rooster crowing outside?

I pushed back my chair and cracked open the kitchen door and poked my head out. Except for the rumble of trucks on Elysian Fields and a train neighing along the river, the day was Mayberry quiet, with even those mulish mechanical sounds muffled under the dome of steamy morning air. Lured by the aroma of roasting coffee courtesy of the Standard Coffee plant two blocks over, I donned the interior coolness and stepped outside, then slipped along the railing to the end of the dependency and hooked a right. In a covered inset facing the yard was a rusty washer and dryer, which like the AC unit protruding through the wall above them still plugged along with unnatural efficacy.

Dismissing the image of the bulging laundry hamper in my bathroom, I leaned onto the railing, allowing the AC to exhale onto my back. Comprising two lots purchased together by the house's original owner in the early 1850s, Georgia's slice of land was wide and deep, a semi-domesticated jungle of plumbago and lantana and banana trees. A path through the middle, effectively barred by two seasons' worth of collapsed banana tree stalks fermenting from yellow to brown, led to a no-longer-working hot tub in the far right corner. Rising behind that was a wooden fence crawling with creeping fig, the forerunner to any number of crooked back-yard separators of diverse composition and heights separating junky patches of ground belonging to smaller houses in incremental stages of decline, most of them shotgun double rentals. In those patches, I knew, lurked all manner of beasts better suited for country living, including a pig that periodically busted out and went charging through the Marigny pursued by its overindulgent owner; a Burmese python that had, according to local lore, escaped from its tank during a hurricane and thrived on the occasional pet while helping to keep the burglary rate down; and a flock of once-domesticated parrots that now came and went as they pleased. The deviant Dr. Doolittle theme carried over into one of the yards a few houses down, where several chickens supplied eggs to their Earth Mother guardian and anyone not reporting her to animal control. However, so as not to attract attention (including of the snake) they were kept behind bars and had never enjoyed the affections of a rooster as far as I knew. To the left, in the other corner of Georgia's yard, a live oak at least as old as the house effectively blotted out sky and earth, its obese trunk a tangle of woody cat's claw vines that quietly strangled their host while splashing its canopy with exuberant dollops of yellow, as if only under duress had the tree discovered its own ability to flower.

I scooted over to the lakeside railing, which was at about the same height as the top of the feather-edge board fence that ran parallel a couple of Seventies car lengths over. Another undulating mass of creeping fig, the fence definitively fortified Georgia's property on the Northwest side while keeping the courtyard below in perpetual shadow, abetted by a row of spindly crape myrtles, which formed a scruffy scrim on their way to the roof line. On the other side of the fence were the shallow yards of five or six houses fronting Royal, also shotgun doubles, whose triangular rear gables zigzagged along the top of the boards. Between the fence and the foliage and fishily placid neighbors, however, it was easy to pretend that nobody lived there. A few blocks over, between the crape myrtles' mottled branches and blossoms, rose the uneven spires of St. Peter and Paul, the American cousin of

Paris' St. Sulpice.

Still, however, no sign of a rooster. And I was about to write it off as a figment of a procrastinating mind when

Cock-a-doodle-do!

And then again:

Cock-a-doodle-*dooo*!

No stranger to symbolism, I hustled back to the kitchen and grabbed a fresh cup—and almost immediately the picture brightened. For while it was true that I had yet to draft any actual reviews, I'd taken copious notes on:

- CC's (Royal and St. Philip)

- Café Rose Nicaud (Frenchmen and Royal)

- Envie (Decatur and Barracks)

- Zotz (Royal and Kerlerec)

- Le Café du Monde (Jackson Square)

Then, with no further ado, I jammed.

Now, with those five reviews in the bag, I'm ready to call it an early night, since tomorrow I plan to really bring it on.

As for Winnie, well, I can't imagine having a healthy child, much less one with a disease for which there's no treatment or cure.

Which, I might add, is one of the reasons I've personally chosen to not reproduce.

That and to demonstrate just how little self control that requires to the millions who have no business having kids in the first place, and who might well refrain were it not for institutionally encouraged ignorance. I mean really, how can any school exploding with hormone-charged youngsters *not* require courses like "Love, Sex, or Just Plain Stupid?," "If You Start Having Kids Now You'll Always Be Poor," "She'll Be Pregnant in the Morning But You'll Still Be Gay," "The Adoption Option," and the list goes on.

But I digress.

Moreover, on my way home this morning post-Lucky Dog I committed to a program of strict abstinence from diversionary inventory-taking.

At least until the first draft is in Winnie's hands.

That's right: *No more distractions.*

(Shut up.)

In the meantime, as for Catfish, well, he knows where to find me.

8

# Storm's A Comin'

**Thursday, August 25, 2005 – 5:30 p.m.**

This day did not go anything as planned, such that I'm now back to square one guidebook-wise as I sit here frenetically freehand journaling. Transforming the landscape of my kitchen table's emerald green top into a mini bone yard is Catfish's collection of Old Paris china, seventeen chipped and hairline-cracked cups and plates with faded gold and apricot bands, plus my long-time favorite: a lidded gravy boat with an ivory acorn knob. For at least the fifth time since I unwrapped the dishes this afternoon I've paid quiet respects to their exquisite remains, as if whatever angels or demons that may repose therein might take pity and possess me with the understanding I so sorely lack, since I can't for the life of me explain the windfall of these dishes or attribute their presence here to anything good.

Still riding the wave of noble intentions I was up and running by 9 a.m., with Rue de la Course and PJ's next on my coffee shop canticle list, both requiring more on-site examination of the foodservice milieu. And because Rue was closer, on South Peters opposite Winnie's building, forthwith I went, braving the street-cleaning machines raging along Decatur; researched, poking my nose into every coffee shop cranny as the reasonably efficient counter guy (who could have lost the linty sock hat and put on a few pounds) pulled me a double-cap; and—after claiming a primo table dead center—proceeded to conquer:

Rue de la Course, French Quarter (South Peters between Bienville and Conti) occupies the ground floor of a mid-19$^{th}$ century brick building that has happily retained many of its original architectural elements, including grooved iron columns and pressed tin ceiling. Spanning the entire width of the block, it is one of the largest coffee shops in the city, with over two dozen marble-top bistro tables spaced throughout. Like other Rues around town, the ambiance is trendy but low-key, with a mildly funky edge and a predominantly younger clientele. However, whereas the Uptown shops are usually crowded with college students spilling over from Tulane and Loyola, this Rue attracts a mélange ranging from professional to..."

That was as far as I got, however, for just as I'd begun to burrow into the full depth of my writing groove the street door gusted open, ushering in a raucous family unit immediately identifiable as Not From Here. Justifiably perturbed, I advised them away from my territory with a fierce yet subtle glower, but to no avail. Paying me no heed whatsoever the doughy-faced daddy plopped onto a chair two tables away as the Mary Kay mommy made a beeline for the counter and the fruits of their loins—three of them, ranging narrowly in age from about six to eight—began running up and down the length of the place in a way that did Communist China's one-child policy proud.

Genetics can be so very unkind, much more so than might illustrate any Darwinian survival-of-the-fittest Nature Channel episode during which, for example, eerily childlike snow monkey babies starve to death over an unusually harsh winter on the Serengeti while photographers rigorously committed to non-interference capture the progression in powerful time-lapse images: going, going, gone. Not that this biped family was in any danger. To the contrary, based on their current exhibition I judged them as easily capable of thwarting multiple attacks if dumped into shark-infested waters simply by confounding the hapless predators with so much activity, what with the kids racing back and forth and the mother darting up and down the service counter going "what's that?! what's that?!" while the hubby squealed unrealistic preferences and picked his teeth—leaving me no choice but to unleash the full force of my observational skills onto the fella, who with his slack cheeks and nasal bray immediately revealed himself as one of those souls bound by destiny to wind up memorialized only by *Unsolved Mysteries* reruns, having been slaughtered in bed with no clear-cut motive, his false teeth grinning inside a glass on the bedside table, the wife uncooperative, the kids too messed up by Dianetics to be of much help. Even crueler, I imagined, would be the cookie-cutter genetic and psycho-social heritage he would have foisted upon his feckless progeny, whose beady eyes and graceless demeanor all but guaranteed that they would one day meet a similarly unlamented fate, their little...

Then I caught myself—doing the inventory-taking thing again—and stopped, and with Desiderata-like forbearance considered this: That they, just like I, had a right to be here.

(Or was that the choirboy?)

Meanwhile, Daryl, Teryl, and—you got it—Cheryl continued to swarm the place like addled wasps, bringing to mind rolled-up newspapers and crunching sounds, and leading one to wonder why some parents think they're entitled to a lifelong slap on the back for something as non-essential as producing a child? It's not like there's a shortage, particularly of starving third-world orphans in dire need of adoption...

*SAMMY!*

I know, I know. And yet *damn*—those kids—buzzing back and forth and back and forth while I tracked their activity over the top of my laptop screen like a spectator at a hellish ping-pong match. There's no way the parents will let this continue, I tried to convince myself, glancing about for a show of solidarity from fellow local patrons. In addition to being on the thin side, however, the other dredges of the mid-morning Rue crowd were clearly less committed than I. Aside from the wasps, was I the only one there without a cell phone ear muff, I was beginning to wonder, when I locked eyes with a phone-free damsel who obviously shared my irritation, because after faux strangling herself purely for my benefit she bagged her own laptop and hit the door while the rest of the hold-outs chatted insensibly on. Needless to say, this collateral damage was lost on the wasp quintet, who continued to merrily desecrate the shrine of my morn. Still, at any moment, I continued to delude myself, they'd ascertain that Rue did not carry Yoo-Hoo or Pop-Tarts or whatever it was they were hoping for, at which point they'd load up on toothpicks and toilet paper and depart. Imagine my astonishment then, when linty-hat guy began piling foodstuffs onto Mamma Wasp's tray.

*Just get up and leave!*

Definitely the choirboy.

And for once we were on the same page.

Without further negotiation I slid my laptop into its case and headed for the door.

Now, let me say this: I've never been 100 percent convinced that those *Children of the Corn* movies are not based, at least in theory, on the actual proclivities of certain youngsters residing in the Midwest. And what happened next lends credence to this suspicion. Because just as I thought I'd safely shepherded myself through the obstacle course of tables and chairs so as to avoid those three frenzied creatures, two of them joined hands and launched themselves at me, shrieking at the top of their lungs.

Instinctively, I clutched my laptop to my bosom and braced for impact. But at the very last instant the two of them released one another, whooshing past so close on either side the slipstream lifted my hair.

Clearly, this was no laughing matter.

Without so much as a look over my shoulder I cast decorum aside and fled. And I was once again feeling confident in my ability to escape when my foot slammed into the base of a bistro table and I almost went down.

By some miracle, I regained equilibrium. And with both eyes on the prize I lurched toward the door, telling myself that I was almost there, almost there, when the third child struck me full-body between the shoulder blades, as if the first two kids were a slingshot and he its belated projectile.

"Umph!" I cried as my laptop twirled out of my hands and landed with a crack by the entrance while I attempted to break my fall with a push-up-like maneuver that left me winded but physio-logically intact.

For his part, it appeared that the devil child had vaulted off one of my elbows and skidded across a table top onto the floor, quiet at last.

But not for long.

"Eee-yewww!" he began to screech seconds later, pointing theatrically in my direction.

What happened next is still something of a blur, what with the blood gushing from Daryl's nose and Poppa Wasp suddenly concerned with nothing else in the world so much as the child's welfare and Mamma Wasp hurrying hither and thither with napkins and makeshift tourniquets and such, at which point a manager materialized. Meanwhile, with neither parent as yet able to extract coherency from their exsanguinating child, I seized the opportunity, scrambling forth to collect whatever might be left of my laptop and then racing out onto the city sidewalk as the devil child's wails achieved an impressive crescendo, its head spinning round and round and round on its bony stalk of a neck, or so I imagined.

Panting like angina itself I ducked behind the life-sized Woldenberg and Child bronzes that face the river and scanned the grassy expanse behind them. Thankfully, aside from a couple of shirtless dudes lobbing a frisbee across the lawn, the coast was not just clear but high-summer deserted.

Belching a sigh of relief I turned back toward the water and collapsed on the granite steps beside the bespeckled philanthropist and his attentive young charge. Although it was only midmorning, the sun was already high and beginning to make the beaded flesh of my forehead sizzle, to such a degree that I briefly considered other seating options. Flanking the stainless steel sculpture I'd just scurried past were two gigantic Queen palms whose fronds air-brushed gray feathers onto the green, while a bit further down the promenade a few donut-shaped benches encircling thick crape myrtles squatted unoccupied, in between shifts of homeless and grunge. But in the end I didn't merit comfort as I unzipped my computer case to inspect the rattle, which involved a wedge of black plastic formerly attached to the monitor and a dented battery pack that refused to remain snapped in place.

I rezipped the case and gazed out at the river, which seemed to be moving faster than usual, as if fully devoted to the task of washing away all of my hopes and dreams. *So this is how the "new career" caper ends*, I thought, feeling foolish to have considered the possibility that I could compose something of worth and perhaps even beauty, even if only within the context of a New Orleans guidebook. The truth was, I couldn't even get a crummy first draft to Winnie on time. And now, this—B. Sammy Singleton self-sabotage at its finest! Even if the computer could be repaired (or at the very least, the hard drive recovered), it could take days to get rolling again, not to mention bounce back from what I couldn't help but view as cosmic retribution for having backslid yet again into judgmental behavior. In the meantime, what was I supposed to do? Horn in on one of Naomi's computers? The possibility made me cringe, not because she'd mind but because she wouldn't. To the contrary, she'd be more than happy to oblige. But between her having periodically dropped by to "check on me" during the weekend jail trauma and her gracious downplaying of the car-scraping event, I was beginning to feel like a charity case, and there's only so much well-meaning supportiveness a person can take.

A few feet away was the nearest in a row of evenly spaced

fleur-de-lis-themed trash receptacles that lined the riverfront like robotic sentries, and with all my might I heaved my laptop into its indifferent slit of a mouth.

Okay, I didn't, but it crossed my mind.

And in that instant something twisted in me as I realized that wasn't an option. Not because of Winnie or Jake or monies paid. Rather, at some point this stupid guidebook had become something more, something I now gradually identified as...a step. Yes, a step. Like my move to New Orleans, a voyage not so much toward one thing as away from another. And yet perhaps because every step is both, those two aims had become entangled to such a degree that now only the motion could be trusted or understood. But not abandoned. Because as was sometimes the case with my journaling, in indulging myself in the dream of that journey I'd felt connected, like a conduit for something more useful than me.

Which, I supposed with a melodramatic sigh, meant plowing ahead freehand until the computer issue could be resolved.

Which now that I thought about it might not be such a bad thing since freehand was, after all, "the only truly organic form of expository writing" according to Catfish, who...

—son of a gun!—

...had the practically brand new desktop computer from his Decatur Street shop stored at his Bywater warehouse.

And who owed me.

Big time.

I mean really, who could argue that this debacle was at least as much his fault as mine, since for going on two weeks he'd managed to derail my creative process, and without so much as a post-incarceration howdy-do. What's more, if there was anyone who hardly ever imposed on him for anything it was yours truly. Quickly reviewing our history I could recall maybe a half dozen times I'd been obliged to do so, such as when (right here on this very Moonwalk, actually) I'd twisted my ankle on the way home from *Moulin Rouge* while trying to hit the high note in "Come What May" and Catfish had *carried* me out to the street; or the time not long after that, on the morning of 9-11, while sitting in Georgia's living room watching CNN with Georgia and Catfish and Naomi I'd started sobbing and been unable to pull it together; or the time a few months ago when, during Catfish's vigil following my hernia operation he'd peeked into the recovery cubicle bathroom just in time to keep me from toppling off the commode in a low-blood-pressure blackout. What's more, while I had no one to blame for this book business but myself, it was Catfish who'd been blowing onto the ashes of my adolescent fantasy of becoming a writer ever since I let that historical tidbit slip.

And yet now, *where* was he?

It was time I found out.

I looped the computer case strap over my shoulder and took off down the promenade, an unlikely breeze Farrah Fawcett feathering my hair as I tried to muster an appropriate degree of annoyance over the man's basic lack of consideration. Instead, however, with mind-numbing sharpness I saw him dropping whatever he was doing and taking charge, pummeling me with words of encouragement while taxi-ing me to a computer repair shop to drop off my laptop, then to his Bywater warehouse to pick up the loaner, then back to my apartment for a one-two-three USB set-up followed by a light lunch at Pizza Kitchen. Come to think of it, make that a hearty one, since in my rush out of Rue de la Course I'd left a perfectly good scone beside the tepid inch of a house blend refill. Yes, a Cesar salad followed by a Pizza Margherita (followed, perhaps, by a crème brulée) should do it, I'd negotiated when I ran into the following sticking point: Assuming I was willing to put life and limb on the line by venturing unaccompanied into the Tremé, what assurance did I have that Catfish would even be there?

None whatsoever, an unfortunate truth that spotlighted how much our visits had dwindled since he'd closed his shop on Decatur back in June. And yet for some reason as I strutted along the levee in the general direction of his house none of that mattered, because I also knew this: that when I finally did catch up with him, he'd be there.

And with his house key on my key ring, I was prepared to wait.

I just hoped the cupboard wasn't bare. By this time my stomach was starting to rumble, and Catfish had never been big on—

"How do?" the gravelly voice rang out.

I glanced back, visually confirming what my ears already had. It was Jonah, one of the local "freelance" pickers. True to form, he was peddling along on his vintage Schwinn, which was all the more impressive in that all of its parts—from its sparkly banana-shaped seat to its chopper-style handlebars—had been remaindered from different bikes. The exception was the enormous wire basket hanging off the front, which was originally used for transporting shrimp to market.

"Hey, Jonah!"

I slowed to a stop and so did the breeze, the damp heat slapping up in its place. As usual Jonah looked like he'd wriggled out of a rabbit hole, which as far as I knew he had since he'd been "temporarily address-less" for as long as I'd known him. Also in keeping with his usual flair, despite the temperature he was sporting a stocking cap pulled down to his eyebrows and several layers of clothing encrusted with dried mud. Although he was about the size of a skinny seven-year-old, he could have been anywhere from fifty to eighty, the only clear signals being the yellowish whites of his eyes and borderline toothlessness. Personal longevity aside, he'd been a fixture of the French Quarter for as long as anyone could remember, like Ruthie the Duck Lady or Jude Acers–Chess Expert, except that his range was not limited to the Vieux Carré. Rather, he was equally likely to be found pedaling through the Marigny or Tremé or Faubourg St. John—wherever and whenever his "duty" took him—a duty that consisted of salvaging "treasures" that would otherwise be "gone for good" from the thousands of derelict 19th century homes all over the city. Sometimes he came up with nothing more than a few marbles or doll appendages or vintage pop bottles dug out from under a house, while other times his pickings were more substantial—a jeweled stained-glass window without many cracks, or a set of hand-hewn cypress brackets, or a courtyard-sized cache of marble bricks. Regardless of street value each item was personally excavated and delivered by Jonah, with most of his goods going to the junktique dealers along Decatur, where he went by several names. The last time I'd seen him he'd been weaving down Elysian Fields alongside Washington Square Park, a fluted porch column suspended across his basket in a balancing act worthy of any Cirque de Soleil.

"How you doing?" I said as he scooted to a stop beside me.

"Oooh…" he inhaled and looked away, a dash of red infusing his cheeks as he took a moment to ponder, as he always did, although I'd never known him not to come back with the same reply, which he proceeded to do. "Can't complain, can't complain," he said, smacking his lips.

"Glad to hear it."

"Yes indeed, yes indeed."

I lifted my chin toward the wide, shallow basket, which appeared to be empty except for a packing quilt lining the bottom. "Traveling light, aren't you?"

He grinned, revealing a tilted tooth. "You got that right! Thanks to Catfish, I'm on vacation!"

My ears pricked up. "Really? How's that?"

He dug into his pocket and revealed the tip of a wad of cash.

"Wow!"

"Um hm. Bought every single thing I had."

"Did he! And, um…when was that?"

Jonah cocked his head to one side. "You know, I can't really say," he frowned following a pensive pause.

"Yesterday? Last week?"

Another period of consideration. "Yes," he finally said, poking the air. "About like that."

I swiped off my forehead with the back of my hand. Between the heat and the unconsumed carbs, I was beginning to feel lightheaded. "Okay. And…where did you see him?"

"Tremé. Over to his house."

"Really? Because I was just…"

A sunbeam splintered against the bike's handlebars, ending in starbursts.

"…on my way over there."

*Catfish threw open the door and smiled.*

Jonah leaned forward. "You okay?"

The lights almost went out.

*Catfish threw open the door and smiled.*

"Hey!" Jonah cried, waving in and out as I caught hold of the basket.

I notched back the dizziness with a few deep breaths. "Low blood sugar," I gasped. "It's nothing."

Jonah squinted at me through his handlebars.

"No, really. This happens sometimes. It's called hypoglycemia."

"You don't say."

"Seriously. I just…need a bite to eat."

"If you say so."

Still braced against the basket, I gulped additional oxygen as Jonah held the V-shaped handlebars stable. On the same plane as my nose his hands were as cracked and brown and constant as the soil they sifted, at once the instruments and the yield. And as this notion congealed I caught a whiff of something wholesome and wild, like a summer field of flowering weeds.

His eyes flitted and fluttered like a moth against glass, then lighted upon my laptop case.

"What you got there?"

"Huh? Oh," I replied with a woeful shake of the head. "I busted my computer. That's why I'm headed over to Catfish's."

Jonah let out a long low whistle, his face pursed in commiseration.

Then, like a sea captain hoisting sail, he reached into his basket and plumped the quilt into traveling mode.

"Hop on," he said.

Which is how I found myself reclining against those handle-bars, more outside the basket than in it as Jonah pedaled toward Catfish's house, no longer concerned about personal safety in the least since being escorted by Jonah through that part of town was like traveling with an ambassador in a foreign land. What's more, as he carted me up Esplanade and across North Rampart, then turned left on Marais and submerged us in the Tremé, even my hyper-awareness of my own clumsiness, which could have at any time sent me tumbling off onto the pavement, began to wane, since Jonah's expertise at transporting ungainly things easily trumped my own innate lack of grace. And sure enough, without fail each time I slipped to one side he swayed to the other, leaving me no choice but to surrender to that hobbyhorse motion as the breeze picked back up, like an infant settling down in its mother's arms, mesmerized by the world unfolding around it, eyelids heavy, peering out at all those houses built right up to the street, close enough to reach out and touch almost, their faded pinks and yellows and greens gusting past like watercolor pictures of what once was or might have been, or dreams that have been sleeping for far too long and which open their eyes the instant you close yours.

As broken and blighted as it is today, the Faubourg Tremé is one of the oldest urban districts in the country and the richest in New Orleans when it comes to black Creole history. Adjacent to the French Quarter and bounded by North Rampart Street, Broad Avenue, Canal Street, and St. Bernard Avenue, the neighborhood's land once belonged to Claude Tremé, a wealthy hatmaker, planter, and real estate developer who arrived in New Orleans from Sauvigny, France in 1783, and whose property was acquired by the city in 1809 and subdivided for housing. Here free people of color—along with African slaves who had purchased, bargained for, or otherwise achieved freedom—were able during the time of slavery to acquire and own property, something that occurred nowhere else in the South but New Orleans. By 1850, a decade before the outbreak of the Civil War, free blacks held over $2 million in prime real estate, much of it right downtown in the Faubourgs Tremé and Marigny. And this equity formed the economic and cultural base of free people of color and freed African slaves (some of whom sued their masters for payment of back wages) that would soon be felt not only in New Orleans but nationwide.

The Tremé of the 1860s also birthed America's earliest civil rights movement. It was here that the first African-American daily newspaper, the *New Orleans Tribune*, sprang up to help document the need for change and the change that was coming. And though it was illegal in the South for black people to learn to read, Tremé residents of that period held regular literary salons and put together *Les Cennelles*, the first published anthology of poetry by African-Americans. A half-century before Rosa Parks refused to give up her seat on the bus, Homer Plessy (whose mother also happened to be named Rosa) did much the same thing, in one of the most celebrated episodes of the many civil rights agitations that took place in or near the Tremé. A native Creole of European and African descent, Plessy was arrested and jailed in 1892 for sitting in a Louisiana railroad car designated For Whites Only based on the state's law mandating racially segregated facilities (a law written in 1890 by state legislator Murphy Foster, grandfather of Mike Foster, who served as Louisiana's Governor from 1996 to 2004). To force the issue into the courts, in deliberate defiance of the law Plessy boarded the first-class white car of the East Louisiana Railway traveling from New Orleans to Covington and, upon refusing to disembark, was dragged off the train and thrown in jail. Claiming that the law violated the Equal Protection clause of the Fourteenth Amendment of the U.S. Constitution, Plessy went to court, and after being found guilty at the state level he appealed his case to the U.S. Supreme Court, which in 1896 ruled against him by an eight to one majority. And while this ruling effectively institutionalized the "Separate But Equal" doctrine of segregation in the United States, Plessy's stand nevertheless set the stage for the modern civil rights movement, culminating with 1954's landmark *Brown v. Board of Education*, which ruled unanimously that racial segregation was unconstitutional.

But the Tremé's history is not just one of struggle, for it is also the home of Congo Square, where African-Americans, both slave and free, performed traditional dances, played old world music, and preserved many of the musical elements that would coalesce into jazz. Ex-slaves, Civil War veterans, Buffalo Soldiers, and Caribbean immigrants all gathered in Congo Square, where the live improvisational music was rich with West African rhythms. It was also here that, when the "White Act" was passed in 1894, causing light-skinned Creoles of African ancestry to lose their privileged status, Creole musicians schooled in European literature and classical music, who had once looked down on the less formal music of Congo Square, were forced to join their darker brethren in order to continue working. Adding spice to the musical gumbo were musicians looking for gigs after arriving on riverboats from St. Louis or Memphis or Chicago, resulting in an historically unique moment when high-energy ragtime, classically structured music, and African-American blues improvisation clashed and clanged into one.

Although jazz historians are at odds over the precise birthplace of jazz, most agree that some of the most important commercialization of this style of music occurred in the Storyville section of the Faubourg Tremé, the area closest to Canal Street, which fell victim to (per Catfish) "a catastrophic example of environmental racism" that culminated with the construction of I-10 along Claiborne Avenue.  Rather ironically, the area was named after white City Councilman Sidney Story, who in 1897 backed city legislation to quarantine prostitution in the black neighborhood, which lacked the political clout to resist, even though the foundation of the neighborhood was its many churches.  As a result of this legislation and the lax drinking laws, Storyville became a red-light district rife with 24-hour bordellos, saloons, and restaurant-bars catering to carousing plantation owners and providing steady work to such early black and Creole musicians as George Lewis and Jimmie Noone, as well as jazz greats like Buddy Bolden, Sidney Bechet, Jelly Roll Morton, and Louis Armstrong.  When politics and local sentiment shifted in 1917, Storyville all but disappeared, however, with most of its important jazz sites—Economy Hall and the Gypsy Tea Room among them—replaced by the Iberville Housing Projects, with only St. Louis Cemeteries No. 1 and No. 2 surviving relatively intact.  From there the blight spread throughout the Tremé, where today most of the houses are so run-down it's hard to imagine the neighborhood will ever recover.

"Want me to wait for you?"

"Huh?"

The bicycle had halted so gradually that it took a moment to register that we were no longer moving, and that all of the houses and pedestrians that had just glided by might have actually been there, and that the house directly in front of us was Catfish's.

"Oh. Yes. Would you?"

I sledded off the basket onto the sidewalk, like an over-sized baby bird being nudged out of its nest. By way of greeting the city heat radiated off the lopsided concrete slab, shimmering Catfish's dwelling into a listing ship.

I surveyed the area. Although the pay phone's battered kiosk was still clinging to the utility pole, the telephone itself was conclusively gone. Even less encouraging, Catfish's car wasn't there.

I coerced a smile Jonah's way, then mounted the sooty box steps and rang the doorbell inside the shallow alcove.

No discernable sound.

No discernable answer.

I pressed again and waited.

Still no answer.

Jonah started to whistle a tune I knew but couldn't name.

I looked over my shoulder and shrugged, then lifted my hand to knock—

—and the door rattled open.

The girl peering out was chubby-cheeked and, if fifteen years old, small for her age, her head covered with shiny cornrows dotted with colored beads.

"May I help you?" she said, more than ready to slam the door in my face if my purpose did not suit her.

Then she caught a glimpse of the person behind me.

"Uncle Bob!" she cried.

"Tera?"

She threw open the door and smiled, then skipped past me down the steps.

"Hey, Darlin'!" Jonah beamed as the girl swayed against the front of the basket. "What you doin' here?"

She put her hands on her hips. "We live here now!"

"You do?" I blurted out from my eagle's nest.

"You don't say!" Jonah continued. "Well, that's just fine!"

"Yeah!" I interjected, seizing the occasion to join them next to the curb.

The girl sized me up while saying nothing.

"I'm Sammy," I offered following a frosty beat.

"Oh!" she cried. "Mr. Catfish friend! He said you'd be stopping by!"

"He did"?"

"Um hm. Left something for you too."

"Really?"

"Um hm."

"And you are?"

"Teresa. But everybody just call me Tera."

"How's your Mamma doing?" Jonah cut in.

The girl traced a coppery toe across the sidewalk. Practically brushing the top of her foot was the white tail of a man's dress shirt, while her grease-spotted vest suggested Popeye's was hiring young these days. "'Bout the same, I guess."

Jonah frowned, then fished under the quilt and pulled out what appeared to be a bunch of undernourished black-eyed Susans.

"Thanks, Uncle Bob," Tera said, receiving the brittle bouquet.

"You're most welcome, most welcome. You 'member what I told you?"

"It gonna take time."

"Yes indeed, yes indeed." He winked at her. "Most things do."

Tera produced a smile.

Jonah appraised her a moment, then thrust his hand into his pocket and worked it back out. This time the catch was a bracelet, which when dangled before us snatched the sun's rays and shot them out crimson. Tarnished to the point of flaky corrosion, it could have been silver or gold, its rectangular links alternating with flat, reddish stones, each engraved with a cameo profile Jonah suggested looked like Tera. "*Oooh*," the girl gasped, "It's *beautiful!*"

Jonah glared upward so suddenly Tera and I followed his gaze.

"What?" I said as he slowly scanned the sky.

"Ow!" Tera cried as if she'd been stung.

But nothing could have been further from the truth.

Because when I looked over she was gaping at her wrist.

And fastened around it was Jonah's bracelet.

"Uncle *Bob*!"

"Hee heee," Jonah went, cackling up the steps of a musical scale as Tera stood cradling her forearm like a sleeping kitten. He wagged a finger between Tera and me. "Y'all good?"

"Um..." I began.

"Yes!" Tera cried.

"Alright then," Jonah said, "'Cause, well, you know, I got places to be."

He lowered his rear tire from sidewalk to street. "Catch you later, Sweet Pea."

"Catch you later, Uncle Bob!"

"Yeah," I joined in. "Catch you later!"

All at once, however, I felt like I was forgetting something.

"Um...Jonah?" I called out after him.

But by this time he was already two houses down, swaying from side to side.

As if to signal a right turn, he stuck out an arm and lifted a finger heavenward.

"Storm's a comin'," I thought I heard him say.

Tera and I inspected the sky a second time, but it was still nothing but blue. And when we looked back at the street, Jonah was gone.

For a long moment we stared at the wrinkle of air that seemed to have swallowed him up.

Then Tera tugged her sleeve over the bracelet and turned toward me and batted her eyes.

"I hope you hungry," she said.

"So is Mr. Catfish not home?" I inquired as I followed her down the slim hallway that ran between the staircase and double parlor which had served as Catfish's poetry salon.

She paused in front of a narrow door under the stairs. "I don't know."

"Oh?"

"Mr. Catfish don't live here no more."

"You mean..."

"He gone."

She pushed through the door and beckoned for me to follow.

Like so many others around town, the adjoining slave quarter Tera and I entered had been grimly retrofitted during the 1950s or 60s, complete with cottage-cheese-panel dropped ceiling and vinyl floor tiles capable of surviving Armageddon. Also, in contrast to the spacious, relatively unadulterated rooms of the main house, where Catfish had staked out his own living quarters, each of the rooms through which we now passed was no more than seven feet tall and no wider than the length of a bed. As redeeming features, each boasted a fireplace and pair of French doors, although in order to keep the cool air in (and it was at least twenty degrees cooler back here) all of the window panes had been covered with black garbage bags. Because of this, the only light came from the bare bulbs of central ceiling fixtures, whose glare amplified the impression of not-just-for-kicks thrift store shopping. At the same time, partially unpacked boxes suggested that the slave quarter's newest tenants hadn't been there long.

"Mr. Sammy here!" Tera announced as she entered the room

at the end of the row, where a bare-fronted air conditioner the size of an SUV rattled and rocked in its cut-out over an olive green stove, competing with a new television balanced on its own box opposite a saggy couch. Partially reclining on the couch was a large woman pillowed by two tiny boys raptly watching *Sesame Street*.

The woman stirred.

"Oh! And Uncle Bob brought you some more a them herbs a his!" Tera continued as she crossed to the bank of appliances and sinktop along the rear wall.

The woman propped herself up.

The girl turned on the tap and stuck a pan under it, then swiveled and addressed the woman on the couch directly. "You okay?"

But the woman wasn't paying her any mind. Instead, she was staring at me.

"Summa?" she said.

I'd delayed in the doorway but now took a step forward. "Dilsey?"

"That her alright," Tera solemnly nodded.

*Oh my God!* I thought. Since the last time I'd seen her, the woman had doubled in size, and between that and the slackness of one side of her face (which brought to mind Winnie's Bell's palsy) I'd not recognized her. To make up for this lack, I hurried over and leaned down for a clumsy hug, followed by an even more awkward thud of silence. Dilsey patted back her hair and mumbled something I couldn't make out.

"She said she took a stroke," Tera obliged.

"Oh my God!" I exclaimed as it dawned on me that, yes indeed. The efficient assistant manager I'd spoken to on almost a weekly basis for years at my and Catfish's rainy day haunt next to Jackson Square had at some point disappeared. How long ago had that been? I automatically tried to place it either before or after the restaurant's having replaced its fresh-baked baguettes with the not-nearly-as-good frozen ones and cut back so disastrously on the pecans in its five-dollar tarts.

"When?" I said.

"'Bout three months ago," Tera replied. She turned back toward the stove and tossed Jonah's herbs into a steaming pan, then lifted the lid off a simmering pot, multiplying the aroma of sausage and beans.

She put a hand on her hip and addressed the boys over her shoulder. "Hey!" she said. "You shrimps hungry?"

They nodded in unison but did not take their eyes off Big Bird as their sister began dishing out steaming portions.

Meanwhile, Dilsey stared expressionlessly off to one side as I tried to think of something to say that would not sound idiotic or insincere.

And yet what, really, was there to say?

Tera tapped me on the arm and held out a dish.


And so it was that, after claiming the corduroy La-Z-Boy next to the couch, I ended up cupping my bowl in my lap, trying to cover up the fact that my appetite had fled by interjecting the occasional question or comment to demonstrate sufficient depth of concern while extracting as much information as quickly as possible about Catfish. Meanwhile, Tera alternated between Dilsey and the twins, helping them manage their food and sharing the details of her mother's stroke and subsequent descent into the ranks of the unemployed. Although she'd worked at La Baguette her entire adult life, there wasn't much use in the busy restaurant for a person unable to work like a dray horse. And when her replacement had stopped by with the money collected from employees and matched by Corporate, telling Dilsey how bad they all felt and asking what else they could do, Dilsey hadn't been able to think of a thing except to give her her job back as soon as she was fit.

So, just like that, Dilsey had found herself facing the prospect of living off public assistance, something she'd sworn she'd never do, much as she'd sworn she'd never let Tera drop out of school or follow her mother's path into the foodservice trade. Tera's fast-food wages had not, however, been enough to pay the rent on their apartment in the Faubourg St. John, not if they were also going to eat, and they'd been on the brink of homelessness when Catfish had shown up on their porch. A few days later—a little over two weeks ago—he'd moved them in here until other arrangements could be made. Since then, however, they'd seen him only once, the previous Friday, when he'd stopped by to inform them that he had good news. Instead of relocating them, he'd decided to add *that* house to his roster of Foundation homes, meaning they could stay right where they were while the main house was being fixed up. In other words, Dilsey cut in, taking over from Tera, a glimmer of her old self coming through even though the stroke had reduced her honey-smooth Creole patois to an almost indecipherable slur, they were doing just fine.

"Ayn thah rah bay!" she called out to Tera, who'd transported a load of dishes to the sink and was now straining from pan to cup the result of Jonah's herbs, a dark green reduction that smelled like licorice sticks.

"Um hm," Tera replied.

She blew across the top of the cup and positioned it between her mother's palms, then stood by as Dilsey took the first few sips—and for a moment, just a moment, the brew was a miracle elixir, one that would cause Dilsey to rise Mary Poppins-like up off the couch and take charge of that kitchen, the same way she used to run La Baguette practically single-handed on the not-infrequent occasions they were understaffed. Instead, however, as I sat there and pretended not to notice, a dribble of green escaped from one side of her mouth and snaked down her chin, and because that side of her face was paralyzed and Tera was back at the sink and it wasn't *my* place, there was nobody there to wipe it off. And because there was nobody to wipe it off the liquid proceeded to crawl under Dilsey's jaw and down her neck until it reached the neckline of her baggy T-shirt, where it paused before poking its wet snout under. At any moment, I kept telling myself, Tera would turn around and take note and act accordingly. But she didn't, and by the time Dilsey had emptied the cup a soggy stain hooked one of her heavy breasts.

"Well..." I said, sweeping up from the chair and transporting my dish to the sink.

Tera took silent stock of the uneaten food, which I'd done my best to compact.

I thanked her and praised the meal heartily, then turned back toward the couch, brimming with thank-yous and get-well wishes and carefully imprecise allusions to future visits. However, although Dilsey had perked up considerably while eating, she was now all but asleep, as were the boys, their half-open eyes still riveted to the flickering TV screen. So instead, our farewell boiled down to this:

"Goodbye, Dilsey."

"Goo-bah."

"I'll try to stop by."

"Ah-wah."

Then I followed Tera back out into the heat and light.

*I'll never see them again*, I thought.

(or was that a hope?)

It most certainly was not! I really would come back, I pee-vishly vowed, even if their problems were a bottomless pit of need. Master of self-deception that I am, however, I couldn't quite pull it off, and by the time Tera and I had reached the foot of the stairs I couldn't wait to get the hell out of there.

And yet, I couldn't just *leave*, because what if I'd missed some all-important clue as to Catfish's whereabouts? Although Tera and Dilsey had assured me they had no idea where he'd been spending his nights, they weren't exactly in Sherlock Holmes mode these days.

As Tera advanced toward the door, I paused at the double parlor and scanned the rooms. Once capable of being divided by grand pocket doors now long gone, the sixty-foot span could have been a snapshot taken during my last visit, from the raggedy drapes dressing the tall crooked windows to the once-sharp kitchenette at the back to the now motionless cobwebs sloping from ceiling to wall. Although the curtains were drawn the way Catfish liked it, water and time and moths had done such a number on the faded green velvet that daggers of light criss-crossed the room like security lasers, impaling familiar components of Catfish's daily life including the peeling veneer top of the pedestal game table where he and Joseph and I had taken many a meal and my trusty divan and the two hideous recliner sofas Joseph had spotted in the window of Hurwitz Mintz when Catfish was in a good mood. Also still present were a few other items I doubted Catfish would abandon, including a baby grand piano stripped ages ago of its ivory keys, whose top sloped in the corner beside one of the street windows, two water-damaged pier mirrors gracing the mantles of the twin marble fireplaces, and two crystal chandeliers that had survived more or less intact inside the circumference of their crumbling plaster medallions despite the intrusion of the elements and any number of looters. I couldn't imagine Catfish would scrap those antiques not because of their monetary value (which despite their condition was not inconsiderable) but because they dated back to the time when his father had occupied the house as a pied-à-terre. In one of the big chestnut armoires upstairs, Catfish had found a number of Frederick's personal effects, including a few Eighties-era changes of clothing, while in a separate cabinet he'd discovered several dresses of a size and style that ruled Tess out. Removing any doubt, thumbtacked at the back of that second armoire was a picture of Frederick with his lady friend, whose skin tone implied something more interesting than purely Caucasian and whose grip on Frederick's arm suggested she understood well enough that he'd never belong to her more than he did then.

*I should go look upstairs*, I thought, turning toward the staircase. While there was still no wallboard, the missing pieces of siding had been patched, I registered—all the more reason to extend the investigation. But then Tera, who'd been watching, backtracked.

"What?" she said, stopping next to me.

"Oh, nothing. I was just—"

"Oh, that right!"

She brushed past me into the double parlor. On the floor next to the baseboard inside the doorway was a milk crate flowering with crumpled newspaper. She prodded the crate with her foot. "This here for you."

"Oh! Right. What is it?"

She hitched up her shoulders.

I leaned down and tugged back a petal of paper—and took a deep breath. Because with that first gold-ringed flash I knew what it was: Catfish's Old Paris.

I frowned at Tera. "Are you sure?"

She nodded. "Mr. Catfish said."

I searched her face, then hoisted the crate onto my belly. "Well, okay then. Are you sure he didn't say where he was going?"

Tera shook her head.

"Or when he might be stopping back by?"

Another definitive shake, then back to the door.

I gave the parlor a parting scan and joined her there.

Tera glanced skittishly back down the hall.

"What is it?" I said.

She shook her head, lips together.

"Alright then…" I adjusted the crate, as in, you may now open the door.

But she did not. Instead she toe-polished the floor as I inspected the furrows between her braids, like freshly tilled soil from which something would sprout.

I exercised patience, then secured the crate with one arm and reached for the doorknob myself.

Tera's fingers darted out and clutched my thumb. "Wait!" she said.

Her eyes flicked down the hallway again, then back at me.

Face flushed, she held up her hand and yanked back the shirt cuff to reveal the bracelet.

"How much you think it worth?" she said.


After the door creaked shut behind me, I stood in front of the house, milk crate under one arm, debating with myself over what to do with Tera's bracelet. Accompanied by a promise to not mention the transaction to Catfish or Jonah, the sixty-three dollars I'd given the girl (all the cash I had on me) had seemed to mean far more to her than the hypothetically much greater "actual value" of the piece, which I'd begun to explain could be appraised by any number of the dealers along Royal Street, although I wasn't sure exactly which ones, feeling more and more ridiculous with each word that exited my mouth since I could imagine the reception she'd get going shop to shop inquiring about the value of a piece of antique jewelry, even if it turned out to be nothing other than pot metal and paste. And so I resolved to do that on her behalf, with the bracelet going to the highest bidder and the money back to Tera and Dilsey, an anonymous envelope through Catfish's mail slot.

This righteous design was, of course, dependent upon my being able to find my way out of the Tremé in one piece, however, which all at once didn't seem like a given. For as I stood there on the porch clutching my box of fine china, something straight out of *National Geographic* rose up around me, a kind of primitive tribal chant that brought to mind legions of naked savages hurtling across dusty plains, faces painted and spears raised,  an encampment of emaciated women and children and revered elders dependent upon the success of the hunt.  And even though there was not a single other creature in sight except a few dusty preschoolers by the phone pole, I found myself heaving the milk crate a few inches higher and gauging its potential effectiveness as a blunt force object.  At the same time, I began making my way toward the end of the block, no longer taking for granted my improbable shrimp basket ride over when—for another reason entirely—my stomach flip-flopped and I rocked to a stop.

Because in that basket, was a carefully arranged packing quilt.

And inside that quilt, my laptop.

"Damn!" I sputtered.

And then, a significantly more emphatic "Screw it!"

Feeling like I deserved whatever I got for being such an absent-minded fool, I started plodding down the middle of Catfish's street, debating whether to continue straight on to North Claiborne or to hook a left toward Elysian Fields since the two routes were equidistant to relative safety.  Pausing at the corner of North Villere, I did a mental coin toss, then opted for Elysian Fields and made the turn.  Almost immediately I regretted this, however, since the street was even more barren than Catfish's had been. And as the few fellow humans I did cross paths with either ignored me or eyed me with a mix of curiosity and amusement I found myself adopting a kind of home-boy swagger, an effect I imagined to be amplified by the bagginess of my Eddie Bauer shorts.  Nevertheless, whereas I'd felt light and transparent on

Jonah's bike, I now felt like an elephant crashing through brush, the china tinkling absurdly as I made my way past one vine-covered dwelling after another. And I'd begun to think it wise to reconsider my route when I realized that the chant had grown louder—quite a bit louder—and was growing louder still. Duly noting the escalation, I resolved to hang a right toward North Claiborne at the next corner and had just hit a fresh stride when two teenagers—both of them every bit as brown as I am white—rounded the bend, riding side by side on bicycles way too small for them, coming at me like arrows toward sheep, intensifying their medley as they approached, crying out and responding and joining together in a manner that started out softly and rose to a crescendo and then started again, like this:

"i"—"i"

"I"—"I"

"I!"—"I!"

"I am"—"I!"

"I!"—"I am"

"I AM..."

"SOMEBODY!"

"i"—"i"

...and so on. And as I stood there frozen in the middle of the street I recalled the many debates about racially motivated fear and hatred in America I'd had with Catfish, who doggedly maintained that it was next to impossible for white people like ourselves to grow up in this country without becoming racist, a notion to which I'd taken heated exception, countering that I for one had been brought up in a household where the n-word was never used (except, I didn't say, in the occasional joke by a coarse family member or friend), and whose father was a Baptist preacher whose monthly outreach included a number of African-American families (none of whom attended our church, but that's how it was), and whose mother felt every bit as sorry for black people as she did for anyone else she perceived to be less fortunate than she (and even more so, I'd once heard her say but also thought it best not to mention, for the "really dark ones" since "you just know they can't like what they see when they look in the mirror").

And so no, I'd argued time and again, *I* was not a racist. No how, no way. And yet now—as the distance between myself and the bicyclists dwindled and the chanting peaked and resumed—I found myself flushed with resentment that these two should unnerve me so, even if this was their neighborhood and their premeditated aim was not robbing and killing—how *dare* they make such thoughts occur to me—*me*—the consummate liberal, who'd chosen New Orleans (a city whose population is over half black!) as his home, who'd chosen to live in a mixed neighborhood, whose mother had cried the day Martin Luther King was assassinated—*what right did they have*?

And so yes, *damn you!* I thought as they closed those last yards of relative safety, my fear now eclipsed by an anger much older than I myself and one that came to a head as my would-be assailants came closer, then closer still.

*I'm running through the Tremé in abject terror, down one gray street after another, hearing the boys behind me even though I can no longer see them, trying to find my way back to Catfish's house, knowing that if I can make it there I'll be safe, that he'll throw open the door and let me in. But all of the houses look exactly the same, dismal and empty and covered with soot. And I all at once realize there's no longer anyone living here, no one at all. That the neighborhood has been abandoned even by its longest-time residents. People who have lived and worked here for generations. Whose ancestors built and paid for these homes. Good-hearted people who would have been willing to help me despite my mistrust. And the harder I try to escape the more futile my flight becomes, until I look down and realize I'm running through water almost up to my knees, and that it's not so much the water that's slowing me down as a layer of mud on the bottom. And though the water at first seems almost perfectly clear, as my feet pound and churn it begins to cloud up, becoming not murky and brown but as white as a pearl. And as this whiteness swirls—now almost up to my hips—I understand that its source is not mud after all, but ash—the finely ground ashes of flesh and bones, which as I forge ahead even more frantically continue to rise. And as the water and ashes rise around me I spy a boat anchored up ahead, a houseboat with an American flag and a wry appellation stenciled across the stern, "The Boat," a name I know well because this is the houseboat my family once owned. And in this instant I also realize that I'm no longer in the Tremé but in the warm waters of the Tennessee River, not far from where Daddy would dock that boat. But then the boat starts to putter away and I begin to call out, then to shout, at first certain somebody will hear me, then beginning to doubt, then to fear. Because not unlike in the deserted Tremé there doesn't appear to be anyone on board. And as the boat's wake fantails around me and its engine rumbles exhaust the gooey water continues to rise until it's up to my neck and I inadvertently swallow a little. And on its way down my throat taste and texture reveal that it's now thick with river mud and ashes alike as the water continues to come up, leaving me no choice but to swim. And I'm all set to take off when I remember, I never learned how.*

Only a dream?

Well, of course it was, but it didn't feel like that when I opened my eyes, gasping for air and not yet registering that I'd arrived safely back home hours before and was lying on my bed fully dressed. Nor did I immediately recall that I'd navigated without incident back to Elysian Fields after the two bicyclists continued past without so much as a glance in my direction. So vivid was the nightmare, in fact, that it was not until the bells of St. Peter & Paul chimed 4 p.m. that reality began to claw its way in.

Now I'm most certainly not one of those people who jumps out of bed bright-eyed and bushy tailed, just glad to be alive and able-bodied. But in this case I was the collective alter ego of all such folk as I lay like a sarcophagus atop the covers, replaying the events of the past few hours, pushing the stop and start and rewind buttons again and again, trying to remember every word Tera and Dilsey had said, or not said, anything to make it possible for me to *stay* back in time, in that chameleon-like state of free-wheeling denial that had heretofore changed its colors to accommodate every out-of-the-ordinary eventuality in my seven-year-long Catfish saga. The moment Tera had surrendered that box of china, however, that lizard had begun to drag its frazzled carcass away, such that I now found myself wondering if I really knew Catfish at all, watching through bleary eyes as the ceiling fan circled over my bed, creaking from some minor but irreparable imbalance, unable to either get up or go back to sleep as the crape myrtles outside my bedroom windows stained the afternoon peach, much as I was unable to stop myself from thinking back on all that had spun me to where I was now, into this domestic cocoon from which I'd no present desire to emerge, recollections that under other circumstances might have been pleasant but in this case were anything but. Because while those memories did indeed light the corners of my mind and at times even manage to make me smile, they also marched me unfailingly back to the same unwanted conclusion: that Catfish was not just busy, or inconsiderate, or anything else.

Anything else, that was, except gone.

# Creole Heart

## November 1998

*Times-Picayune* in hand I hesitate at the intersection of Chartres and Dumaine, facing the entrance to a shop in a slim
brick townhouse. Unevenly suspended overhead is a hand-
painted sign with the script "Creole Heart Antiques & Objets"
encircling a wobbly heart that could pass for the Valentine's Day
expression of a lover too bereft to maintain a steady hand. Set
back behind an iron column in a slice off the corner of the building, the shop's door is ajar—to tap into the idyllic late fall weather, I presume. Even so, as I peer inside I'm not sure the place is
open, since the jumble of rustic tables and chairs, many of them
in an advanced state of distress, suggests repair as opposed to
display. Backlighting the pile is a muffled puzzle of sunlight,
which sparkles across a membrane of dust before repeating on the
pock-marked red brick floor, where it combines the furniture
silhouettes into the outline of a slumbering beast. Clinging to
every inch of the opposite wall are shelves loaded with books and
newspapers and colored bottles with raised inscriptions, some of
them still partially full of earth. Although the shelves are flush
with the inner wall, they seem to be bulging into the narrow path
leading toward the dim rear of the store, where a library lamp
ladles light onto a waist-high counter. Consuming the meager

serving of illumination is a sheet of paper so heavy it might cascade to the floor were it not for the cradle of fingers pressing it down.

Dismembered from its owner by the sheer band of light, a hand sweeps a second sheet over the first with a *rattle-snap-crack* that startles me into opening my mouth.

"Are you open?"

"Oh! Yes. Hold on."

A miniature solar system of halogen spotlights does a reverse eclipse. The master of this universe is tall and angular, his rumpled button-down crowned by a halo of reddish-gold hair. The centered counter, running half the width of the shop, is an equally weighted scale with a cash register on one end and a computer monitor on the other.

"Looking for anything in particular?"

"Sorry to interrupt you. Would you be able to spare some change? For the pay phone?"

"Sure."

The man side-steps to the register and pops it open, then frowns. He slams the drawer and thrusts his hands in his pockets but also comes up empty.

"Looks like I need to get to the bank."

He picks up a cordless phone and tilts it toward me.

"I don't want to bother you…"

"It's no bother."

"Thanks, but I actually need to make a few calls…"

"Help yourself."

He brushes off my thank-you as I navigate to the rear of the shop, then returns straightaway to his drawing, an architectural blueprint with a purplish cast. Not wanting to distract him any further, I transport the phone to the end of the counter and turn toward the street, clutching the receiver between shoulder and chin as I unfold the paper.

"Charming slave quarter with LOTS of history plus central air!" announces listing No. 1.

I rejiggle and dial and get a machine, then leave a message that fatally garbles the call-back part and neglects to include a name.

"Already rented," I'm told with regard to listing No. 2 ("Large Swimming Pool") by a human with an equally mechanical tone.

Not wanting to abuse the telephone privileges, I turn back toward my host. "Just one more. Are you sure you don't mind?"

"Be my guest."

"HELLO?" replies the creaky voice representing listing No. 3—"Secluded Garden Apartment Paradise"—which is not only my last hope for the day but Choice No. 1. As such, it's of course almost certainly long gone. Except that it apparently isn't. Because right off the bat the woman (?) on the other end of the line begins shouting questions suggesting I could be in the running as long as I hold the receiver a few inches off my ear and promptly shout back and slow it way down:

"NAME?"

"B. Sammy Singleton."

"YOU'RE GONNA HAVE TO SPEAK UP."

"B...SAMMY...SINGLETON!"

Inwardly cringing but still craving garden seclusion I peer

over my shoulder.  The man glances up from his blueprint and grins.  I grimace and mouth the word "sorry."

"AGE?"

"38."

"MARRIED?"

"No."

"COME AGAIN?"

"NO, SINGLE.  I'M SING…GUL."

"NO NEED TO SHOUT!  PREVIOUS ADDRESS?"

"29 WEST 37th STREET.  NEW YORK, NEW YORK. 10011."

"OKAY.  AND BEFORE THAT?"

"Oh.  College."

"WHAT?

"COLLEGE!  I WAS IN COLLEGE!"

"THAT'S OKAY.  WHERE?"

"New Haven."

"THAT'S A COLLEGE?"

"Oh.  No.  Yale."

"YOU *FAIL*ED?"

"NO, *YALE*."

"NEVER HEARD OF IT.  PROFESSION?"

"WRITER."

"EMPLOYER?"

"I'm a freelancer."

"HUH?"

"I'M SELF-EMPLOYED."

"AH. SO YOU DON'T HAVE A JOB."

"Well, actually…"

"PHONE NUMBER?"

"I'M STAYING AT THE DAYS INN ON CANAL STREET."

Silence.

"Hello?"

Click.

"HEL-*LO*?"

I refold the paper and tuck it under my arm, then turn and sneak the phone into its stand, all the while relying on a faulty cloak of invisibility. The man looks up and smiles sympathetically, a gold medal accomplishment of blue eyes and cheek bones and a heart-shaped mouth, with a pale upper-lip scar that looks like a tiny fang and which combines with the rest into Dangerously Cute.

"I'm sorry," I mutter, my face an inferno.

"No problem, but, uh…" he feigns a shiver, "the Days Inn on Canal?"

"Uh-huh. Thanks again. I appreciate it."

"Catfish."

"I beg your pardon?"

He extends his hand. "That's what people call me. The nice ones, I mean." A wink that makes tiny crow's-feet flash.

"Ah." I give his fingers a polite shake during which my hand tingles. "Sammy. B. Sammy Singleton."

"So I heard. What's the B for?"

"Nothing."

"Right."

"Really. It's just an initial. It's a family thing."

"So then, just...B?"

"But everybody calls me Sammy."

He regards me a moment, then shakes his head as if genuinely amazed. "Wow. Just B."

"Yep."

"So, B. Why New Orleans?"

"I don't know. I...I don't know."

"You're gonna fit right in." Another one of those smiles. "Do you have a few minutes?"

"Um..."

"Because I may know of a place." He flops the top drawing around to display the façade of a big two-story house with a cast iron balcony. *River House*, the label reads. "What do you think?"

"It's beautiful..."

"It's got four one-bedrooms in the rear dependency and one of them's available. I'm about to head over there to drop these drawings off. It's only a few blocks, in the Faubourg Marigny. I just need a couple minutes to finish up."

"The Faubourg...?"

"Marigny. It's the next neighborhood over. Would you care to join me?"

The collection of oval portraits on the front wall of the shop have veneer frames with convex glass and subjects from very dark-skinned to almost white. Dating from over a century ago to 1940s, a few are charcoal renderings but most are hand-colored photographs, and their linear arrangement suggests a chronological and perhaps familial progression: a "mammy" on a rocker holding a white infant, a man (her husband?) clutching a straw broom whose knotty handle is almost as tall as he, three generations of soldiers in military attire, a morose teenage boy burdened with a starched collar and ribbon tie, a young woman with a tilted head and quizzical smile. Illuminated at an angle by the spotlights, the pictures flash in a manner that makes viewing them tricky, since with a slight change of position the bubble glasses become mirrors behind which their subjects duck. It's an effect that comes in handy as I wait for "Catfish" to finish, since it allows me to casually inspect my own appearance. In anticipation of my new life Down South, I've recreated myself by shedding enough pounds to not appear pudgy in the wavy glass, a hard-won sleekness accentuated by an East Village crew-cut, courtesy of a now fondly recalled St. Mark's Place stylist who described my grayish eyes as hazel and my mousy locks as "almost classic auburn." For purposes of apartment-deserving first impressions, I'm also decked out in my favorite black polo shirt and khaki dress shorts, with a pair of yellow Keds contributing a madcap dash of the young at heart. The overall effect isn't too shabby, I conclude as the visage of my self-appointed real estate agent repeats itself in the picture glasses.

"Beautiful, aren't they?" he says to the reflection of me as I realize he's right behind me, almost a full head taller and so close I catch a whiff of printer's ink.

I agree that they are.

I lift a finger to one of the stickers the portraits have in common. "What's 'N.F.S.'?"

"Not For Sale."

"Ah."

"I'm having a hard time letting them go."

"I can see why. They look like they belong here."

Half a bicycle tire edges through the shop's front door, which is as far as it can go since suspended between its handlebars is a broad wire basket with a number of items strapped on, including a dented watering can and a weather-beaten plantation rocker missing a runner.

"Anybody home?" a gravelly voice calls out.

Catfish spins away in multiples in front of my eyes. "Jonah! How you doing, fella?"

"Oooh…" a sigh and a pause. "…can't complain, can't complain."

Catfish's blueprints are rolled up inside a cardboard tube, and as we make our way down Chartres and across Esplanade, he uses the carrying case as a pointer while gracing me with a rundown of both the neighborhood and the property that is our destination. As the story goes, the Faubourg Marigny was founded by Bernard Xavier Philippe de Marigny de Mandeville— "the last of the great Creoles"—who inherited the family fortune and then frittered it away on gambling and the good life of New Orleans. To make ends meet, de Marigny was forced to sell off bit by bit his enormous plantation, which ran the length of the Mississippi from Esplanade to Franklin, creating the second official "suburb" of New Orleans (after the Faubourg St. Marie at the opposite end of the French Quarter, which is now the Central

Business District, or CBD). The first houses in the Marigny were built around 1810, with the neighborhood's earliest residents including a mix of Spanish, French, Free People of Color, Italians, Germans, and Irish, a diversity that continues to this day, along with a robust Kinsey scale mix. The Marigny also remains one of the best-preserved sections of the city, with a hodge-podge of architectural styles ranging from Creole Cottage and Southern Shotgun to Greek Revival and early Victorian—although as Catfish and I cross Elysian Fields and enter the seedier section known as "the Rectangle" (the more genteel part being "the Triangle") many of those houses look like they're ready to tumble.

"Here we are," he announces, hanging a left onto Marigny Street and gesturing toward a hulking structure in the middle of the block. A far cry from the grand residence of his drawing, the house we cut across the street toward looks more like a barn, the few bits of architectural detail that have survived on its façade further shortchanged by a palette of dingy beiges and greens. With its supporting cast of sagging double shotguns, the house might even pass for derelict were it not for a single true-to-the-blueprint feature: a sidewalk-width covered balcony frothing with flowering plants and vines winding up and through the cast iron columns and railing, with enough left over to occasionally drizzle down to the street. In the flap of shadow under the balcony are two shuttered windows and two carriageway entries, one wide enough to afford entry to a car, the other about half that width and apparently serving as the residence's main point of entry. Both of the carriageways are secured with metal security gates, the smaller of which has been enhanced by a number of items wired on from the inside, including a rusty bicycle wheel and the ash-encrusted grate of a barbecue grill.

Catfish stops next to the gate and rings one of five or six yellowed plastic buzzers, then ducks back out into the middle of the street and motions for me to join him there. A minute later, a head pokes through the overhead flora, the purple and green striped scarf looped around its neck fluttering like a sea anemone in the river breeze.

"Hey!" Catfish calls up.

"Well hello there," the person replies, a bit short in the enthusiasm department, it seems to me.

Catfish lifts the cardboard tube like a cavalry sword. "Voila!"

"Oh my goodness…that's right."

"Is this still a good time?"

"Certainly."

"There's somebody here I want you to meet!"

"So I see. Are you with key?"

Catfish digs into a faded jean pocket. "I think so...yes!"


The contrast so many New Orleans homes flaunt strikes me the instant I clear the gate in that the exterior and interior of this house are diametrically opposed, the outside teetering on the brink of neglect, the inside reflecting a sense of self-expression edging toward excess. The present articulation comprises a masterful mélange of green, gold, and purple in tones that alchemize the abject tackiness that combination almost invariably exudes into a vibrantly insouciant backdrop for life. As I wait for Catfish to relock the gate I peer back into what appears to be an enormous compound, down a brick carriageway overhung with gas lamps, its distant end broadening into a glowing rectangle of courtyard shaded by a procession of red-blossomed crape myrtles brushing the side of another house behind the one whose threshold I *thought* we'd just crossed. Rather than entering that front house, however, we're still outside, or at least semi-outside, in one of those uniquely in-between spaces peculiar to New Orleans, where the closing of a shutter or the unfurling of a blind can take one in a heartbeat from outside to in, such that the two spaces remain at all times inextricably mingled, the people occupying them lolling quite happily somewhere in the middle.

"Well?" Catfish smirks, bumping my shoulder and motioning for me to follow him into the heart of the place, a cavernous two-story breezeway connecting what I'm now able to confirm are in fact two otherwise separate structures. Here a staircase curves up and around toward parts unknown, uncharted territory toward which Catfish ascends. With him leading the way, my view is fragmented by the dark cut-out of his body, such that the only way I can see past him is by angling to one side or the other between the two banisters, whose once-rounded rails have been worn flat by a century and a half of fingertips that now include my own. As a result, I first hear, rather than see, Catfish's friend on the landing.

"So..." the distinctive voice floats down, a modified drawl mostly absent the South. "Who have we here?"

"Hey, Sweety," Catfish replies, mounting the last steps onto the landing, where he and the person exchange double kisses. He steps to one side and makes an introductory gesture. "This's my friend Sammy. Sammy, Georgia."

The person shoots a quizzical look at Catfish, then lowers a wrist. "Georgia Moore. Pleased to meet you."

I reach up and shake the hand. "B. Sammy Singleton. Nice to meet you."

"The B doesn't stand for anything!" Catfish chimes in. "Isn't that fabulous?"

"Utterly."

He edges aside enough for me to step up onto the landing next to the person to whom I've been introduced, whose fawn linen pantsuit almost tames the scarf into a tie. Gracefully long-limbed and maybe sixty, she has skin the color of roasted pecans and salt-and-pepper hair pulled back into a braided bun and lips that glisten beneath a fresh coat of clear gloss.

"Is April gone?" Catfish inquires.

Georgia nods. "She is indeed. Two days ago."

"Praise Jesus."

"Now Charles..."

"Just kidding. Sort of. Anyway, that's why we're here. Sammy's looking for a place."

Our hostess stiffens.

"Is it available?"

She glances at me, then touches Catfish's arm. "May I speak with you?" Then, to me: "Would you please excuse us?"

"Of course!" I oblige, mildly mortified as Georgia draws Catfish across the breezeway, where the two of them engage in a brief but intensive exchange beside the railed cut-out of the staircase. Running along what I estimate to be the back of the main house are six pairs of French doors facing a row of windows on the opposite wall, which appear to belong to the rear dependency. A moment later they're back, the sheepish look on Catfish's face strongly implying additional familiarity with budget lodging.

"I am so sorry…" Georgia begins.

"No…" I cut in. "*I'm* sorry to barge in on you!"

She shakes her head. "Oh heavens no. Any friend of Charles is always welcome here. The thing is…well…April just moved out and I wasn't really planning—"

"It's *fine*," Catfish says.

"It is," I confirm.

Georgia ponders a moment, then shakes her head. "No, it's not," she sighs, her eyes moistening. "It's rude. I'm being terribly rude and I apologize."

Catfish reaches over and joggles her wrist. "You are not," he says. "Are you okay?"

"I'm fine." She swipes a tear with a coral-tipped finger. "It's just that…well, you know how I worry. I mean, there's no way that van of April's going to make it all the way to Cozumel!"

Catfish rolls his eyes. "Oh, come on. This is a woman who knows how to build a staircase."

Georgia stares at him a second, then bursts into snickers. "True," she says, dabbing at her eyes so as not to smear her mascara.

"Okay, fellows," she says, turning back to me. "Let's take this from the top."

"Are you sure you don't want us to come back later?" I offer.

"Positively." She holds her hand out and smiles warmly. "Georgia."

I give it a dainty tug. "Sammy."

"Welcome to River House. I'm afraid it really is a mess though."

"I beg your pardon?"

"The apartment. I'm giving you fair warning."

Catfish claps my shoulder. "Yes!" he exclaims. "You're gonna love it."

Georgia taps a fingernail against his blueprint tube. "We won't be long. Why don't you put those inside?"

"Oh. Right." He crow's-feets me again. "See you in a bit?"

"Yes…"

"This way," Georgia says.

And it's the funniest thing. Because even though the place is so sprawling I can barely tell left from right and the apartment itself has yet to be seen, as I cross the broad deck connecting front house to back, worn smooth by a century and a half of footsteps that now include my own, something tells me I'm home.

The first house on the block between Chartres and Royal, 623-25 Marigny Street was built in the 1850s for a German immigrant named Henry Blaese. No doubt factoring in the ever-present threat of flooding, Blaese situated his family on the second floor of the house, whose uncomplicated Creole-style configuration is that of a square divided by a Roman cross of walls, the four rooms originally connected inside by plain panel doors and outside by a narrow gallery surrounding the house on all sides. In keeping with the custom of the day, this was not only where Mr. Blaese lived but also where he conducted his business, a booming wholesale grocery trade powered by the Mississippi. Most days of the week horse-drawn carts would arrive from boats docked at the end of the street, piled high with goods brought in from as close as the local plantations or as far away as the Orient, to be unloaded directly under the upstairs rooms, between rows of rough-hewn bracketed columns now mostly hidden inside subsequently added walls.

Upon his arrival in New Orleans, Mr. Blaese married a woman named Catherine, who was born here to a German family named Reich. And as soon as their home was built and the business established, Catherine and Henry began a family that would grow to include six children. Among them was their eldest son Henry, who was educated at the Virginia Military Institute and graduated from the Locustdale Academy in Louisiana. When the senior Blaese died in 1872, his widow married Mr. C. Potthoff, a local paint dealer for whom Henry Jr. had begun to work as a boy and in whose employ he'd remained for twelve years before opening his own supplies shop in 1890. According to *Louisiana Biographical and Historical Memoirs* (1892), Vol. 2, Henry Blaese Jr. was:

> ...a prominent and successful dealer in paints, oils, glass, etc. [who] has been established in his present business, 72 Camp Street, since 1890. His stock is full and complete, while prices are governed by moderation and the best satisfaction is guaranteed. He is popular as a business man, and enjoys the confidence of all having dealings with him... and [has] thus far enjoyed an unsullied reputation and has materially helped the general interests and standing of New Orleans. He is a clear-headed man of business and an excellent manager of all affairs which he has under his control. He is a young man of good habits and is a member of the Young Men's Gymnastic club. Under his able management his business promises to

become one of the largest of the kind in the city.

Along with his brothers and sisters, Henry was born in the house on Marigny Street, which grew along with the family, with first one and then another two-story *garçonniere* built back to back behind the main house, with one side facing the Mississippi and the other Lake Pontchartrain. By historical standards, however, the residence remained in the hands of the Blaeses for only a short while. In 1889, Henry Jr.'s mother died and was buried in St. Louis Cemetery No. 1 beside her second husband. And following her death her estate was auctioned off and the proceeds divided among her children, with the 8,000-square-foot house and dependencies fetching the tidy sum of $2,500. After the Blaeses, 623-25 Marigny St. passed through a series of owners and a number of sometimes crude architectural modifications. Among these was the enclosure of the first floor of the main house to create two street-level apartments, and the conversion of the second floor side galleries into interior hallways. At some point, most likely during the 1930s, a number of small bathrooms were added, including four at the rear of the *garçonnieres*, which were subdivided into the flats Georgia now rented out, two up and two down on either side. In most cases, however, there are no records to indicate when the alterations occurred or to account for certain anomalies, such as the fact that the style of the main house's French doors predates its construction by thirty years, suggesting the doors were salvaged from an even older property (perhaps the Marigny plantation itself). What's more, the cultural significance of the building site is older and more cryptic still, with a pile of Native American artifacts unearthed during a plumbing excavation implicating the site as a Choctaw burial ground.

Even without the short list of small but life-altering cosmetic adjustments that have begun to sashay through my mind, the apartment's a dream, and as I wait for Georgia to go "scare up" some keys I have plenty of time to review its merits. All but waltzing back and forth from one end of its 40-foot length to the other, I also have time to trample the distinct impression that Georgia is less than desperate to rent the three-room flat, since while whisking me through she's made it a point to highlight its every imperfection, having no idea that—in the eyes of this midtown Manhattan refugee—each one of these "flaws" only adds to the place's heart-stopping charm. Among these: multiple French doors "that make the place a bit drafty in the winter" (*French doors!*), a side balcony with "a few rotten boards" (*a balcony!*), floor heaters inside the fireplaces "you have to be careful with" (*fireplaces!*), a number of sounds that "might take some getting used to," such as the fog horns on the river (*it's that close?!*) and the bells of St. Peter & Paul, whose uneven towers can be seen from my bedroom windows (*a view!*). There are also several pieces of furniture that I'm "free to use," including a bed with matching nightstands and dresser in the bedroom (all of which April has not just left behind but *made*), a futofa in the living room (also courtesy of April—full van), and a high-Deco chrome and Formica table with jewel-tone top and matching chairs in the kitchen, as well as sheets, towels, pots, pans, silverware (not plastic), and numerous other household items I'd otherwise have to run out and buy—all for the bargain-basement price of $275 a month. Nor do I view as anything more than trifling the potentially awkward implications of taking up residence in a place Georgia has just referred to as "a communal environment," telling myself that getting along at her River

House will require nothing beyond doing what I do so well and so automatically most of the time anyway—avoiding people—made all the easier by the place's maze-like configuration.

In other words, I conclude as I circle back to the kitchen for the third or fourth time, I'm ready to sign on the dotted line.

Still no sign of my landlady-to-be, however. And with no forewarning my excitement flip-flops into fear. What if she's changed her mind, with her protracted absence involving not a search for keys but for the proper words to nullify our whisper-thin verbal contract?

*Be patient!* the choirboy squeaks.

And I try, except that now as I steer myself through the procession of rooms I feel like I'm standing on a NYC subway platform as the train I thought was a local flashes past.

I poke my head outside the kitchen door, then mount the two steps onto the breezeway. About halfway down, the mint green shutter into Georgia's apartment is open. And following a brief but savage battle inside my head during which the choirboy is temporarily slain I skulk along the stair rail in that direction. Dead and all, however, the choirboy continues to counsel faith. And with his soprano chiming so guilelessly from the grave I'm about to retreat when other voices drift toward me:

"Are you sure you're okay?"

"Of course. Just a little tired. Could we do it next week?"

A cell phone rings, sending me fleeing back to the apartment that may or may not be mine.

A moment later, Georgia appears in the kitchen doorway and holds out a set of keys that includes a *skeleton* key.

"Here you go," she says.

"Wonderful!" I gush. "Thank you so much!"

She issues a few basic security directives and turns to go.

"Excuse me?" I interject.

She spins back. "Yes?"

I expose my checkbook. "Would you like a deposit or the first month's rent or something?"

"Why? Are you planning to skip out on us?"

"Oh...no! I just thought..."

"I'm joking, Son. We'll catch up with you."

Another exit attempt.

"Um...excuse me?" I venture again, already beginning to feel distinctly high maintenance.

Another about-face, this time accompanied by an arched eyebrow. "Yes?"

"Is Catfish...?

"Oh for heaven's sake!" she cuts in. "I almost forgot. He had to run. He told me to tell you to stop by the shop."

10

Welcome to River House

## November 1998

Dickie... Naomi... Peter... Fanning... Edgar... Rusty... As glorious as my new digs are, within 48 hours of United Cab-ing it from Georgia's back to the Days Inn for my suitcase I'm beginning to question whether they're worth the price, not in dollars but in terms of real and potential strain on my anorexic social skills. My first encounter with a fellow tenant comes less than a full day after I've unpacked my bags, when I'm awakened by the sound of my doorbell buzzing with such persistence that not even I can ignore its auditory sting. Nevertheless, for several minutes I attempt to do just that, burrowing down in my pillow and pitting my will against that of whoever is cretin enough to ring *anyone's* doorbell before 10 a.m.

Finally throwing in the towel, I drag myself up off of April's futofa, feeling as though a shovel blade has been wedged into my back. I attribute this handicap directly to an earlier interlude on April's "bed"—a four-poster platform affair that hasn't evolved far from raw lumber, topped by a slab of dry-rotting foam—abandoned at some indeterminate point in the middle of the night.

As the doorbell drones on, I creakily maneuver into bathrobe and moccasins, then shuffle out into the breezeway, resolving to reward my morning caller with a healthy dollop of attitude. As I round the curve of the stairs, however, I register that the door to the apartment beneath mine is open. And as I continue past and swivel gingerly to the left I note that the security gate at the front of the carriageway is also ajar, propped open with what looks like a human foot.

"Hello?" I call out.

"Hell-ooo," a cheerful-sounding voice calls back.

"Who is it?"

"Why it's special delivery for a—just a minute!—Mr. B. Sammy Singleton!"

Hm.

I inch forward, weighing the fact that whoever is out front knows my name against the open door and what is indeed, I have by this time confirmed, a foot—a wide and capable-looking one—with a thick tuft of hair on top and curly yellow nails.

"Why, I do declayah!" the voice exclaims, bringing to mind hoop skirts made out of drapes that have seen grander days. "If it isn't a Northstar Supreme Serta Perfect Sleeper!"

*Oh my God!* I think, remembering. During the wee hours of the morn, having ascertained that April's erstwhile futofa was even crueler than her bed, I'd also maneuvered myself into the kitchen and dialed 1-800-Mattress on the wall phone next to the fridge, which no one had bothered to disconnect, making the perky sales girl's cheerful "24-hour-delivery—maybe sooner!" pitch seem even more surreal.

"Coming!" I call out as I proceed up the carriageway, vaguely disconcerted by the idea of a barefooted delivery person, which even by NOLA standards seems a bit casual after Labor Day. To be on the safe side, instead of immediately pulling the gate open,

I attempt to peer out through the narrow opening, an ill-fated act that makes my neck spasm. "Damn!" I groan, barely managing to step out of the way as the gate rocks in and the foot's owner reveals itself—not a delivery person by any stretch (although my plastic-wrapped Serta is indeed leaning against the front of the house) but rather a creature that looks like it just stepped off the set of a high school production of *Mommy Dearest*.

"Do you have any fucking idea what time it is?" it roars, eyes wide, as in both big as doorknobs and disconcertingly far apart, conditions exaggerated by remnants of eye liner and a beanbag-shaped face caked with what smells like expired Noxzema. Like me, the creature is wearing a bathrobe, although that one is emblazoned with a Hampton Inn logo.

"Um..."

"Nooooooo," it cuts me off, brandishing a Magic Marker. "I don't believe you dooooooo. I don't believe you dooooooo because if you diiiiiiid we wouldn't be standing here right now, now woooooooould we?"

I shake my head and take a step back.

"Do you know who I am?"

Shake shake.

"Okay, then listen up," it says, "because this ain't a dress rehearsal and there ain't gonna be no repeat performance. This...is *me*," it says, poking a stubby finger at one of the buzzers next to the gate—the one with the numeral "1" and what I gather must be its name beside it—*Dickie Grand*—engraved in flowing calligraphy on a scalloped brass plaque, "And this...is *you*," it continues, pointing to another buzzer—the one with nothing other than a no-frills "3" beside it. "Got it?"

I mutely nod.

"NoIdontthinkyoudo," the creature snarls. Using its teeth, it snaps the top off the Magic Marker and clamps it there while writing my name in inch-high letters onto Georgia's siding along with a thick red arrow curving to my buzzer. "There!" it leers, recapping the marker and thrusting it back in its pocket. "Do I make myself clear?"

"Yes. Sorry."

"As you should be," it agrees with a great lift of the eyebrows, blowing past me through the gate and up the carriageway. And I've just begun to bless its retreat when, about halfway back, it stops and effects a theatrical turn that causes its bathrobe to flare out, then executes a perfect curtsy accompanied by a feather-light hand motion culminating palm up.

"Oh, and one more thing," it says with a proper British accent.

"Yes?"

"Welcome to River House."


That afternoon there comes a determined rapping on my kitchen door, the first of five pairs of French doors that line my balcony, a configuration that affords the happy advantage of being able to utilize the gallery as an outdoor extension of the apartment by opening the doors in and the shutters out. On the down side, it also makes it easy and not conclusively inappropriate for people to enter my living space unannounced, as someone has apparently done. My morning encounter still all too vivid, my first thought is that I must have in some way incurred the wrath of Mr. Grand again, even though I've endeavored to be considerate by waiting until past noon to flop April's foam down the stairs and push/drag/slide my new mattress up.

On the other hand, perhaps it's Georgia, whom I've not seen again since we met.

Regardless, I'm in no mood for afternoon callers.

I'm busy.

As any moving-in person would rightly be.

Still decked out in bathrobe and moccasins I am, more specifically, trying to wrangle the plastic cover off my new plush yet extra firm mattress.

*Rap-rap-rap*!

I abort the enterprise, and when I do the mattress slumps against the wall, creating a triangular passage between floorboard and pillow-top.

*No way*, I think.

But then the knocking repeats and, well, what can I say?

Assuming a macabre crouching position I hit the floor and scuttle on all fours under cover while trying to ignore the tremor of pain in my shoulder, telling myself that any degree of physical discomfort will be worth it if it means not having to make the acquaintance of another neighbor right about now. And indeed, a false sense of security has just begun to envelop me when I remember that, aside from the kitchen door (which I intentionally left closed, hoping to send a signal to anyone who might happen by that B. Sammy Singleton was not in fact open for business) all of the other doors have been thrown open onto the glorious afternoon. As a result, should the interloper proceed, there will be nothing to shield me but the complimentary Quaker lace tablecloths that have been retrofitted by Georgia as curtains.

Another knock.

Another pause.

"Hullo?" The voice is as resonant as an oboe middle C, and, I'm pretty sure, neither Dickie's nor Georgia's.

I compress myself between mattress and wall, willing the person to go away, but this is not to be. Instead, a series of tiny earthquakes shudder through all twenty digits as the trespasser advances, stopping at one door, then the next, fee-fi-fo-fum.

"Hullo?" the person calls out again, by this time so close I can smell the patchouli.

Not a peep from yours truly. And for a few seconds I think I might pull it off.

Then my left calf cramps, forcing me to extend my leg.

*CRACKLE-CRACKLE-CRACKLE!* snaps the mattress wrapper.

"Hul-*lo*? Is somebody there?"

*Huh-uh huh-uh huh-uh*, I strive to convey psychically. But to no avail. Because the next thing I know, following a brisk series of thumps on the floor, a head appears in the light-filled space in front of me, with a silhouette effect that emphasizes what appear to be two floppy ears.

"Hey!" the head exclaims. "Whatcha doing back there?"

"Hello!" I reply through a smokescreen of maximum perkiness. "Oh...well...you know...it's this darn mattress. I was just trying to..."

Before I can finish, however, my cover swings up and away, making me feel like a roly-poly that's had its rock kicked as I blink at the girl-woman before me, who's at least a foot taller than I, with enough extra bulk to make me feel petite. Not that she's what one could call fat with absolute accuracy, since any broad-brush characterization along those lines would fail to take into account her wiry upper body. On the other hand, and in rather dramatic juxtaposition, from the waist down she's amply proportioned, with a dimpled rear end and thighs that quiver like a wheelbarrow load of brains bursting with notions and desires eager to be expressed. For their part, the two Spaniel ears are actually pigtails into which all of her bushy brown hair has been bound in a rather juvenile configuration, although her clothing— khakis, docksiders, pink cashmere sweater with pearl-shaped buttons—are Wellesley all the way.

Her rump swaying precariously close to my nose, she heaves the mattress up on one end and accordions the plastic sleeve down, then hauls it over to April's bed (which short of a chain saw or exorcism is apparently here to stay) and levers it into place. In the meantime, I scramble up off the floor while trying to keep my neck aligned.

"Thank you so much!" I enthuse as she swings back around.

She shrugs and sticks out a palm. "Naomi," she says. "Naomi Plant."

I give it a shake. "Sammy. B. Sammy Singleton."

"I know," she nods. "You're the writer."

"Yes," I reply, forgoing the "business" qualification rigorous honesty usually requires I tack on.

She flips back a pigtail and shifts her weight from foot to foot in a manner that simultaneously brings to mind chewing tobacco and an orphan hoping to be chosen from among dozens of more appealing ones.

"Oh my Gosh!" she exclaims after a sober moment. "I almost forgot!"

She pounds over to the door and scoops up a foil-covered dish off the dresser opposite the bed, then pounds back and shoves the dish into my hands.

"What's this?" I inquire as several red flags rocket up.

"A pumpkin pie. I made it myself."

"Oooh!" I coo, peeling back the foil and taking a delighted-seeming whiff. "That's just so *nice* of you!"

"Yeah, well, I wouldn't get your hopes up. It's my maiden voyage."

"Really?"

"Uh-huh. Well, me and *Martha Stewart Home for the Holidays*. Praise the Lord!"

I smile, attempting to edit out that last comment.

She studies me a moment, then tilts her head to one side. "Do you know the Lord, Sammy?"

"Um…"

She cups her hands on my shoulders. "I mean…have you accepted Jesus Christ as your Personal Lord and Savior?"

I meet her gaze and do what I have to do. "My father's a Baptist minister."

Her mouth drops open. "No!"

Oh yes.

She gapes at me a few seconds, then erupts into an ear-to-ear grin. "Well then Praise God!" she rejoices, giving my shoulders a good hard squeeze.

"Ow!" I shriek, almost going down.

"Oh my God!" she cries, rescuing the pie and delivering it to my bedside table. "Did I do that?"

"No," I groan, clutching my neck. "I—*ow!*—slept on it wrong."

"Want a back rub?"

"Huh?"

She motions toward the bed. "You know. A massage."

"Oh. No. Thanks."

"It's fine. I'm certified."

"That's okay."

She pats the mattress. "Lay down."

"Naomi..."

"Oh come on, silly. I don't bite."

"But..."

She wiggles her fingers in front of her face. "Get over here, Mister. They don't call me Nirvana Naomi for nothin'!"

By about midway through what I must confess is a rather divine feat I think it's fair to say that I've been thoroughly introduced to the person straddling me, since after I've effectively parried a few additional inquiries into the state of my soul Naomi has begun sharing the trials and tribulations of her own. Coming as a bit of a relief is the revelation that it's only been a few months since she's "seen the light," since this suggests there might still be hope for the woman, along with the fact that she's at the young and impressionable age of at least ten years my junior. Equally reassuring, instead of ingesting her congregation's "literal interpretation of the Bible" hook-line-and-sinker, she's confronting head-on a number of quandaries involving certain particulars of her new-found faith. Is there or is there not, for example, a place in the Kingdom of Heaven for a woman like Naomi, a woman with no clear-cut preference for either gender? Equally problematic is the issue of her livelihood, a budding e-commerce biz specializing in top-notch paraphernalia for plus-sized women, a natural outgrowth of a booming massage therapy business targeting that same underserved segment of the population with "intimate self-realization." Certainly, taking that garden-variety device and scaling it up with those incredibly handy extra inches, not to mention the seasonal colors, was a stroke ("wink!") of inspiration. And no matter what the folks over at Body of Christ might have to say, she finds it hard to understand how something that's bringing so much joy to so many large women could *not* be God's will. As a result, rather than abandon the business altogether she has dropped from her PayPal-enabled website anything that could be remotely construed as pornographic and begun "retooling" ("wink!") her inventory with a limited-edition set of religious-themed gadgets featuring (hopefully) glow-in-the-dark package art by that "Painter of Light" guy. The two names she's kicking around for the new line are "Holy Holy" and "He Is Risen," which in any case will showcase products with functional yet theologically resonant fish-like shapes.

"Which name do you like best?" she asks, kneading gently.

"Gee, I don't know," I confess, groaning softly. "I kind of like them both."

Naomi grunts, kneads.

A few seconds later, my head pops up. "How about one for Christmas and one for Easter?"

"Oh my Gaw—I mean, Praise the Lord!" she gasps, thumping my back.

"*Ow*!" I wail.

"Sorry!  Are you okay?"

"Yes.  I mean, I think so.  Just…don't stop."


"So," Naomi ventures a few minutes later.  "When's the bash?"

"What bash?"

"The 'Welcome to River House' bash.  Georgia always throws one.  Usually right after somebody moves in."

"Really?  Huh.  I don't know.  She hasn't said anything yet."

"He."

"What?"

"Georgia's a man."

"Oh."

"He just chooses to express himself as a woman."

"Ah."

"Except in bed.  Not that that matters.  What about you?"

"Um…"

"Never mind!  That's just *so* none of my business!"

"That's okay."

"Plus, who cares, right?  I mean, I'm no New Testament scholar, but that Paul contradicts himself left and right: I hate the Jews, I love the Jews; women are equal, women are doormats.  Plus the man's like *totally* homophobic.  *If* he even wrote those parts.  Which is of course wide open for debate since MEN have been sticking things in and yanking things out of the Bible for like two thousand years.  Meanwhile, Jesus never said anything about *any* of that. I mean, we're all God's children, right? John 14:2: 'In my father's house are many dwelling places...'"

I lift my head a few significant inches. "Naomi?"

"Yes?"

"I love Martha."

"Really? "Oh my Gaw—I mean, Praise the Lord! Me too! When she's talking to Jesus? And he says—John 11:25, I think— 'I am the resurrection and the life'? Well, I get shivers."

"No," I gently correct. "The *other* Martha."

"Huh? Ahhh," she sighs, extending my ear flaps. "Well who doesn't? I mean, she's a saint, too. Am I right?"


Late that night, as I lay atop my new mattress tracking ceiling fan revolutions and thinking up catchy yet discrete marketing slogans, an enigma of sounds from the garden draws me Pied-Piper-like up from the bed and into the bathroom, the only room in the apartment with a window facing the back. At this time of year it's not uncommon for the river fog to roll in smoky waves over the levees, but it's the first time I've experienced this phenomenon first hand. And as I stand barefoot in my awesomely authentic claw-foot bathtub, it's as if I'm watching a Fellini-directed dream sequence. Contributing to the surrealism is the fact that, in my delight over the apartment, I've not yet gotten around to exploring the yard, which is strung with colored lights now magnified by the fog into softball-sized orbs.

Under such conditions there's no reliable way to separate fact from fiction, but I want to believe that what I'm seeing is real, or at least possible. Because rising out of the ground at the rear of the garden is the largest, most perfectly proportioned penis

I've ever seen. I close my eyes and open them again and…yes! The penis remains, one of those perpetually semi-tumescent slabs with an affable swing, angled sliding-board-like in precisely the right direction at all times despite an inherent preference for the North. On the other hand, I gradually realize as I finally tear my eyes away, the bearer of this remarkable specimen is—how shall I put this?—distinctly less remarkable, a skinny guy wearing a pork pie hat, with glasses and flesh even whiter than my own, who all at once slides completely out of sight, as if his entire body has been deep-throated by the earth itself.

"Is it hot?" a sultry female voice calls out from what sounds like right beneath me. And sure enough when I look down there's a head sticking out of the bathroom window of the first-floor riverside unit, its raft of hair hanging down almost to the ground in a nattily Rastafarian jumble.

"Veeery!" Penis Man sniggers back, his head briefly materializing at ground level through rising steam, which along with the context clues of his verbal exchange with Rasta Woman suggests there's some manner of hot tub involved.

"Alright, then!" the woman announces. "He-ah ah come!" And sure enough, a sinewy female promptly lunges through the window and proceeds to do a Mariachi-style half-dance, half-crawl along the garden trail, undulating and growling as she goes, snapping her fingers over her head to her own primitive, warbling a cappella accompaniment, naked but for a beaded hula skirt and two sequined swags capping her breasts, as Penis Man encourages her with cat calls and clapping until she reaches the place where he disappeared—at which point she rises up on her haunches and lets loose a terrible roar, then plummets forward into the low-lying mist, followed by splashing and more applause and throaty laughter. Having a pretty fair idea of what's about to ensue and already feeling like a Peeping Tom, I'm about to relinquish my post when the man lets out a long low whistle, inciting an enormous beast to bound through Rasta Woman's window and follow her path, ending in a splash followed by giggles and fresh grunts of delight.

"Hey, Sammy," calls a third voice from directly to my right, causing me to duck instinctively back inside.

"Sammy?"

Damn.

Ever quick on the draw, I nab a washcloth and maneuver back outside and start swiping at the glass as if I didn't hear a thing.

Naomi leans out of her bathroom window. "Can you believe this?" she sighs.

"Huh? Oh! Hey, Naomi." I roll my eyes. "I know. These windows are *filthy*."

"No, silly." She motions toward the rear of the yard as the hot tub romp is dually punctuated by a high-pitched squeal and a guttural moan. "Fanning and Peter. They live beneath me. They're in a band."

"Oh?" I say, primly daubing my window.

She crosses her elbows on the windowsill and puts her chin down. "They're out there after every big gig."

"Ah."

"It's not usually this foggy."

"No?"

"Uh-uh. And it doesn't matter one bit. They're like *totally* uninhibited. Like Adam and Eve before the fall."

As if to confirm this, a new round of sounds, low and anima-listic but clearly human, rises into the night. Naomi fixes me with a sideways gaze. "I mean you tell me. How can that not be healthy?"

A few seconds later the dog meanders out of the mist and lays down off to one side, head on paws.

"Is that dog orange?" I say.

"Oh yeah," she confirms, almost defensively. "Fanning dyes it. Green for St. Patrick's Day. Pink for Valentine's Day. Right now he's orange. Halloween."

"Wow."

"I know. I hate her. She's so freakin' creative."


Naomi's ministrations notwithstanding, the next morning I'm awakened by an even more severe degree of neck and back woe, forcing me stick-man-like out of bed at the inhuman hour of 6:32 a.m. in a frantic but fruitless search for a bottle of aspirin. In no condition to explore convenience store options, I briefly consider knocking on Naomi's door but then delete that option, not wanting to send the wrong kind of signal. If I'm to survive in this seething petri dish of humanity I'm going to have to navigate on my own, not to mention establish a few prudent boundaries early on, such as no more late-night bathroom window chit-chat, no cups of sugar and, in this case, no analgesics. Despite my high threshold for physical pain, however, my condition is going from bad to worse. And when I attempt to sit down on the toilet I find that I'm unable to do so without unleashing a fresh paroxysm of misery. Fortunately, my most pressing need is of the liquid sort, a function I'm able to execute standing up.

Because the only tolerable position neck-wise is to keep my chin perpendicular to the floor, there's no way to direct the flow with any degree of precision, so after giving up on that hygienic goal I just stand there and splatter in the general direction of the bowl, attempting to turn my head to one side or the other, like a mechanical doll in need of oil. Finding it impossible to twist my head more than an inch or so to the right without triggering a new spasm, I switch directions, somehow managing to effect almost a full 90 degree turn that has me once again consorting with the infamous window. Outside the fog has begun to glow with the rising sun, as has the steam from the hot tub, which is all at once plainly visible in the shifting mist, tenderly bubbling.

No way, I tell myself, snapping my head back around.

At which point a concomitant explosion of agony begs to differ.


A few minutes later I'm tiptoeing down the stairs en route to the garden, silently cursing each creaky step and fully expecting at any second for some door or window or trap door to fly open and a jack-in-the-box head to pop out cackling maniacally until every resident of the house (a small army, no doubt) is gathered at the head and foot of the stairs, snickering and whispering conspiratorially. Although I've managed to toe my way into my moccasins, getting into the bathrobe has proven impossible. So after abandoning it in a pool on the floor I've boldly decided to set foot outside wearing nothing but my sleeping garb: a pair of polka dot boxers and a Fruit of the Loom T-shirt, with one of April's left-behind bath towels slung over my shoulder. In other words, for the first time in my adult life I'm venturing outside virtually naked, the kind of stuff chronically recurring nightmares are made of. But desperate times call for desperate measures. And it seems unlikely I'll run into anyone that early in the day.

So far, so good, I congratulate myself as I reach the central landing. Effectively out of range of the other second-floor residents, I must now pass directly only one more apartment—either Fanning's on the riverside or Dickie's on the lakeside. Emphasizing the potentially life-altering consequences of this decision is the staircase itself, which is actually two staircases sharing a number of central steps, such that it's possible to start up or down on either side and cross over in the middle. Given my run-in with Dickie the day before, the risk assessment process is not complex, albeit partially dependent on the hypothesis that Fanning and Peter will be deep in the sleep of the wicked.

In the old days ships carrying cargo downriver to New Orleans from places like St. Louis and Memphis would be loaded with great flat stones known as ballast, which were used to help balance the freight. Once the vessels were down-river, however, the stones were of no use to the boatmen. So at that point they would be cast aside onto the banks of the Mississippi, where they would be carted off by the locals and used as pavers. And after passing Fanning and Peter's apartment without incident, I find myself following a path of such stones down the riverside courtyard, where the fog lingers between the house and a high wooden fence. Lining the fence is a tight row of gnarly wild elms, which are alive with orchids and Spanish moss interspersed with philodendron, whose scalloped leaves reach toward the house like amphibious hands seeking solid land. Luckily for me the path winds back to the tub, since even though the fog is beginning to burn off, the courtyard is so thick with vegetation that it's impossible to see directly from front to back, a limitation I judge to be advantageous to whomever, like myself, might desire some modicum of privacy. Of course, I'm also well aware that it's possible to see over the tops of those plants and straight down into the tub from the second-floor apartments, leaving me little choice but to trust that Naomi too will be fast asleep, or if not, a good deal less interested in my jacuzzi antics than those of our infinitely more agile neighbors.

Upon reaching the clearing at the back of the yard I kick off a moccasin and stick a toe into the hot tub while noting that its overall aesthetic is rather impressive, with natural flagstones both rimming its broad opening and supplying steps and seating. On the other hand, floating jelly-fish-like in the center of the water is an unsavory patch of yellowish foam, within which swirl a few sequins and a tuft of orange fur. I hesitate, wondering what else Fanning and Peter (and God knows who else) might have deposited there. And yet, I chide myself as the steam beckons to me with phantom fingers, have I come this far only to be thwarted by a few decorative elements and a bit of hair? Certainly not, I conclude, a whiff of chlorine bolstering my resolve as I shake off the remaining moccasin and maneuver myself down.

Every once in a while, more by chance than design, we human beings get something right. And as I sit back in the tub I can't help but feel that this is one of those times as I experience for the first time the sounds of the Marigny: the bucolic chorale of birds, the quiet clacking of railroad cars behind the floodwall, the harmonica-like foghorn bursts of vessels bound for the sea. At the same time, all of my troubles and cares, not to mention my neck and shoulder pain, seem to be absorbed almost instantly by the water roiling around me—which with the push of a button has begun to churn like a witch's cauldron, causing what's left of the foam (minus the sequins and hair, scooped out with a leaf) to become one with my watery world, with everything that is good and right about this mortal life of ours. Already beginning to regain full mobility, I lift my arms onto the coping stones, then allow the rest of my body to slide deeper into the water as the air bubbles inside my shorts effect their escape, exploding atop the surface in applause-like bursts, giving thanks to the universe for the relief I feel. I close my eyes and groan, experiencing a sudden profound empathy for people like Fanning and Peter, for those River House brothers and sisters who revere the elemental mysteries of water, whose humble human forms need soothing just like mine, fellow travelers on this sometimes treacherous road of life whose torsos have traced the contours of these very same stones, whose toes have spread fan-like against these same jets, against this same fleshy—

"Yo!" a voice cries out, causing me to yank my foot back, my reveries dissipating faster than noonday mist.

"Sorry!" I say a bit too loudly to the grinning head atop the water across from me, overcompensating for the light roar of rushing water. "I didn't know..."

"No biggy," the young man replies, his deep brown eyes wide with amusement as droplets of water sparkle along his long lashes. "I thought you were asleep! You looked so out of it."

"I almost was," I confide. And for a few precious seconds we just sit there and smile at each other, serenaded by the husky bray of a passing barge, the morning sunlight white against my mysterious companion's skullcap of straight black hair, the sun's Eastern origin mystically heralding his obviously Asian heritage, until finally I find myself looking dreamily away, counting my blessings:

First, a man called Catfish with a great smile and even greater apartment tidings.

Now...this.

Maybe there's a God after all, I humbly sigh, trying to catch my tubmate's reflection in some of the larger bubbles while attempting to dismiss the impression that he's a bit on the young side (twenty-six? twenty-seven?)—then cavalierly casting all such limitations aside while speculating as to the possible significance of the additional towel on the ground next to the tub.

My heels aligned against the step upon which I'm perched like the praying hands of a parochial school girl, I lean my head back against the stone and regard my companion through casually angled eyes. "You live here?"

He nods, patting the water.

I do a rapid domestic survey but come up empty.

"Where?" I inquire, my desire to know outweighing my fear of coming across as nosy.

He makes a water pistol out of his fist and aims for a lizard inching its way up a clay pot. "Front house."

"Oh. Beneath Georgia, you mean?"

"Yep."

"I didn't think anyone lived there."

He interrupts what he's doing to make a "ta-da" motion, then goes back to targeting the lizard.

"Sammy," I say, holding a wet paw out over the water in a shamelessly gratuitous gesture.

He replies with a courteous shake. "Right. You're the new guy."

I nod, thrilled to have been heard of by this stalwart Oriental prince and longing more than ever to know his name, something exotic and sing-song I presume, and yet already fearing I might have overstepped. Feeling the heat rising into my cheeks I avert my eyes to the new foam formation in the center of the tub, which is perfectly white and, it seems to me, distinctly swan-like.

"Ehd-gur!" somebody screeches from the direction of the house. I look that way, a tad startled, then back at my friend, who grins and puts a finger to his lips. Concurrently I can swear I feel his toes brush against my foot, although in the swirling waters there's no way to be sure.

"Ehhhd-guuur!" the voice comes again, closer and louder.

"Shhhh!" Edgar insists with imploring eyes. Then he takes a deep breath and plunges into the foam, at which point something definitely brushes up against my foot.

A man about my age emerges from the garden and hurries up to the tub, his perfectly knotted tie bouncing against his button-down shirt, which curves over a paunch into a pair of starched Dickies dress slacks. Thick, wire-rimmed glasses add a pseudo-scholarly flair, and I immediately peg him as the kind of person who would never, under any circumstances, discard a paper clip, not to mention *way* too old for Edgar.

"Oh," he says, regarding me like a kitchen ant. "You must be the new guy."

I nod. "Sammy. B. Sammy Singleton."

"Rusty," he says, not warmly. "Have you seen Edgar?"

So much for niceties, I think, my lips melding into a tight line, as in bamboo shoots shall draw no confession here.

At that moment, however, my acquaintance bursts up out of the water, laughing and sputtering.

"What do you think you're doing?" Rusty demands, teapot-like.

"Oh, lighten up, wouldja!" Edgar says, standing up to reveal broad, sinewy shoulders and a narrow brown chest streaked by gleaming rivulets *d'eau chaud*. Following a momentary mental synapse, I wrench my eyes chastely back toward Rusty.

"You're going to be late," the cradle-robber scolds, tapping his watch.

"No, I'm not," Edgar quibbles, hypnotically twisting his upper body from side to side while sliding the flats of his palms across the top of the water.

"Get out of the tub."

"But Thorn said—"

"I don't care what Thorn said. Let's go."

"But, Da-ad..."

"Move it!"

Edgar moans and slaps the top of the water one last time, then follows orders, blue surfer trunks and all.

"Later," he says to me, flicking a few drops of water at Rusty and scampering off.

The father figure snatches the boy's towel off the ground and blots his tie, then glares at me. "He's only seventeen," he says, his eyes brimming with contempt.

"But—"

"Talk to the hand," he says, thrusting one forward like the stop sign of a middle school traffic monitor, then huffing back into the forbidden garden.

11

Certain Things

Are Better Left Unsaid

## November 1998

Within 72 hours of unpacking my bags at 625 Marigny Street, any reservations I may have about fitting in there have been trumped by the concern that this may not be an issue after all. Not only have I yet to receive word of any welcome "bash," I've not seen hide nor hair of Georgia since he handed over the keys. With each passing day, I keep thinking he'll at least stop by to check up and collect the rent. But he doesn't. And as I struggle to account for this nonappearance I pass through a series of emotions closely tracking the stages of grief, commencing with denial that I could be lucky enough to have a landlord who's never around, followed by a spate of anger over his not officially welcoming me into the fold, leading into a period of bargaining that if I remain patient that may yet occur. By the time my 96th hour has come and gone with still no sign of Georgia, however, I've weathered a squall of depression over the thought that the only possible explanation for the absence is that he instinctively loathes and is about to evict me, then entered into a dull mode of acceptance, consoling myself that at least there won't be much to pack. Of course, these gloomy imaginings are magnified at least a thousand-fold by the fact that I've also not seen or heard from Catfish since he discarded me there, and not for lack of effort on my part either. Per Georgia's suggestion, I've stopped by Creole Heart a half dozen times at various hours, glorious thank-you phaelaenopsis in mossy cachepot in hand, only to find the place consistently closed. Compounding the unpopular new kid theme, following the neighborly onslaught of the first couple days I've yet to encounter (or re-encounter) anyone else, including Naomi. Instead, a kind of lull-before-the-storm calm has descended, as if everyone knows there's no point in pretending the new guy's going to work out. Meanwhile, unable to muster a sufficient level of concentration to dive into Earth-Friendly Incontinence Products (my next Handy Stats topic), to help while away the hours I've been endeavoring to accentuate the shadow line beneath the furrowed chrome edge of my kitchen counter with a hair-thin wisp of red. This pursuit's ability to distract is limited, however. And my mind has just begun to wander in the direction of abandoned boxcars when the doorbell buzzes.

"Damn!" I hiss, almost going outside the line as I automatically associate the sound with Dickie Grand, whom I by now know to be a perennial headliner at a reasonably popular local "cabaret."

Then a second possibility hits me: Catfish, perchance?

I slip my mascara-applicator-sized brush into a cup of paint thinner and race downstairs.

A few seconds later I'm trudging back up wondering two things: why UPS men wear dark socks with shorts, and what to do with the box I'm carrying, which despite the buzzer intrusion is addressed to George Moore and marked "Special Delivery—Keep Refrigerated!" Having previously puzzled at length over the first conundrum, I turn my problem-solving skills to the latter. And by the time I reach the top of the stairs I've narrowed the choices down to two: 1) put the parcel in my fridge and wait for Georgia to come by (which some tiny part of me still insists he will, if for no other reason than to serve me with eviction papers), or 2) view the package as, if not some sort of sign, at least a valid reason to take the bull by the horns and go knock on Georgia's door, putting an end to my mental torment once and for all. Briefly considering that sheltered torment is perhaps preferable to homeless serenity, I pause at the top of the stairs, then make my way over to the pair of French doors through which Georgia previously came and went. Like the other pairs, this one is shielded on the inside by voluminous silk drapes, and after a brief sequel of second-guessing I tap on the glass.

"Hello?"

To my surprise, the drapes part almost instantly and the door flies open.

"I'm here!" Georgia practically shouts—although at first I'm not sure it's him despite the ample exterior light. A far cry from the elegant personage who'd greeted Catfish and me, this afghan-draped individual looks like he's coming off a week-long binge.

"Oh," he groans, "it's you."

"Georgia?" I say, attempting to mask my dismay.

He spots the UPS package. "Is that for me?"

I nod and lift.

"Oh thank God!" he cries, snatching the box and banging the door closed.

With my expulsion from River House clearly imminent,

there's no point in continuing with my kitchen upgrade. But for the next two and a half hours continue I do, imagining how one day in a not-so-distant future in which I've settled into my destined role of literary lion, an osteoporosis-hobbled Georgia Moore will discover my little line there, at eye level, and realize what a terrible mistake he's made in having banished an individual with—among so many gifts—flawless taste, cursing his barely mobile self as he traces the inspired crimson trail with a gnarled fingertip, all alone in that big old house, with one progressively more unremarkable tenant after another having moved on, as he now understands a fiercely loyal nester like that Singleton fellow would never have done had he not been so brutally expunged from *la Maison de Fleuve*, one more bit of lint in the vast dustbin of former River House tenants deemed not quite up to snuff in the hypercritical eyes of Georgia Moore. The only thing is, a slight tremor in my hand seems to be preventing me from following the ruler of masking tape I've applied with unflagging precision. Plus, the fumes from the spirits are beginning to get to me.

I've therefore just concluded a 30-minute break, during which I've opened my kitchen door to let in some air and whisked up a pitcher of Crystal Light, when I realize my landlord is standing right behind me—a rather nerve-wracking discovery that causes my paint brush to jag decisively outside the line as I straighten up with a start. Since our previous encounter he's gone through a substantial makeover, one involving cocoa butter and a kimono-like robe of baby blue silk and a good (though slightly crooked) wig of flouncy gray curls. At the same time, he still seems pretty out of it (is that pot I smell?), his eyes bulbous and blurry atop his gaunt, ashen face. Most egregiously, there's no missing the shadow topping his lip, although the rest of his face is as hairless as an egg.

"Oh dear!" the new-and-improved Georgia exclaims. "I didn't mean to startle!"

"No problem!" I reply, feeling like I've been caught taking down a wall with a sledge hammer.

"What, pray tell, are you doing?"

"Nothing."

He leans to one side. "Nothing?"

"Oh *that*..." I snatch up a cloth and dab gingerly, signaling that the entire business can be removed with purely minimal effort. "Just a little touch-up. Gosh, I hope you don't mind."

He registers a puzzled look, then pulls out a pair of reading glasses and leans down. "This? But...I can hardly see it."

(Yep, the man reeks.)

"It's subtle."

He fixes me over the top of his glasses. "It certainly is," he all but chuckles.

"It's an *accent* stripe," I clarify. "I'm sorry. I should have asked first."

He considers me a beat, then sighs. "We need to talk."

"Oh. Okay. Just let me—."

"Five minutes. My place."


One would presume that people who after a long period of uncertainty have been sentenced to death for some crime they didn't commit, while no doubt aghast, must nevertheless feel some measure of relief, a certain inner calmness in simply knowing that their fate, dismal though it may be, has been determined. And it's in this spirit that I head over to Georgia's lair, deriving a measure of satisfaction from my prescient foreboding of impending eviction since I am by this time at least partially prepared. At the same time, I must confess, I'm also curious to see exactly where, and how, the Georgia lives, knowing that with knowledge comes power, and confident that insight will cement my already strong suspicions about just how selfish and misguided a creature he really is. Given the laxness of his appearance and his failure to grasp the understated exquisiteness of my shadow line, anything's possible, I tell myself as I cross the breezeway, preparing for what will almost certainly be a horrific assault upon the senses from which I may never fully recover, envisaging myself weaving dizzily along a suffocatingly narrow trail cleft between dusty piles of objects heaped floor to ceiling—the accumulated possessions of former tenants too traumatized to cart them off or ever return for them, as I now understand the erstwhile April must have been—on my way to the three-by-five patch in which the sad fellow actually lives, where any day now a frayed hotplate cord will burst into flames, engulfing both the rag rug upon which he routinely passes out and the tragically disturbed Georgia himself.

In actuality, the residence of Georgia Moore consists of four gracious rooms with beaded board ceilings soaring high overhead, whence tiny flakes of age-old paint flutter down just often enough to make it seem like Christmas is always right around the corner. Aside from the aroma of what smells like some very good weed, what strikes me first as I peer in the door he's left open is the practically overwhelming impression that somebody lives there, an effect I somehow never quite managed to achieve in the Manhattan apartment I'd spent over a decade in and one I all at once doubt I ever will—or if so most certainly not in the quirky but unselfconscious manner that now presents itself, that perfect balance of personal yet inviting that no degree of professional assistance can create. In this case, it's a balance that also somehow manages to accomplish a feat I'd heretofore considered to be virtually impossible, this being to seamlessly interweave formal and casual while integrating elements from disparate eras. Directly in front of me, for example, is a Louisiana cypress table overhung with a globed chandelier, its glow doubled by the gold-leaf mirror tilting atop the mantel of the fireplace to my right, the plaster cherub at the mirror's peak hovering rapturously near the ceiling, creating the focal point for a room straight out of the 1850s. On the other hand, from my station by the door one need only glance across that table to be rocketed gently forward a hundred years. For in the adjoining front room the design theme shifts unapologetically into a brave new world of Danish modern sofas and end tables and space-ship-shaped lamps, of Formica and bakelite and nubby textiles with geometric prints and, in one corner, a glass-topped Seeburg jukebox with a backlit plastic banner announcing "Music for Everyone!"

At the other end of the dining room, to my left, a broad archway opens into a galley kitchen. And as my eyes complete the circuit I realize I'm being observed by Georgia, who's hovering in the archway holding a tray.

"Well don't just stand there," he says, spider to fly.


Appearances notwithstanding, the material of the sofa upon which I've been directed to wait while Georgia returns to the kitchen with unspecified intent is not scratchy but soft, as are the pleated throw pillows and the indirect light from the trio of French doors before me, whose rusty persimmon drapes have been puddled back to reveal the flowering forest of Georgia's front balcony. But I refuse to be lulled into a false sense of security, instead remaining perched on the edge of the couch like a junior Hindenburg ready for launch. On the triangular coffee table in front of me lie the ruins of the UPS box, and next to that a fiddle-shaped ashtray with half a joint in it. Flanking the ashtray are two ravishingly retro glasses of what Georgia has identified as iced tea, the occasional bead of condensation trickling down their ringed surfaces. And as I sit there watching those teardrops fall, waiting for Georgia to come back and cut me loose, my mind begins to race in new and unwelcome directions, driven by a lash-like sense of impending doom in a form far more lethal than I've thus far considered. What, after all, do I really know about this Georgia character, or for that matter Catfish? I peer discreetly across the coffee table into the adjacent room, where an abnor-mally narrow staircase forms an extreme angle leading up to a hatch-like ceiling trapdoor that appears to be padlocked shut. Although it's common knowledge that they almost always work alone, there are I believe at least a few documented cases of serial killers pairing up—that father and son team with the Hispanic last name, for example. And all at once it seems perfectly logical that Catfish and Georgia are in cahoots, with Catfish luring the prey over to Georgia's with the promise of too-good-to-be-true apart-ments and Georgia taking it from there, engineering a series of slick abductions now extending to yours truly, who will soon find himself chained up in the attic among a host of former victims in odd poses and various stages of decomp, including whatever's left of the once resourceful April, barely able to breathe between the discolored dish towel duct-taped into my mouth and the dangling grove of pine-tree shaped automobile deodorizers, staring through swollen eyelids at the row of common household implements aligned atop one of those fold-up picnic tables avail-able at Wal-Marts nationwide as one "family member" after another slips in and out to ogle and prod while waiting for the real fun to begin.

In other words, there's no way I'm touching that tea.

Georgia reappears and lands like a brittle leaf on the edge of the Eames chair to my left, knees together. "Sorry to keep you waiting," he says.

"No problem," I smile, attempting to ignore both the craters surrounding his eyes and the dark crumb adhering to his upper lip.

He picks up his tea and tilts the glass my way. "To new friends."

"What? Oh…yes!" I hoist my glass and clink, then take a sip that barely moistens my lips.

"And well…" he continues, "you're just going to have to excuse the disarray."

"What are you talking about? This place is like a museum!"

He sweeps a slim finger up and down his front. "*This* disarray," he sighs.

"You look fine."

"Please. I've been a bit under the weather."

"Oh. I'm sorry. Nothing serious, I hope."

He pats his tummy. "Just a little nauseous. Somebody told me some pot might help."

"I've heard that."

"Would you care for some?"

"What? Oh. No, thanks."

"You don't smoke?"

"Um…actually, no."

"I didn't think so. I bet you don't drink either."

I smile and shake my head.

Georgia nods approvingly, then slips a cellophane tube of cookies out of the pocket of his robe. "My weakness," he confides. "Would you like one?"

"Oh...no thanks."

"You don't like Oreos?"

"No, I do. I just...ate."

"Well you've got a lot more willpower than I do. Do you mind?"

"Not at all!"

He liberates a cookie and takes a dainty bite, then closes his eyes and chews slowly. A moment later he opens them. "Oh my God," he groans as the lip crumb tumbles. "This must be why they call it the munchies. Are you sure you don't want one?"

"Yes, but go right ahead."

He takes another bite and washes it down with a sip of tea. "So," he dabs at his mouth with the edge of a cocktail napkin, "how's the apartment?"

"Wonderful! I love it."

"So then...you'll be staying?"

"What? Oh...yes. I mean, *yes*."

"I feel just terrible," he says, rolling his eyes. "Like I *abandoned* you over there."

"Not at all."

Georgia lifts a palm to his chest. "Oh!"

"What?"

"Nothing. Just a slight sugar rush."

"Are you sure you're okay?"

"Never better. Have you at least met some of the others?"

"Actually, yes. Naomi. Dickie. Everyone seems really nice. Oh! That reminds me..." I pull out my wallet and scissor a folded check toward him.

He rewards the gesture with a blank stare.

"The rent?"

"Ah!"

He receives the payment, then dons his glasses and reads out loud: "B. Sammy Singleton. New York, New York." He glances up and appraises me as if impressed. "My my my," he says. "You've come a long way, haven't you, Son?"

I shrug atop an impromptu burst of emotion, all at once feeling that, if ever I tripped and skinned my knee, this was the person I'd want to bandage it up.

He studies me a bit longer, then glances spacily about the room. On top of the jukebox is an elegantly framed head-shot of a pretty lady with huge brown eyes, and it's there that Georgia's gaze lands and remains during a long silence in which he seems to forget I'm there. I am in fact beginning to wonder if it's time to excuse myself when he reaches over and clasps my hand and gives it a shake.

"Charles is a wonderful person," he says.

"Um...who?"

"Catfish. His real name is Charles."

"Oh, that's right. Yes, he seems really nice."

"Have you two...?"

"What?"

"Connected?"

"Oh. Um, actually, no. I mean, not since the other day. I stopped by a few times but the shop was always closed."

"Oh dear," Georgia says, dropping the cookie tube onto the table.

"Is something wrong?"

"Probably not," he shrugs. "It's just that, well, I worry about him. Especially lately, what with this ridiculous grave-robbing affair. I mean, between the surveillance and the police raids and the interrogations…"

"Grave robbing?"

"He didn't say a word, did he?"

"No."

Georgia flicks the crumb off his lap. "Of course he didn't. That's what worries me. He keeps everything bottled up. Which is the *worst* thing a person like him can do. I mean, one way or another it's going to come out. And he's got the scars on his wrists to prove it!"

"Uh…"

"Oh it's fine," he says with a wave. "I mean, thanks to Tess the fact that Charles tried to kill himself when he was in high school, *twice*, is practically universal knowledge."

"Oh. Um…Tess?"

"His mother. She's, well, don't get me started."

"Ah."

"Which I suppose is where I come in. Or *try* to. It's not easy. I think I have some idea how James must have felt."

"James?"

"Charles' ex. Back in San Francisco. You look like him. Charles and I moved here from there."

"Oh. So you and, um, Charles…?"

"What? Oh heavens no! Not at the same time. I moved here a year before he did. Nineteen ninety-one. I knew James in San Francisco but not Charles. Charles and I met here. If it hadn't been for his architectural genius and contractor connections this place would still be a ruin. Anyway, that's part of why I worry. I don't think he ever got over Frederick's death."

"Um…"

"Charles' father. They didn't get along too well either. But there was going to be a reconciliation. But then Frederick's plane went down en route to see Charles…and James and Charles split up…and Charles moved back to New Orleans…and he and Tess starting going at it (again) and, well—you get the point—it was just all too much. Who wouldn't have swallowed a handful of barbiturates?"

"You mean…"

"Number three. Right downstairs. In Dickie's apartment. Before Dickie moved in of course. Thank God April was still trimming that bed. She's the one who called the paramedics. But now, like I said, this police investigation…"

"Wow."

Georgia nods. "That's why I have a favor to ask."

"Oh?"

"I'm afraid it could be a bit awkward."

"What is it?"

"The next time you see Charles—do you even have his phone number?"

I shake my head.

"Remind me to give it to you. Anyway, the next time you see him—you are planning to see him again, aren't you?"

"Sure. I mean, I hope so."

"You're not mad at him, are you?"

"Why would I be mad at him?"

"For disappearing."

"No. Of course not."

"Because he does that. It has nothing to do with you. He's just...busy."

"I'm fine."

"Good. So," Georgia lowers his voice a notch, "the next time you see him, I'd prefer you not mention that I look like death warmed over."

"No you don't."

"I appreciate that. But I saw your face when you dropped off the package. Please. It will only alarm him. Plus the last thing I need is to have Charles fussing around here worrying about me."

"I won't say a word."

Georgia touches my knee and smiles. And when he does I wonder if he's really as out of it as I'd thus far presumed. Because in contrast to the rapid-fire ramble of personal information just unleashed, his demeanor is now measured, his eyes perfectly lucid.

"Thank you," he says, rising in a manner suggesting I'm to follow suit. "Besides, certain things are better left unsaid, don't you think?"

12

With A Cross Over It

**Friday August 26, 2005 – 2:30 a.m.**

Can't sleep so here I am, propped up in bed, the AC heaving as reliably as an iron lung. How ironic that Catfish got me started with this whole journaling thing, with the gift of a book called *The Artist's Way* dropped off the day after my command performance poetry reading. Even though it languished unopened for almost five years, once I got going I couldn't stop, with the book's recommended "morning pages" gradually morphing into "anytime pages" I've been piling up ever since. As a result, a small Everest of black-and-white-marbled-cover notebooks now graces the shelf of my bedroom closet, each of them crammed full of words that often say little but whose mere transcription on the page almost always makes me feel better. Indeed, with AA meetings now pretty much a thing of the past, I sometimes feel like this seemingly endless string of syllables is the only thing keeping me tethered to Planet Earth. "You lie, you die," my first AA sponsor drilled into me early on with his Harvey Fierstein rattle. And while that may have struck me as a bit severe (as, for that matter, did the heavily pierced Justin in general), I've since come to believe that we alcoholics really are, as he insisted, "as sick as our secrets."

…and yet, all these years later, here I am.

What a joke.

What's wrong with me?

I don't know.

I don't even know if I want to know.

All I know is that everything else seems preternaturally clear right now, in this purgatorial pit between awake and asleep.

Of course, I've been here before, plenty of times.

And yet...not. Not even close.

So for want of a better option, here goes: A fearless and searching moral inventory of all I've thus far chosen to ignore with regard to the well-being of my so-called best friend.

As if that really could make some kind of mystical difference.

And yet, right now the alternative feels like death.

So, where to begin with a lie as long and winding as this?

At the beginning, I guess.


"Hey!" Catfish waved, blowing through the restaurant door toting a bottle of California Red. Two days after my powwow with a cannabis-infused Georgia, Catfish and I had finally hooked up. And with the blossoms prematurely caramelizing on the gift orchid, I'd alternately expressed my gratitude with a dinner invite. "Some place nice," I'd gently prodded, insisting the choice be his but thinking along the lines of Arnaud's or Antoine's. Instead we'd landed at Mona Lisa in the lower Quarter, a hallway-width place with a couple dozen budget renditions of the namesake painting lining the walls and a bunch of half-dead succulents in the window.

"Hey!" I parroted as he lighted across from me and centered the bottle between us.

"They don't serve alcohol here," he explained, blithely unaware or unconcerned that he was ten minutes late.

I nodded but held up a palm as a tiny Turkish waiter darted forth and thrust a wine glass my way.

Catfish cocked his head to one side. "No?"

"No, thanks. But go ahead."

"You sure?"

"Absolutely."

Taking the cue, the waiter opened the bottle and poured for Catfish and went to get me a Diet Coke.

Catfish twisted the stem of his glass next to a fat crimson votive fitted with plastic net, the buttons on the cuff of his pink Brooks Brothers glowing. "So…you don't drink?"

I shook my head.

"May I ask why not?"

"Let's just say that I've already consumed at least one lifetime's worth of booze."

"Ah. AA?"

"Over three years."

"Good for you!"

"And you."

He grinned. "Why, were you a wild one?"

"No, just a drunk one." I motioned toward his glass. "It's okay. Really."

He wrinkled his nose. "I can take it or leave it."

## Chapter 12

The waiter returned with my soda. "Are you ready to order?"

Catfish peered at me over his menu. "May I?"

"Sure."

"Are you carnivorous?"

"Hopelessly."

"Two Mardi Gras pastas with extra andouille," he instructed the waiter, handing over the menus. "And a large garlic bread."

"Anything else?"

He scooted the wine glass and bottle to the edge of the table. "Yes," he said. "I'll have a Diet Coke."


Two house specials later we'd covered such first-date (in the Aladdin's lamp of my mind, at least) basics as hometowns and universities and the fact that we both spoke French (he way better than I) and were beginning to edge beyond, into territories of discussion I normally avoided but on this night was more than willing to explore as long as the crow's-feet kept dancing, even if it did seem like I was doing most of the talking and blurting out seldom shared information, such as the details of my parents' recent sudden but tidy divorce.

"So..." Catfish picked up the conversation as we awaited baklava. "A real-life preacher's kid."

"Yep."

"Any brothers or sisters?"

"One sister. You?"

He shook his head. "What about you and your folks?"

"What about us?"

*The Coffee Shop Chronicles of New Orleans*

"Do you get along?"

"Sure."

"What do they think about your being gay?"

"Good question.  Hm…I'm actually not sure they know."

"Really?"

"Why, is it that obvious?"

"Well to me it is."  An exculpatory wink.  "No, it's just that, I mean, you never…?"

"I don't really see the point," I shrugged.  "They're both pretty old.  And it would only hurt them.  My father especially.  And for what?  I hardly ever see them.  Plus, now that they're divorced…  Besides, I'm pretty sure my mother already knows."

"Why's that?"

"Well, uh, okay.  What single straight guy asks his mother for a chenille quilt for Christmas?"

"True."

"From Pottery Barn."

"Yikes."

"A year in advance."

"You're right.  The woman knows."

"What about your family?" I said, casually sipping my Coke.  Silence.

"What?"

"Nothing.  It's just that…" he rolled his eyes, "this is *such* a cliché."

"Oh, come on."

"You remind me of someone."

"James?"

"Huh? How did you…? Oh. Of course. What *else* did Georgia tell you?"

"Not much."

"I bet."

I worked my straw into the ice in the bottom of my glass. "How long were you together?"

"Uh…almost twelve years."

"Wow. Do you still talk?"

"He's in San Francisco," Catfish shrugged, yanking on a cover of nonchalance. "What about you?"

"What about me?"

"Have you ever, you know, been in a long-term relationship?"

The waiter bopped back, baklava in hand.

"This looks delicious," I observed.

"Yeah," Catfish agreed.

"No," I said, picking up a thread I might have left dangling had it not been for the unanticipated absence of life from his eyes. "I never have."


Now while I take full responsibility for what happened after that since it was I who invited the man in after he insisted on walking me home, it was nevertheless Catfish who kissed me first, catching me off guard in the breezeway as I finished locking the gate. Dry and garlicky and slightly off center, there could have been no better indication than that first kiss that there could be no worse romantic combination than he and myself. Yet something not immediately responsive to logic had apparently been set into motion because the next thing I knew we were stumbling through my kitchen door and across my living room and onto my new plush mattress, propelled by a series of rather desperate attempts at tender kisses and passionate gropings, discarding our clothing as we went. Nor did matters improve once we took to the bed. Because not having had a "date" in longer than I cared to calculate and cosmetically encouraged by the relative darkness I eventually found myself in one overambitious configuration too many, at which point a jolt of excruciating pain caused me to let loose a shriek and crash down onto the mattress like a felled sequoia, effectively putting an end to any fantasies I might have harbored about his step-dancing home the next day howling "Son of a Preacher Man" into a make-believe microphone.

Instead, he spent the rest of the night stepping back and forth to the refrigerator for ice to press against my aching groin, his long white body slipping wraith-like in and out of the room as I watched him fade and reappear, his naked skin pearlescent in the late night light, its prominent arteries and fine veins forming an obscure map beneath the flesh. "You okay?" he'd inquire every so often as we lay there on the mattress beside one another, flickering beneath some candles he'd scrounged up somewhere as he angled up on an elbow and looked down at me, his blue eyes so pale I could hardly look back, the lip scar a tender smile, the vertical lines that began at the upper edges of his freckled brow merging between the reddish hairs of his lashes like an arrow indicating his gravest concern, making me silently curse the morning light when it finally crept through Georgia's lace tablecloths.

*The Coffee Shop Chronicles of New Orleans*

*Chapter 12*

"How'd you get those?" I said in a near-whisper, in not just for a penny and sensing that he was about to make his last run to the kitchen. For the past little while we'd been lying awake on our backs, breathing, the low hill of my body next to the flat plain of his, naked and relaxed beneath Mother's quilt. His eyes followed mine to the exposed underside of his forearm, where a row of pale stripes tracked from elbow to wrist like partially submerged railroad ties.

"Big ol' cat," he said, curling his fingers into claws and letting out a soft "grrr."

"No, really." I eased up onto one side and bumped my fingers down the tough ridges of skin.

"Okay," he confessed. "It was a tiger."

"Catfish..."

He shook his head. "It was a long time ago, B. I'm not proud."

I nodded and tried to let it go but couldn't. "Why?" I said.

He puffed out a sigh. "I don't know. I didn't like who I was, I guess."

"Who were you?"

"A Beaucoeur."

"What's a bo-cur?"

He checked to see if I was kidding, then smiled and shook his head. A moment later he leaned over and kissed me on the forehead, hovering a few seconds before dropping back down.

"I like you, Sammy," he said. "You're innocent."

"No I'm not."

"Yes you are."

"No, I'm not."

"Yes, you are."

"How do you know?"

"Because only the innocent claim categorically not to be."

"I'm as guilty as sin. You have no idea."

"Really? Of what then?"

"Trying to seduce you?"

"I'm pretty sure it was the other way around."

I floated a Mona Lisa smile of my own.

"Seriously, B. I'm sorry. I never should have—"

"You didn't answer the question."

"What?"

"What's a Beaucoeur?"

A beleaguered exhalation. "*I'm* a Beaucoeur," he finally said. "B-E-A-U-C-O-E-U-R."

"Oh. Um…beautiful heart?"

"Yeah. Right," he scoffed. He jumped up from the bed and disappeared into the living room. "I like it like it is, Sammy," he called back.

"Okay," I replied, gingerly sitting up. "It's just that…"

He appeared in the doorway, shirt in hand. "What?"

"What about now?"

"What *about* now?"

"Do you like who you are? I mean, you're still a Beaucoeur, aren't you?"

He glowered at me, then pulled his shirt on. "Yes, Sammy," he said. "I still am."

"So then..."

"Look," he said, stepping into his pants. "I'm fine, alright? Regardless of whatever Georgia may have told you. I mean, I love the guy dearly but—"

"He told me what happened downstairs."

"You're kidding."

I shook my head.

"Jesus Christ!" he groaned. "That was an *accident*!"

"Okay."

"And it was a long time ago."

"Okay."

"I have to go now."

Although it would be another week before Georgia gave me the full run-down, what happened downstairs was that Georgia had found himself unable to awaken Catfish one morning back in 1993. Theirs had been a friendship from day one, that being an afternoon less than a year after Catfish had moved back to New Orleans, when Georgia moseyed into the Chartres Street shop wearing a pair of Betsey Johnson knickers and slapped down the San Francisco expat card. By that time, Catfish's life was a book open to anyone reading the paper, with the court case just settled, while Georgia, plain and simple, needed an architect. Yet it was far more than that. For with both parties grieving the loss of a loved one, there had been a connection of the kind only pain can forge, immediate and intense and not fully intentional. Nevertheless, while Georgia had been able to remount that ever-slippery slope of despair, pulling himself up with the lifeline of the house's endless demands, for Catfish the going had been less certain due to what Georgia called the "triple whammy" of his having lost his father, parted with James, and fallen out with Tess (again) virtually all at once. And indeed, less than three months after Catfish had offered to help with Georgia's monumental restoration, the incident in question had occurred, following one of the not infrequent nights Catfish had ended up all but passing out from exhaustion in one of Georgia's unfinished flats, too bushed to make the walk back to his temporary digs over the shop. And while Catfish maintained to this day that the overdose had been accidental, Georgia remained unconvinced.

Meanwhile, and how very convenient for me, I declined to choose sides, lacking as I did sufficient first-hand perspective, the flesh-and-blood evidence of Catfish's earlier traumas notwithstanding. And not just that. For despite Georgia's early warnings and what I could see for myself, I elected to believe that Catfish was over all that, convincing myself that not bringing up the topic ever again was the only kind and proper thing to do, our hasty intimacy notwithstanding. And in all fairness, that one night had been a departure, both in the sense of my having jumped (literally) into bed with someone I'd just met (or had long known, for that matter) and in the sense of my having felt comfortable enough to pose such deeply personal questions to a person I barely knew. The truth is, the following morning I could hardly believe I'd committed said acts, although the fact that I spent the next few days hobbling around did serve as a reminder that my groin, at least, had been fully engaged. So did the fact that almost a week passed before either Catfish or I saw or spoke to one another again. Clearly something had happened there, something that made me feel both special and a little uneasy, not unlike the two *pains au chocolats* that mysteriously appeared on my kitchen table while I slept, in between Catfish's early a.m. departure and his apparently very quiet and very short-lived return. And though I failed to grasp fully what that was, I nevertheless fancied it would always bond us in some substantial, private way that connected Catfish with no one else. In the full arrogance of that denial I also fantasized that our exchange would have the magical effect of purging him of any lingering demons and keeping him safe, partially because the opposite was unthinkable, and partially because, truth be told, I didn't want to deal with it. After all, weren't conversations of the sort Catfish and I had had that night (of which I'd admittedly had few) supposed to be cathartic? Wasn't that what therapy (the idea of which made me cringe) was supposed to be all about? In any case it didn't take long for me to get the unspoken message that whatever had happened between us had been a one-time deal, a natural conclusion I gamely attributed to basic lack of compatibility and one that also, I must confess, carried with it a measure of relief. What's more, as time went by, I came to understand that as emotionally in sync as we might have been on that accidental night and sometimes were thereafter, we could just as easily and with no discernible pattern disconnect, especially since Catfish tended to drop out of sight for days at a time, unexcused absences I felt absolved me from any greater responsibility.

While I may have refrained from any additional direct inquiry into Catfish's psyche, however, I did not restrain myself when it came to looking into the Beaucoeur family name, which post spelling bee seemed to be popping up everywhere, including on the fronts of Southern art museums and children's hospital wings. And most certainly, through what turned out to be a rather obsessive degree of digging through the stacks and archives of the public library's Historic New Orleans Collection, I was able to find out plenty about the Beaucoeurs of yesteryear, compiling a virtual history book that I liked to pretend, as much for my own sake as for Catfish's, was far more thorough than any family history he himself had ever read, a book I completed, and closed, and then carted around without once reopening until, well, now.

Jean-Pierre Phillipe de Beaucoeur arrived in the New World in the mid-1700s with a land grant arranged by Roman Catholic cardinal André Hercule de Fleury, successor to the Duke D'Orléans and chief advisor to King Louis XV. And Beaucoeur was among the first both to monetize the agricultural potential of the land running alongside the Mississippi River, which through thousands of years of flooding had formed its own high banks sloping into fields dark with silt, and to capitalize on the strategic position of the fledgling Nouvelle-Orléans as an international shipping crossroads. Even for the wealthy, however, life in early southern Louisiana was a struggle, with scores succumbing to yellow fever and malaria and dysentery in the swampy, mosquito-ridden wilderness, and with scores of others blown or washed away by the unpredictable whims of violent storms and rising waters, as was the case in 1723, when a hurricane lasting three days destroyed much of the earliest settlement at the river crescent. Nevertheless, Jean-Pierre was determined to make his own fortune. And after a number of trials with various crops he eventually settled upon the one that would become the mainstay of the Beaucoeur clan for generations to come: sugarcane.

Starting a few miles outside New Orleans, Beaucoeur land-holdings once amounted to over a hundred thousand acres, spreading out west along the Mississippi River from Jefferson Parish through Ascension Parish, and east through St. Bernard down into Plaquemines. Some records show that these holdings continued all the way to the Gulf Coast. But it was the higher ground along the river between Baton Rouge and New Orleans that yielded the most bounty, with relatively modest plantings of cotton and corn and indigo supplementing the core crop—vast seas of sugarcane that wound along the river mile after mile and extended back from its banks beyond the reach of the naked eye. Throughout the fledgling nation and the Old World it was known that from those fields came the table sugar of the King of France, who was rumored to have petitioned God for the fertility of the land and whose own investments in the territory were extensive. And for many years it seemed that the King's prayers had been answered, with each season's crop breaking the previous year's record.

By 1763, when France ceded the territory to Spain in the Treaty of Paris, the Beaucoeurs were already established as an economic bloc in the region. And they continued to thrive throughout the period of Spanish rule, as they did when the territory reverted to French sovereignty in 1800, and then was sold to the United States in 1803, with the family fortune growing as abundantly as the cane. By the 1840s practically every plantation along the River Road belonged to one of Jean-Pierre's sons or grandsons, or to a planter who had married into the Beaucoeur family. And with the fields long since cleared and the swamps drained and the grand homes glittering along the landscape, life in Southern Louisiana was good for the Beaucoeurs, who came to be famous for their Creole hospitality and uncomplicated taste— only the best that money could buy!—from cosmopolitan balls and sumptuous feasts on the plantations during the summer, to lengthy retreats to city townhomes during the winter, to annual shopping trips to world capitals, followed by a stream of shipments from far-off places, until the houses were so full of furniture and fine art and silver that making room for the next wave of luxury became the foremost preoccupation of many a Beaucoeur wife.

Not everyone in the Beaucoeur circle was blessed, however, for revolving around the bright stars of these privileged daughters and sons, nieces and nephews, was a galaxy of souls but dimly lit, although it was their hands that had built the Beaucoeur manors and worked the Beaucoeur fields, and cooked the Beaucoeur meals and raised the Beaucoeur children—theirs and those of their daughters and sons, who had done the same, as had the next generation, and the one after that. At the peak of the Beaucoeur empire in the 1850s, the extended relations lay claim to over 700 slaves, none of whom were allowed to own property or have surnames other than those of their masters, the first restriction due to law, the second based on a convention not uncommon among southern slaveholders, in whose view allowing slaves to have family names was folly, especially since slave trading tore husbands from wives and parents from children. With little else to pass along, it was therefore the first names that these slaves handed down like precious heirlooms from one generation to the next, women's names like Louisa and Linder and Henrietta and Rose, Caroline and Hester and Rachel and Di, Marian and Eveline and Dilsey and Rose; and men's names like Samuel and Joseph and Erwin and Ben, Wilson and Wesley and Baptiste and Caleb, Solomon and Washington and Jacob and George. And as I sat there breathing the fine dust of those seldom read files, deciphering cursive ledgers of nineteenth century French, it was names like these that came up again and again in tracing that other Beaucoeur legacy, initially unable or unwilling to believe what was laid out before me.

Then one day, during the course of a blustery December afternoon at the Williams Research Center on Chartres Street, I came across the Library of Congress's *Born in Slavery: Slave Narratives 1936-38*—more than 2,300 first-person accounts of former slaves collected under the aegis of the Federal Writers' Project of the WPA, whose agents had, in painstakingly compiling those records, done their best to reproduce the vernacular of their interviewees; and then—tipped off by the well-dressed white lady behind the reference desk—a similar archive specific to the Mississippi River Valley, in which dozens of former slaves told their stories, including a 95-year-old "retiree" named Bitsy Baker:

*I was bon a slave on de big Beaucoeur place in St. Bernard Parish by de big ben in de river. My daddy's name was Anthony and my momma's name was Emma but I don member dem cause I was so lil when marster Beaucoeur gave me way to his in-laws up to Natchez. It was Chrismus and dey tol me to stop blubberin and go stan by de Chrismus tree. When de missus came in she clap her hands and say I was de bes present she ever had! She was nice to me too—sen me straight to de kitchen for a fin Chrismus dinner. She was sickly tho, and when she die the lil missus made me go work outside.*

*I worked in dem fiel many a day, a hoein and a plowin and a pickin. And when I got too tired de overseer let me rest beneef a tree and he nebber whip me cause he fraid I run off. I nebber did run off tho cause I know dey catch me and sen me back, and den mebbe sell me off some place wust! Dey neb-*

*ber did like me too much tho cause I nebber would give dem no babies. I nebber did get married and I nebber did have no childern. But I gots brothers and sisters somewheres, I knows dat much.*

*I's still fraid to talk about when we was freed but I guess it's good we was. Lots of niggas up and lef but I stayed right here on de farm, raisin up childern, washin, ironin, scourin, patchin, cookin—dere ain't nothing what I ain't done! Nebber did take no assistance neither. Sometimes I think bout tryin to fin some of my kin but I'm tired and don know where to look. Mebbe one of dem read dis and fin me! I got enough money for dem to bury me.*

The upholstered library chair in which I'd been sitting was cushy and warm, but after closing the book on Bitsy Baker I no longer felt comfortable there. So after returning a few rough-edged volumes to the woman behind the counter I shoved off into the wind, which rushed across the library's granite steps with the force of a city bus. As it was for the earliest settlers in the region and all those who have lived here since, being that close to the river was both a blessing and a curse, between the floods in the summer and the chill in the winter, and I was all at once a full-fledged member of the club. The light coat I was wearing had been selected under the Yankee misconception that it never got cold in New Orleans, or certainly not cold enough to daunt a former New Yorker. But this was a day for casting illusions aside, so after clutching the collar of my jacket to I launched myself down the steps in the direction of home.

Although 'twas the season to be jolly I was feeling anything but as I passed in front of one gaily painted storefront after another, most of them posh antique shops or art galleries, their gas-lit doorways draped with fresh-cut pine wound with ribbons, their interiors shimmering with holiday lights. While I'd read through only the tiniest fraction of the slave accounts, I'd uncovered a dark thread that seemed to coil up and around me as I marched down those delightful French Quarter streets, the wind gusting behind me as if to say *run, run!* Issues of physical fitness aside, however, there was no way I could run that fast. And if I couldn't escape, how could I possibly have done what I did, that being to quietly expect—no, to demand—that Catfish break free, that he discreetly disentangle himself from that thread, a thread with which his being was stitched through and through? What's more, not until now—as I sit here scribbling these words—am I finally getting around to articulating this: Isn't it possible that, on more than one occasion in Catfish's past, it was in the very process of trying to unravel himself from that infinitely malignant thread that, in that form of despair most desperate, he alternately wove it into a noose?

Of course it is, I have no choice but to conclude, knowing him as I have come to through the years.

And knowing the rest.


Nowhere had it been recorded in so many words. But it hadn't been hard to piece together that sugarcane had not been the only Beaucoeur crop. When the further importation of slaves became illegal in 1808, those who relied upon slaves for their livelihoods became fearful that the "natural increase" would not be sufficient. And with demand for slave labor still on the rise, a few entrepreneurial planters entered into a new kind of business.

While most of the resultant surplus came from states too far north to produce cotton profitably, such as Kentucky and Maryland, it was the Beaucoeurs who set the bar in the South. You could, for example, count on a Beaucoeur slave to be strong and clean, with not a mark upon his or her well-exercised body, the only exemptions being those who had tried to run away or learn to read (and even they were judiciously whipped only across the back). The other exception to the Beaucoeur's no-mark rule was the curly "B"—about one-inch high—that was branded into the neck of every Beaucoeur slave upon the first birthday—a "B" that made it possible for a slave born and bred on the Beaucoeur place to fetch a price well above the market average: over $1,000 a head for a male under 30, and significantly more for a female able to bear children. For very good clients it was even possible to pay the Beaucoeurs a social visit, where across tables laden with food and drink one might request that certain slaves be brought together. Because of this it was a rare occurrence for a Beaucoeur slave to be spotted in the great slave emporium of New Orleans, whose nineteenth century streets were lined with hundreds of showrooms, depots, and auction marts from Esplanade Avenue to the CBD, where outfits including "T. Hart, Slaves" and "Charles Lamarque and Co., Negroes" processed tens of thousands of blacks during the four decades leading up to the Civil War. The Beaucoeurs were also unusually generous with the slaves themselves, making sure that they were well fed and properly sheltered and clothed. And because of considerations such as these the family was lauded far and wide for their Christian goodness.

At the same time, every young Beaucoeur slave dreaded the day when the bill of sale bearing his or her name would be tendered and the child or young adult loaded onto a wagon and carried away, never again to be seen or heard from, since it was another strict Beaucoeur rule that related slaves sold apart not be allowed to socialize. Although this may have seemed harsh, it was in reality an act of kindness, according to the Beaucoeurs and their admirers, since allowing slaves to indulge their familial instincts ultimately made them unhappy and unmanageable. For this same reason, co-habitating slave couples were shuffled, slave marriages were forbidden and broken up if discovered, and mothers were relieved of their babies after the first month, at which point the infants were transferred to a different property, where they were raised by slave women not related by blood. Balancing such considerations was hard work, but the Beaucoeurs felt it their responsibility to not inflict undue anguish upon those God had in His great wisdom assigned to their charge—assuming of course that the poor savages were capable of such emotions, a question that was hotly debated at that time but which a number of circumstances suggested might be the case.

There were, for example, the women who upon finding out that they were with child went into the woods and ate strange herbs or paid visits to hoodoo men, or who threw themselves into the racing river waters while clutching their newborns. While the males were generally less likely to get carried away with such displays, there was also the occasional tale of a buck refusing to be sold away from his secret wife, if by no other means than cutting his own throat. In some instances, children who'd been sold or given away would sneak back to the Beaucoeur estate, only to find their own kin hostile and more than willing to turn them in. Then of course there was the usual sulking and carrying on that often accompanied separation. Still, like the more dramatic incidents, this was more likely an instinctual response as opposed to proof that the brutes felt the same kinds of emotions their owners did.

Yes, I learned all of this within my first month as an official resident of the Big Easy—and then proceeded to not think about it. Since Catfish didn't want to discuss the specifics of his family history any more than the scars on his wrists, it was none of my business, I told myself, chalking up his occasional disappearances and gloomy moods to southern eccentricity rather than some potentially perilous imbalance. Nor was that all I'd handily chosen to ignore. Rather, that first sip of denial had unleashed a beast that continued to swig while lumbering on, all the way up to the door of Catfish's house less than 24 hours ago—and then attempted to carry on! To put as much distance as possible as quickly as possible between B. Sammy Singleton and such developments as Catfish's abrupt relinquishment of both his home and the dishes his father had cherished enough to stash at the Tremé house, in a wooden box bearing a single word of Frederick's flat flowery script: "Mother." And, truth be told, had the house and china been all, I might have succeeded in denying their implications. But they weren't all, but rather the clarion atop a mountain of boulder-sized signals not only that something wasn't right but that something was *wrong*, from Catfish's decision to call Tess from jail, to his subsequent absence, to his lack of enthusiasm over the near certainty that he was about to inherit enough to infuse new life into the Beaucoeur Foundation for years to come. And I knew why, too. At least I thought I did, based on any number of times he'd tried too hard to convey the opposite: that at some point between the day we met and the present he'd begun to give up on the probability of reparative justice for the sins of his fathers, a change of heart I didn't exactly oppose since, after over a decade now, what really had his Foundation accomplished beyond housing a few poor people? What, really, was the point of even trying in a country that not only had yet to issue an apology for its centuries-long history of Crimes Against Humanity but was dead-set on covering them up, a country in which—outside academia—even the liberal media were more interested in Catfish's social standing than in delving into such topics as a Jim Crow legacy that manifests itself every second of every day in the disproportionate rates of incarceration, unemployment, life expectancy, and infant mortality among those of African descent, an unabashedly self-interested society whose priorities had crystallized for Catfish a few years back when *Vanity Fair* had retracted an offer to "tell the real story" when he'd refused to pose shirtless next to a cotton gin. In other words, now—as I sit here in my bedroom craving the amnesiac whitewash of morning light—what it boils down to is this: For seven years I've lived in full awareness that my friend was unhappy and becoming more so. And while yes, the line between faith and denial is hair-thin, and more often than not blurred beyond relevance by the dependency of the former upon the latter, I know which side of that line I come down on, and that my only response to Catfish's heartache has been to tread ever more lightly.

Even so, after two and a half hours of journaling following my post-Tremé nap, I'd thought myself capable of out-maneuvering such thoughts, aided by a DiGiorno and the TMC complicity of *Remains of the Day*. And no doubt, under normal circumstances anything with either Emma Thompson or Anthony Hopkins in it, much less both, would have been enough to whisk me away. In this case, however, as I sat there trying to commiserate with Miss Kenton and Mr. Stevens, Dilsey and Tera and Jonah kept storming onto that Merchant Ivory set until I was finally forced up off the couch and into a kitchen-cleaning frenzy.

And then, quite unexpectedly once the kitchen was spic and span, over to see Naomi.

Okay, not that unexpectedly, since when the going gets tough, I sometimes do go to Naomi (who always seems to be halfway waiting for that, by the way). But unexpectedly in the sense that I had no desire to engage in a conversation that would almost certainly lead back to the weekend of Catfish's incarceration, during which Naomi alone had witnessed my feverish state as I waited for Infinity to call me back with the latest update, unable to clear my mind of jail cell horrors long enough to catch more than twenty minutes of shut-eye at a time.

When I poked my head in over at Georgia's a few hours ago, however, the place was dark. And perhaps because the prospect of returning to the sepulcher of my own apartment held no appeal, an exhortation that had been shadow-boxing in my brain ever since I'd left Catfish's landed a hit: Call Infinity and terminate the speculation once and for all! True, by that time it was almost 8 p.m., so it was unlikely she'd still be at her office (the only number I had since I'd shredded her cell phone number following our row at City Hall). And true, if she *was* in her office the conversation would not be breezy. But as the slats of the mini blind in the window of Naomi's lab sliced my reflection like a sourdough loaf, I could no longer evade the fact that Naomi, unlike me, had caller ID—which was significant since my first anxious call to, and thus first call-back from, Infinity had been from Naomi's office. Nor could I continue to decline the smarmy incentive that, regardless of whether I actually connected with

Catfish's attorney, I could console myself that I'd tried. All of these balls midair, I had one foot in the door to Naomi's old kitchen when I heard a car door slam in the carriageway and Dylan's chatter through the gallery railing.

And then the hoarse cough of Georgia.

And Naomi's ho-ho-ho.

And well, sorry but there was just no way.

Two minutes and thirty-seven seconds later, according to the digital clock in Naomi's former bedroom, the three mounted the stairs as I crouched under the window next to the bed. And as I peered through the gap between window ledge and blind, I had to stifle a groan at the sight of Georgia, who was supported on one side by Naomi. Because while he was gallantly smiling and dressed to the nines, he'd lost so much weight this time that he could have been the grim reaper himself.

*Go say hello!* the choirboy pleaded.

*Shhh*, the selfish bastard replied.

One hour and twenty-two minutes later, after the lights had gone out across the breezeway, I crept back to my apartment and slipped into bed. First thing in the morning, I promised myself, I'd pay Georgia a visit, then head over to Infinity's for a self-sacrificial face-to-face in lieu of a phone call I no longer felt equipped to make. Like I said though, I couldn't sleep, and after two hours of pretending otherwise I rose and started pacing the length of my moon-lit apartment as a riverfront train clacked through the Marigny and Bywater—from bedroom to kitchen and back again—just as Catfish had gone back and forth on that long-ago night as I lay there not doubting his certain return. And because I now had every reason to doubt, as I criss-crossed that heart pine floor I found my mind beginning to dart, then crawl over every inch of the place in search of something to ensure his return, something he'd left behind and would be unable to do without. But aside from the Old Paris on my kitchen table, which gleamed coldly in the under-counter fluorescent light, I couldn't think of a thing he'd held dear that hadn't slipped through his hands or been deliberately released, a series of relinquishments that had just expanded to include his home. And with no such reassurance forthcoming I was about to give up when I spotted the edge of a box under April's bed, a box I'd forgotten about, a box of books. In helping Catfish to pack up his shop, I'd been invited to take as many as I liked, which had felt awkward since many of them had his familiar "N.F.S." penciled inside. In other words, while there was no way those castaways could qualify as important enough for him to come back for, like the china and his long-gone collection of bubble-glass portraits and yes, Joseph, the books had, for a time at least, meant something to him. And so after repositioning my bedside lamp on the floor, I dropped to my knees and slid the box out and picked up the top volume—*The Grapes of Wrath*—and began flipping through. And as I did this, I discovered that many of the pages contained passages that had been underlined, such as this:

> And the great owners, who must lose their land in an upheaval, the great owners with access to history, with eyes to read history and to know the great fact: when property accumulates in too few hands it is taken away.

And then, a bit further along—

> There is a crime here that goes beyond denunciation. There is a sorrow here that weeping cannot symbolize. There is a

failure here that topples all our success.  The fertile earth, the straight tree rows, the sturdy trunks, and the ripe fruit.

And—

…in the eyes of the people there is the failure; and in the eyes of the hungry there is a growing wrath.  In the souls of the people the grapes of wrath are filling and growing heavy, growing heavy for the vintage.

I lifted out a second book—*You Can't Go Home Again*, a real tome—and opened it up:

I believe that we are lost here in America, but I believe we shall be found.  And this belief, which mounts now to the ca-tharsis of knowledge and conviction, is for me—and I think for all of us—not only our own hope, but America's everlast-ing, living dream.  I think the life we have fashioned in America, and which has fashioned us—the forms we made, the cells that grew, the honeycomb that was created—was self-destructive in its nature, and must be destroyed.  I think these forms are dying, and must die, just as I know that America and the people in it are deathless, undiscovered, and immortal, and must live.

"Yes, Professor," I mumbled, acidly amused that even in his absence Catfish had managed to find a way to proselytize, to shove in my face the never-ending woes of the world.  At the same time, I felt an almost irresistible compulsion to go through every book in the box line by line, as if they might contain some clue to his whereabouts or state of mind—and then all the more so when I realized that several of the books had not been chosen by me but slipped in by Catfish without my knowledge.  Among these was an oversized hardcover with a black dust jacket, which was one second leaning against the inner wall of the box and the next minute clenched before me, rigid with menace. For in the black-and-white photograph vertically bisecting its cover, a young black man dangled from the branch of a tree, his face tilted upward against a luminous sky as a crowd of white men and children posed under his toes.

*Damn*, I exhaled.

I tilted the book and read the name on its spine: *WITHOUT SANCTUARY - Lynching Photography in America.*

*Put it back*, the choirboy advised.

And truly, I wanted to.

But for some reason, I could not.

Or would not.

Or just plain did not.

I don't really know.

Instead, I carried the book into the kitchen and cleared a place on the table.


Although Catfish and I had, rather artfully, managed to skirt the nitty gritty of his family's involvement in the Louisiana slave trade, we'd spent hours discussing that peculiar institution he called the American Holocaust. No stranger myself to the occasional obsession, I'd decided early on to indulge him what I'd come to view as a reasonable mental fixation, thinking it therapeutic to let him go on, and on, and on, on the topic, which he did ad infinitum. As a result I'd spent many a long and cheerless hour being educated on just about every aspect of slavery in America, as well as its social and psychographic impact upon black Americans before, during, and after the Civil War, all the way up until the present, by a person who was an expert in the field, at times in matter-of-fact college-style lectures, at times as the single-member audience of a "work-in-progress" poetry reading, at times in various casual situations, such as when he'd lean over during a movie and whisper some little-known horrible factoid into my ear, or Amazon.com me a book I had to read, or show up on my doorstep with a DVD in hand.

And so it was that I too gradually became a virtual encyclopedia of information about slavery in America, learning for example that the number of African slaves imported into the Chesapeake Bay area in the first decade of the eighteenth century was more than double the total for the seventeenth century, due in part to the Royal African Company's losing its monopoly in 1698. That during the peak period of slave importation from Africa from 1740 to 1760, there were over a hundred thousand new arrivals on American shores, flowing into Eastern seaboard states like Maryland and Virginia and South Carolina, with Rhode Island and Charleston hosting major ports. That it was not uncommon for a sizeable percentage of the catch to die or kill themselves during the crossing, and that those slaves who did survive were often something of a disappointment, since they were so traumatized that they failed to deliver the much hoped for increase. That during the daily antebellum slave trade, more than two million slaves were sold in interstate, local, and state-ordered exchanges as the business edged steadily southwest, resulting in one of the largest forced migrations in world history. That of the two-thirds of a million interstate sales made by slave traders in the decades before the Civil War, 25 percent involved the destruction of a first marriage and 50 percent the demolition of a nuclear family. That the value of slaves tracked that of cotton to such a degree that the price of a slave could be calculated by multiplying the cost of cotton (around seven cents a pound) by ten thousand. That by 1860, there were almost four million slaves held in the fifteen states in which slavery was legal, representing approximately one-third of the residents. That with this growth in the African population, whites became mightily afraid of their slaves, enacting increasingly severe measures of repression, which were eventually formalized into state-enforced "slave codes" under which the routine torture and killing of human beings was in effect condoned under U.S. law. And the more well-versed I became in the subject of slavery, the more I realized how ignorant I'd been, as well as how unconscious most people are about the two hundred years of atrocities upon which America was built, atrocities that were—as Catfish had hammered into me again and again—every bit as sociopath and terrorist as those carried out by Hitler or Pohl Pot, and yet atrocities seldom thought about, much less talked about, in this country today.

Even though I'd been born and raised in Kentucky, where for generations crops including tobacco and corn depended upon slave labor, I could not recall having ever given that chapter of U.S. history more than a shrug or a sigh. I had, after all, grown up in the 1960s and '70s, when many Caucasian Americans, including my parents, were busy congratulating themselves for their sympathetic views with regard to blacks and for the advances being made in civil rights, a term I did not then understand but which I at least knew stood for a cause that was supposedly noble and good—yet one Catfish was more likely to characterize as white people racing toward unearned redemption. By jumping on the JFK and LBJ bandwagons and cutting back on their use of the word nigger, he said, all those rednecks and crackers and peckerheads, as well as the doctors and lawyers and judges and juries, who not so long ago had stood on the sidelines and watched as a fellow human was hanged or burned alive, people who had *been there* and not said a word, a whole generation of whites had found an easy way to wash their souls clean.

Nor was the deliberate failure to own up to our nation's past restricted to places like Kentucky, Catfish went on to point out, but a transgression also endemic to the North, including in the most prestigious bastions of higher education. Was I aware, for example, that the contribution to the American slave industry by alumni of my own alma mater went far beyond the 1793 invention of the cotton gin by Eli Whitney (Class of 1792). That despite its proud roster of abolitionist alumni—from anti-slavery leader James Hillhouse (1773) to Frederick Douglass speech editor John W. Blassingame (1870)—Yale's first professorship was endowed by Philip Livingston, one of New York's leading importers of slave labor from Jamaica and Antigua during the 1730s and 1740s, whose donation to Yale College occurred at Livingston's slave-trading peak. Or that Yale was also the alma mater of the likes of John C. Calhoun (1804) and Samuel F.B. Morse (1810), two of the most rabid slavery advocates of their day, with the former boasting four decades of political leadership as a proud slaveholder (including two terms as Vice President), and the latter not just inventor of the Morse code but also an outspoken Northern activist who published tracts describing slavery and its precepts as "indispensable regulators of the social system, divinely ordained for the discipline of the human race in this world...with the great declared object of the Savior's mission to earth." Or that Yale University had chosen to name ten of its twelve residential colleges after slaveholders or ardent pro-slavery leaders, not in the time of slavery but in the 1930s and 1960s. Or that Yale continued to honor all of these men today, with the university's tercentennial issue of *Yale Alumni Magazine* lauding unequivocally both Calhoun and Morse.

Okay no, I'd granted, *lux et veritas* notwithstanding I'd earned four years of credits from the place in the late 1970s and early 1980s and not heard word one about any of that. And okay yes, I'd conceded, he had a point—it was important to own up to one's past, including the collective past of the nation. *But* wasn't it more important to deal with that which was right at hand? Didn't he have to admit that those terrible things had taken place a long time ago, and that enormous strides had been made since then? Surely not even Catfish would disagree with the notion that America was a nation in which anything was possible for those willing to pull themselves up. Plus, none of *my* ancestors or relatives had ever owned slaves or abused blacks (as far as I knew). And even if they had, what did that have to do with me, a dewy-eyed Democrat uncomfortably sensitive to the ongoing plight of the African-American? Catfish had of course strenuous-ly begged to differ. And yet nevertheless, his inherent gentleness had shielded me from some of the ugliest truths about the legacy of slavery in this land I so love. Until now. Because by placing in my possession the book spread open before me he had annihi-lated once and for all any illusions I might have still harbored about the basic decency of our forebears, while also exacerbating the fears that had begun to take root in me.

A popular practice in the South during the first few decades of the 1900s was to reprint lynching photographs not only as pictures, but as postcards. And as horrifying as the image on the book's cover had been, it was but the first in a series of 98 plates I'd felt compelled to look at one by one, images I found myself turning to again and again even though they made me lightheaded and queasy, such as the one showing a crowd of craggy-faced white men flanking the charred remains of Jesse Washington, a black 17-year-old who'd been burned alive before a crowd of ten to fifteen thousand cheering Texans, on the back of which was the handwritten message: *"This is the barbecue we had last night. My picture is to the left with a cross over it. Your son, Joe."* And as I lifted one heavy-stock page after another, reminding myself that I was free to stop at any time, I was initially at least able to tell myself that all of these burnings and lynchings and maimings had taken place somewhere other than my old Kentucky home, surely much further south, in places like Texas or Mississippi. However it wasn't long before I arrived at a picture snapped in Cairo, Illinois, and then another in Wickliffe, Kentucky, and one in Sikeston, Missouri—towns less than an hour away from Paducah—making it impossible to pretend that these atrocities had occurred in some distant land, because well, here were the picture postcards to prove it. And yet even then I continued to harbor some hope of deliverance: the distance of time. But as I went back through the prints, that too dissipated because those hangings, those burnings, that castration and dismemberment had been charted not in some far-off past but all the way up through the 1960s, with nearly 5,000 blacks murdered by lynch mobs between 1882 and 1968, and with two or three black Southerners hanged, burned to death, or quietly slaughtered every week in the late nineteenth and early twentieth centuries. So popular was the practice of lynching in the South during this period, the book informed me, that it was often conducted in a carnival-like atmosphere, with the press announcing beforehand the time and place of the event, excursion trains arriving filled with spectators, employers letting off workers to attend, parents writing children passes from school, and families attending together, the kids perched high on their daddies' shoulders. During the time of slavery, the book said, whites had resorted to public burning, lynching, and decapitation to illustrate that resistance was futile. Post emancipation, however, when blacks were no longer shielded by their own monetary worth, the violence took on a new dimension of sadism in order to slake the emotional thirst of the crowd, becoming *"a participatory ritual of torture and death, a voyeuristic spectacle prolonged as long as possible (once for seven hours) for the benefit of the crowd."*

By this time it was after midnight, and yet there I still sat, turning the pages of the book Catfish had left behind, reading the words and looking at the photographs, avoiding the faces of the people in the trees and the people on the pyres, hating the faces of the people in the crowds, the ones to whom I knew I was so closely linked, by race and by privilege and by ignorance and fear:

People who bludgeon an elderly black man and paint his face clown-like and glue cotton to his head, then prop him up in a chair like a "good ol' darky."

The ones who make a drawn-out spectacle of lynching Sam Hose, who strip him and chain him to a tree; who cut off his ears, fingers, and genitals; who plunge knives into his flesh and skin his face; who apply the torch and watch as his skin sizzles and his eyes bulge out while he cries "*Oh, my God! Oh, Jesus*"; and then, before his charred body has cooled, cut out his heart and liver and slice them into souvenirs for the crowd to scuffle over.

Those going after Mary Turner, who at eight months pregnant vowed to find those who lynched her husband and who for this insolence is taught a lesson by a Georgia mob of several hundred, who tie her ankles together and hang her upside down and burn off her clothes and use a hog knife to split open her abdomen, from which her unborn child falls onto the ground and begins to wail until a member of the mob crushes its head beneath his heel as hundreds of bullets are fired into its mother's body.

And so yes, no more than an hour ago, there I sat, no longer feeling like I had much choice, looking at those photographs and reading those words, trying to take it all in, knowing enough to understand it was impossible to, and eventually closing the book on what was already beginning to seem more like a bad dream than anything that could ever have actually occurred.

And then, allowing my thoughts to go a little astray—any place other than where they were—I thought about Catfish and all he hadn't shared. I thought about his fine fingers and his anguished arms and the inheritance he'd been carrying since the day he was born, an inheritance he'd chosen to spare me from. Or perhaps it was his way of sparing himself. There was really no way for me to know that now. For in ways I'd meticulously hidden even from myself, I'd been more than happy to let him travel that road alone.

And then, because it was there, I guess you could say, and so lovely, I reached across the book and picked up the gravy boat. And after cradling it in my hands long enough to warm it through and through, I peeled back the tape securing the lid and lifted it off.

And when I did a ruffled edge of yellowed paper rose.

*Oh my God!* I thought, puffing up with equal parts hope and dread at the thought Catfish had left some kind of message behind.

Then deflating just as suddenly.

For upon unfolding those handwritten pages, I found not a note, but one of Catfish's poems:

### Old Glory

*Hey, you old cloth of liberty*
*A flappin' in the breeze,*
*I had scars and stripes aplenty*
*When they hung me in the trees,*

*From straight across the courthouse square*
*Beneath this moss-draped bough,*
*I hailed to you, the proud, the fair,*
*Thinking it might help somehow,*

*See, the knot they made was way too tight*
*And so it wouldn't slide,*
*Which is why I flailed around all night*
*Before I finally died,*

*And as I did I flashed back on*
*What brought me to this turn,*
*I saw it all as clear as dawn—*
*Oh, how I tried to learn!*

*Now, I know the things you stand for*
*Clearly never stood for me*
*'Cause the men behind your folklore*
*Also strung me up this tree,*

*Still, I'd like to tell this story*
*—it will surely be my last—*
*It's not great nor full of glory,*
*But hey, all I got's the past.*

*I never knew my mama*
*Who like me was born a slave*
*On a big ol' spread by Houma*
*That we used to call White Wave,*

*With A Cross Over It*

*Her name was Matty Claiborne,*
*She was beautiful, I'm told,*
*A few days after I was born*
*The Missus had her sold.*

*My daddy was an African*
*Who dreamed of being freed,*
*He spent his life in chains a man*
*Made like a dog to breed.*

*Light-skinned like me my sister*
*Lived up inside the big house,*
*I once saw the Master kiss her,*
*She was frightened as a mouse.*

*At night I'd watch her by the rail,*
*Or in the yard by day,*
*One time I waved and she turned pale*
*And looked the other way.*

*My older brother Willie*
*Was the one I answered to,*
*Sometimes we'd get right silly*
*After all the work was through,*

*The Coffee Shop Chronicles of New Orleans*

*But one day Willie disappeared*
*And when I went to look,*
*I found him dead where I'd been steered*
*Beside a gurgling brook,*

*They'd stripped him bare and bound him tight*
*With pieces of barbed wire,*
*And set beneath his heels alight*
*A steady little fire,*

*For even though he barely knew*
*The ones who'd run away,*
*He'd lied and stalled a day or two*
*To help them on their way.*

*And so they burned off both his feet*
*—a lesson to us all—*
*They would not tolerate deceit,*
*He rotted there 'til fall.*

*Now I know all this is no excuse*
*For what I did that night,*
*I don't say I don't deserve this noose*
*Or think that I am right,*

*The Coffee Shop Chronicles of New Orleans*

*It's just I'd like to riddle out*
*What leads a man to kill,*
*What this old life was all about:*
*Just destiny? God's will?*

*It all started when my sister*
*Stepped outside into the yard,*
*She said something to the Master*
*And he slapped her real hard,*

*I happened to be passing*
*By the place he'd laid his gun,*
*And when I started shooting*
*Everyone began to run,*

*I shot Master twice in the head*
*—it was just like in a dream!—*
*Without a word he fell down dead*
*And Sis began to scream,*

*Right in time I turned around*
*And saw the overseer,*
*He too dropped dead onto the ground*
*His eyes were full of fear,*

Chapter 12

*When the Missus ran outside*
*There was nothing else to do,*
*With gun in hand she quickly died,*
*But still, I wasn't through,*

*What happened next I can't explain*
*I guess I just went wild:*
*I charged the house like a freight train*
*And shot their only child.*

*If there had been one bullet more*
*It would have been for me,*
*I pulled that trigger and I swore*
*I'd finally be free,*

*But the gun chamber was empty*
*And my soul felt the same way,*
*Which is why I didn't fight, you see,*
*Or try to get away.*

*Of course there wasn't any trial*
*—my deeds spoke plain and loud—*
*They just beat and whipped me for awhile*
*Before an angry crowd,*

*The Coffee Shop Chronicles of New Orleans*

*With A Cross Over It*


*Then hauled me half-dead through the town*
*Into this public park,*
*And strung me up as the sun went down*
*And everything went dark.*

*Well that, Old Glory, is my tale,*
*And this is where it dies,*
*Just like you wave to no avail*
*Before these empty eyes,*

*'Cause as for me, who's never*
*Gonna see the Promised Land,*
*I've got scars and stripes forever*
*You will never understand,*

*And though you may so proudly wag*
*O'er the righteous and the free,*
*You ain't nothing but a blood-soaked rag*
*To a lot of folks like me.*


*—Catfish Beaucoeur*


*The Coffee Shop Chronicles of New Orleans*

## AFTERWORD

This book often blends fact and fiction. So it's important
to be clear on one point: All of the statistics presented here
relating to America's history of slavery and Jim Crow are
factual. Like Sammy, I stumbled across *Without Sanctuary: Lynching Photography in America* (Twin Palms
Publishers, 2000). And like Sammy, I felt compelled to
spend time with it, looking at those picture postcards one
by one. They affected me acutely. I leaned heavily on
*Without Sanctuary* for my descriptions of the lynchings of
Jesse Washington, Sam Hose, and Mary Turner, as well as
for my account of the "spectacle" of lynching in America.
Thanks especially to James Allen, whose postcard collection appears in the book, and to Leon F. Litwak, whose
"Hellhounds" essay is drawn in part from his book *Trouble
in Mind: Black Southerners in the Age of Jim Crow* (Al-
fred A. Knopf Inc., 1998). The Washington, Hose, and
Turner lynchings, along with many others, are also documented by many other sources, including the NAACP's
*Thirty Years of Lynching in the United States, 1889-1918*
(New York, 1919), as well as by newspaper accounts of the
day. I found Walter Johnson's *Soul by Soul: Life Inside
the Antebellum Slave Market* (Harvard University Press,
2000) especially insightful with regard to the business of
slavery in the Deep South and in New Orleans; and I relied
primarily on The Amistad Committee's 2001 *Yale, Slavery
and Abolition* report for relevant information on Yale
University and its alumni.

I have taken liberties in two instances: the account of Bitsy
Baker and the description of the Beaucoeur family. Both

are composites of individuals and families of their time. Bitsy's story combines elements of several of the slave accounts in the Library of Congress's *Born in Slavery: Slave Narratives 1936-38*, which contains more than 2,300 first-person accounts collected under the aegis of the Federal Writers' Project of the Work Projects Administration (WPA) (http://memory.loc.gov/ammem/snhtml/). The fictional Beaucoeur family would have been among the largest in terms of slave and land holdings, but the specifics of their treatment of their slaves are in accordance with the norms of the times. The branding of slaves was, for example, not uncommon. And while some would deny the existence of slave breeding, there is clear evidence that this practice was widespread following the prohibition of the African slave trade in 1808.

I am deeply grateful to my editors and friends, Susan Bergman and David Sprinkle, who gently steered me from what I thought was a book—but which was actually only a draft—to here. I also thank Julia Cameron, from whose *The Artist's Way* sprouted the first lines of this book. But without my life partner and "executive editor" Csaba Lukács, there would be no Sammy, no Catfish, no chronicles, and certainly no River House, which Csaba continues to create and re-create each day to our extreme delight. Thank you, my *mindenem*, for believing in me more than I could.

David Lummis
New Orleans, May 2010

**COMING IN WINTER 2010:**

*The Coffee Shop Chronicles of New Orleans*
Part 2

**AND, IN SPRING 2011,**
**THE CONCLUSION:**

*The Coffee Shop Chronicles of New Orleans*
Part 3

**River House Publishing**
**www.riverhouseINK.com**